HOR.

GU00792192

There's One Born
Every Minute

Books by the same author:

They Must Have Seen Me Coming

In the Shadow of the Brontës

There's One Born Every Minute

Louise Brindley

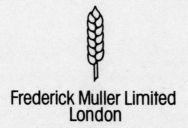

Frederick Muller Limited
London

For my parents, Sarah Elizabeth and
William Hembrough, who stumped up a
penny a day for notebooks and tiger-
nuts, comics and aniseed balls, and
never counted the cost. A small
return for a great deal of love.

First published in Great Britain in 1982 by
Frederick Muller Limited, Dataday House,
Alexandra Road, London SW19 7JZ

Copyright © 1982 by Louise Brindley

British Library Cataloguing in Publication Data
Brindley, Louise
There's one born every minute.
1. Brindley, Louise   2. Great Britain – Biography
I. Title
941.085′092′4   CT788.B/

ISBN 0-584-31154-0

Printed in Great Britain by Billing & Sons Ltd, Worcester

Chapter One

April had just wept a few more of her girlish tears, and I wished she would stop, because I hadn't a free hand to hold up my umbrella as I walked from Carnelian Bay Station lugging two enormous suitcases, my portable typewriter in its zip-up case, two plastic carrier bags, with my shoulder bag slung round my neck to stop it slithering down my right arm, and April's girlish tears dripping down my neck and soaking my woolly muffler.

I should have taken a taxi, but there wasn't one in the station yard. Besides the sun was shining when I got off the train, and I remembered that it was only what Amelia Beatty would have called a 'hop, skip and a jump' to the bus stop in the main square. Not that I felt capable of hopping, skipping or jumping anywhere as I plodded on with the rain dripping from my hair.

And yet my heart felt as light as a red balloon as I turned the corner into the square and saw the central statue of a Victorian gentleman in a tight frock coat with a cheeky pigeon perched on top of his head, and revelled in a sense of homecoming. Into each life a little rain must fall, I consoled myself. It mattered little at that moment that I seemed to be getting mine all at once.

'Is this the Tootington bus queue?' I asked a stout woman with a face newly pink from a hairdresser's dryer, and her coiffure beginning to sag under a purple chiffon headsquare.

She admitted grudgingly that it was, then, as I dumped my suitcases on the wet pavement, she went on, 'You'd think they'd build a bus-shelter wouldn't you? I've a good mind to write a letter to someone about it. It's that lot in the Town Hall, you know!'

1

The queue turned to stare at us. A thin woman in a nylon mackintosh voiced her opinion that if 'they' did build a bus-shelter, people would only write rude things on the walls. The ensuing grumbles floated over my head as I looked round at the pretty seaside town which had changed so little since I was head over heels with Nelson Eddy in *Naughty Marietta*.

Memory, I knew, could play tricks. I had been almost afraid to look in case they had changed Carnelian Bay beyond recognition; in case some johnny in the Town Hall had demolished that lovely row of Georgian houses near the Roxy Cinema, or the Red Lion Hotel with its wide archway and cobbled mews. But they were still there, just as I remembered them.

I sniffed rapturously at the tangy salt air with its indefinable scent of seaweed borne up from the sands beyond the promenade, as the Tootington bus lumbered into view, and stopped with a squeal of brakes.

'About time too,' grumbled the woman with the sagging coiffure, 'Five minutes late as usual. I shall write a letter to someone about it!'

'Where to, Miss?' The driver rested his hand on the ticket machine as I struggled aboard the bus.

'Bagdad Corner,' I said, trying to find my purse.

'Are you having me on?' He pushed back his cap and scratched his head. 'This ain't blooming Turkey you know. There ain't no such place as Bagdad Corner!'

'But there used to be when I was a little girl,' I said anxiously. 'I know exactly where it is.' The scene was painted vividly in my mind's eye. 'There's a big triangle of grass – a sort of common – with a shop on one corner and a pub on the other. It's about two miles out of Carnelian Bay, along the coast road to Fulmar Bay.'

'Aw, you mean Bagby Lane End!' The driver cast an amused look at my belongings. 'Sure you wouldn't sooner wait for the next magic carpet? Looks as if you could do with one to carry that lot!'

Someone gave me a shove from behind and slung my plastic carrier bags in after me as I paid my fare, and sank down on the nearest seat.

The driver was now taking a proprietary interest in me as

2

he called over his shoulder, 'Hope someone's meeting you at yon end. It's a fair hike down to the village from the lane end.'

'No.' I said, unwinding my sodden muffler, and wiping the back of my neck with my handkerchief.

He grinned. 'Huh, thought mebbe the Caliph of Bagdad would be sending one of his eu-know what's with a handcart.' He was enjoying himself hugely now, and so were the passengers judging by the titter that ran round the bus. 'How far are you going then?' He obviously possessed a true Carnelian nose for news.

'To April Cottage.' A shiver of happiness tickled my spine as I said it. 'It's a little way down the lane, opposite the common.'

'Can't say I know it . . .'

'I do,' interrrupted a deep voice from the seat behind. 'That was Miss Beatty's place. She died a while back. Heard tell she left the cottage to the lass who came to get over pewmonia. But that's going back a bit. Must be all of thirty years ago.'

'Actually,' I said, turning round as far as I could without strangling myself with the strap of my shoulder bag, 'it wasn't pneumonia, it was mumps.'

'You mean you're – *her*?' The man in the seat behind stared at me disbelievingly. 'Well, who'd have thought it! I would never have known you.'

'I was only ten at the time,' I reminded him.

'Well, I'll be dashed. Pleased to meet you again, I'm sure. Don't say you don't remember me?' He leaned over, grabbed my hand, and pumped it up and down.

I gulped as the strap of my shoulder bag dug into my Adam's apple. 'No, I'm afraid not.'

'I'm Bert Rumbold, the lad who led that old Galloway for you to ride. You always wanted to ride a hoss and I fixed it up with Farmer Appleby. Eh, I can see you now, a fat little lass with one sock up an' one sock down. What a carry on to get you on that hoss. As fast as I shoved you up on one side you slid down the other. Had to stand you on the fence at the finish. By gum, I've had many a laugh about that since I can tell you.'

'That's as may be. But it didn't have a saddle, did it? There was nothing for me to hang on to except the mane.'

'And you sure hung on to that,' he chuckled. 'Danged nearly wrenched all the hairs out of it. Well, I never.'

More years than I cared to remember had passed since I rode

that sway-backed Galloway, but I could still feel its rough hide under me, recalled the dust that flew up and made me sneeze when I patted it, and my consternation when, having given it a treacle toffee for a treat, it promptly spat out one of its large yellow teeth in the roadway.

'I'm getting off at Bagby Lane End as well,' said my mentor, 'so I'll give you a hand with your luggage. Let me see, your name's Ruby, isn't it?'

'Sally,' I murmured, aware that the entire bus was now hanging on the conversation, 'Sally Shelton'.

'Well, I never . . .'

I smiled to myself as I looked out of the window. April had switched moods again in her usual unpredictable fashion. Bright sunshine was now filtering through flitting clouds. As the bus left the straggling outskirts of Carnelian Bay and laboured up a steep hill, my heart did a somersault for joy as I saw the wide expanse of sea beyond the cliffs, touched here and there with brilliant shafts of light.

April had changed her tears to laughter to welcome me home. There below the cliffs nestled the town I remembered with so much affection, a steep little town with fishermen's cottages clustered near the harbour, climbing in a series of twisting streets and alleyways to a grey church on the hill, and there was the lighthouse on a spit of rock near the harbour mouth.

I little dreamed all those years ago when my mother sent me to stay with her friend, Amelia Beatty, to recover from my mumps, that one day Amelia would leave me her cottage and a few hundred pounds into the bargain just when I needed help.

I felt a chewing sense of excitement as I recognised familiar landmarks – Farmer Appleby's stack-yard, a cluster of farm buildings with smoke rising, flattening and dispersing in the capricious April breeze, a smithy, a garage, and a stone edifice marking the source of the stream that flowed past April Cottage.

Inevitably there were other things which hadn't been there in my younger days: long wooden chicken-houses crowned with what looked like Roman legionnaires' helmets, a grey-bellied grain store, and an outcrop of caravans on a grassy headland.

The bus slowed and stopped. 'Well, here you are, Bagdad Corner!' The driver grinned. 'Give my regards to Ali-Baba!'

Bert Rumbold clambered down behind me and, as the bus trundled away, we were left mounting guard over my pile of luggage.

'I'll hump the big cases,' he said, 'if you can manage the carrier bags and that other contraption. What is it, a portable typewriter?'

'Yes.' I gazed lovingly at my battered Olivetti in its zip-up case.

'You a writer, then?'

'No, but I'd like to be one.' This wasn't the time or place to go into the hours I'd spent trying, and the rejection-slips I'd received for my pains.

'Miss Beatty was always on about you,' Bert puffed, his shoulders sagging with the weight of the cases. 'Thought the world of you, she did. Used to show the missis an' me all your letters and Christmas cards.'

'Did she?' A lump came into my throat.

'Aye. You should've come to see her a bit more often.'

'I know. I wanted to.' This wasn't the time or place either to go into the reasons why I hadn't. I didn't want to mention Hugo, my difficult ex-husband.

'Well here we are!' Bert dumped my cases near the wooden bridge leading to April Cottage.

'Thank you,' I said, 'you've been a great help.'

'Aye well,' he puffed out his red-veined cheeks with sudden emotion, 'what are neighbours for? I live next door, so just call on me if you need owt.'

Could this really be the skinny lad who had led that old Galloway down the lane for me to ride? I remembered that he had once possessed a thatch of fair hair that spouted like a fountain near the crown. Now his hair was grey and wispy under his flat checked cap. But then no wonder he hadn't recognised me either, for the 'fat little lass with one sock up and sock down' was now turned forty – not exactly fat – but what my mother would have termed 'well made'; though my hair hadn't changed much. It was still fair. Not as golden as it used to be when I rode that old 'hoss' on Tootington Common, more honey-coloured now, but at least I hadn't had to resort to dyeing it. My eyes were still grey-blue, and my face was just fat enough not to have sagged, wagged, bagged and dragged too drastically. It wasn't a young face any longer – it simply looked comfortably live in – like a little house with lights in the windows.

'Of course the cottage is a bit run down now,' Bert went on. 'Miss Beatty couldn't manage to keep it up in the end, but she was a proud old girl and wouldn't ask for help unless she was forced to.' He blew his nose on a handkerchief the size of a tea-towel. 'The garden's in a heck of a mess, but you'll soon lick that into shape I shouldn't wonder.' He stuffed the hanky in his breast pocket. 'Are you any good at gardening?'

'Gardening? I've never actually done any,' I confessed, 'but I'm willing to have a go at it.'

He lumbered off to his own cottage, and I looked round at the scene of so many childhood memories; Tootington Common, freshly laundered by the spring rain, the cottages on the far side of it, the pub and the corner shop.

Amelia and I had once had tea in the garden of one of those cottages – a cream tea with scones and jam, a brown earthenware teapot and cups with roses.

Tootington Beck tinkled past Bert's cottage, mine, the one next door to it, and continued on its sparkling way past other groups of cottages leading down the lane to the grey Norman church just visible through burgeoning beeches and sycamores.

After the church the road widened and swung away in a curve past green meadows, and there the beck became a river crossed by a hump-backed bridge. And wasn't there a house near the bridge? A Georgian house with high windows, and lawns sloping down to the water's edge?

I looked at April Cottage. It was just as I remembered it except that the ivy had grown much thicker, and the seedling lilac in the tiny front garden was so high that its branches now tapped what used to be Amelia's bedroom window.

I walked resolutely over the creaking bridge and fitted the key into the lock, thinking of Hugo.

If I'd still been married to him, he would have wanted me to sell April Cottage to the highest bidder, and I would have complied rather than face a first-class row.

Now that there was no Hugo, tall and domineering, wearing horn-rimmed glasses, to point out the folly of incarcerating myself in a run-down cottage in a village near a backwater seaside town, my heart lifted like a bird as I stepped over the threshold and saw, with delight, Miss Beatty's little sitting room with its chenille-covered table and the paraffin lamp she used to light me to bed with, the horsehair sofa near the fireplace, and the print of Leigh Holman's 'Light of the World' above it.

I half expected Amelia to come bustling into the room as I stared at her piano with the brass candleholders, and the corner cupboard filled with her Sunderland lustre jugs and Goss china ornaments.

The two doors facing me led to the dining room and kitchen, the one on the left to an enclosed staircase leading up to the bedrooms. I walked up it and saw that my small bedroom had been turned into a bathroom.

In the old days I'd bathed in front of the sitting-room fire. A vivid memory of Amelia scrubbing my feet with Monkey soap assailed me, and ladling hot water over my head to get the sand out of my hair, scolding and loving me in the same breath.

I opened the velvet-topped piano stool and looked at her music: selections from *The Desert Song* and *Lilac Time*: tenderly touched her books, *Pilgrim's Progress*, Mrs Gaskell's *Life of Charlotte Bronte*, *Enquire Within Upon Everything*, the Bible, and a set of Arthur Mee's *Children's Encyclopedia*.

That homecoming was all April. April Cottage linked to that lovely poem by William Watson:

> April, April,
> Laugh thy girlish laughter;
> Then, the moment after,
> Weep thy girlish tears.

Chapter Two

'Where's tha' going to start, then?' Bert leaned on his side of the fence and looked over at me, wearing the self-satisfied smile of a man whose bit of 'This earth, this realm, this England' is doing very nicely, thank you, when yours is not.

So far as I was concerned he had just asked the jack-pot question, and I wasn't going to win the sixty-four thousand dollars because I didn't know the answer.

Hugo had been anti-soil, pro-concrete. The only concession to growing things in our smart detached town bungalow were a couple of shrubs in tubs near the front door – because shrubs looked right with pseudo carriage-lamps. He wouldn't even give house room to real Christmas trees because of the needles, so I'd had to make do with silver-paper ones that folded up like umbrellas after the festive season.

Now, faced with a sea of nettles that looked like eager junior executives so intent on getting to the office that they hadn't bothered to shave, I shoved my sweat-band an inch up my forehead, feeling like Bjorn Borg before a Wimbledon final. I didn't know where I was going to start. All I knew for sure was that I was going to perspire.

Bert was wearing his leaning-on-the-fence-asking-daft-questions get up; a pair of faded dungarees, a striped flannel shirt with the back and front studs sticking out – apparently hopeful that one day he'd anchor a collar to them – a woollen muffler where his collar should have been but wasn't, and a flat cap which gave him the appearance of a bookie's runner who hasn't the least intention of running anywhere.

'I'd come over and give you a hand,' he said, 'except that I'm going to fix the roof. But you can holler if you need any advice.'

'Thanks very much, but I'll manage – I think.'

'Let's have a look at your tools,' he said.

'Tools?'

He pushed back his cap. 'Aye, tools. Spades, forks, hoes, trowels, them kind of things. Though what you really need is an arrer.'

I stared at him. 'You mean – a bow and arrer?'

'No! Bloody hell! An 'and arrer!' He was fast losing patience with me.

Light dawned. 'Oh I *see*! You mean a hand harrow?'

'That's what I said.'

'I don't think I've got one of those,' I said apologetically. 'What I have got is this, and this.' I produced a rusty fork and spade from Amelia's garden shed, 'and there's something Old Father Time left behind him somewhere, a sort of scythe with a long handle.'

'Hmmm, well that'll do for the nettles,' Bert conceded, 'only mind you don't cut your feet off with it! Tricky things, them scythes.'

He stretched his arms above his head, flexed his muscles, did a few limbering up exercises, snapped his elastic armbands, and said, 'Well, ta-ta for now. Don't forget to holler if you need any help.'

What he means, I thought despondently, is if I need an ambulance. Then I perked up. I'd always enjoyed a challenge, and Amelia's garden was certainly that. But Bert had a point when he said, 'Where's tha' going to start?'

Perhaps I'd better make a slow careful reconnaissance first, approach the job methodically the way Hugo would have done. But I'd never been much of a one for method, I was more of a get in there and slog it out kind of person, which was one of the reasons why Hugo and I hadn't seen eye-to-eye at times.

I turned to survey my domain. April Cottage possessed a kind of lean-to conservatory which Amelia had always referred to proudly as 'The Loggia'. I could see that the loggia had been a bit of Italianate one-upmanship forty years ago, and I remembered it as a miniature Crystal Palace, full of her carefully nurtured geraniums, but so many winters had passed by since then; so much snow had landed on the wooden interstices and cracked glass panes, that Amelia's pride and joy was now little more than an eyesore full of bamboo peasticks, empty plantpots, mouldering seed-boxes and rickety garden chairs.

And yet we'd often had tea out there on a little bamboo table, and watched the birds sitting in the branches of the apple tree. Well at least the tree was still there, a bit gnarled and grouchy-looking now, as if it had rheumatism in its lower branches, but Amelia had been so proud because she had grown it from a pip.

The loggia ran in an L-shape past the dining-room and kitchen windows, and the wall of the next-door cottage. Not Bert's – the one on the other side, and I hadn't met the occupant of that house yet.

They must have queer plumbing in Tootington, I thought, because there, inside the loggia was a drain with a round grating over it, and a pipe disappearing through the wall of the next-door cottage.

I remembered that Amelia had been very particular about that drain, and wouldn't let me play near it in case I caught 'the fever', though which fever – scarlet, yellow, spotted, brain or just drain – I had never troubled to enquire.

Once a week she would go out with a woollen 'zit cap' pulled well down over her ears, and with what looked like a yashmak covering the lower half of her face, looped over her spectacles with elastic bands, to pour half a bottle of Jeyes fluid through the grating. Then she would nod her head in satisfaction and say in muffled tones through the yashmak, 'There, that'll show 'em!'

Capability Brown obviously hadn't taken a hand in design-ing Amelia's garden. It was long and narrow, carved up into dozens of segments with meandering paths edged with fluted Victorian tiles which reminded me of rows of decaying teeth sticking up out of the ground.

Many a bite those toothy tiles had taken out my ankles in the old days when I'd hoochy-koochied past them, bouncing a rubber ball. I smiled inwardly as I remembered Amelia's precise voice explaining to me as she dabbed Iglodine on my wounds that I must learn to walk along those paths. 'Mine is not a runny kind of garden,' she said.

The area outside the loggia had been concreted over years ago. Now, cracked and mottled with little tufts of grass poking through the cracks, it looked all forlorn.

10

Two rusted clothes-posts had been sunk deep into the concrete. I had very nearly garrotted myself on the washing-line strung between them. Amelia had parted with the little plot of grass she had been so proud of, for practical reasons, most likely because she could no longer cut it, and because she had figured that her feet wouldn't get so wet on concrete when she hung out her clothes to dry.

Opposite the loggia door, which slid along on metal runners, was a rockery which depressed me intensely. Running riot with lank green ferns, it was abutted by two concrete pools full of murky water. God only knew what those pools contained. I'd let out a scream when the water had swirled suddenly and a tail disappeared into the dismal depths. Whatever was lurking down there would have to be fished out, but I jibbed at the notion of netting what might prove to be a school of baby alligators.

Tucking my hair firmly under my Bjorn Borg head-band, I looked past the rockery and broken concrete to the confusion of shrubs clinging together like frightened old ladies in a thunderstorm.

It was a right mess of a garden and no mistake. Perhaps an 'and 'arrer was the only possible solution, and yet my foolish heart decided otherwise. I loved Amelia's apple tree and imagined it as it would look eventually, a veritable bridal bouquet of creamy pink blossom. Why, it was beginning to stir with life already.

An impish notion struck me. One of those notions which Hugo would have dubbed 'babyish'. I nipped indoors, found a useful-looking bread-knife, walked up to the clothes-line, cut it through the middle and declaimed in a loud voice, 'I have pleasure in declaring this garden open' at which point I looked up to see a hostile face glaring at me over the next door fence.

'Well, really,' snorted a disapproving voice. The owner of the voice sniffed in high dudgeon, threw up her chin and stalked back to her own cottage.

'Just a minute,' I called after her, but it was no use. As I hung over the fence brandishing the bread-knife, she disappeared with a flurry of her pleated brown tweed skirt and slammed the door behind her.

* * *

11

The corner shop, I was thrilled to discover, had scarcely changed at all. The march of progress hadn't got its boots over *that* threshold, although the pink sugar mice had gone from the goodies window.

I supposed that 'they' – the manufacturers – didn't make pink sugar mice any more. Kids these days didn't want the things I used to buy, sherbert dabs and kali, tiger nuts and aniseed balls. They wanted chocolate bars that wouldn't ruin their appetite between the beef-burgers and fish-fingers.

An indefinable blend of bacon, cheese, cooked ham and firelights hit me as I entered. A scent that nobody had ever succeeded in bottling. Chanel No 5 came nowhere near it. This was Eau-de-Corner Shop par excellence, evocative of Reckitt's Blue Bags, and Zebo grate polish.

I wondered, as I used to when I was ten years old, how one small shop could contain so many shelves and counters. What was the name of the lady who owned it? Ah yes, Mrs Nugent. That was it! I remembered her as a tiny lady with greying hair, who wore a halter-neck pinny over a black jumper and skirt. She'd be in her eighties now, if she was still alive. I hoped that she was still alive. I'd love to see Mrs Nugent again, staring at me over her pince-nez spectacles and weighing currants in blue paper bags.

A neat grey-haired lady appeared from the room behind the shop, and stared at me over a pair of pince-nez spectacles. She wore a black jumper and skirt and a halter-neck pinafore.

'Mrs Nugent,' I said before I could stop myself.

'*Miss* Nugent, if you don't mind,' she said crossly. 'You're mixing me up with my mother! People do say we're alike, but Mother's eighty-two now, so I don't know whether to take your mistake as a compliment or not.'

Trust me to put my foot in it! 'I'm terribly sorry,' I said, 'of course you don't look anywhere near eighty-two. You look exactly the way your mother used to when I was a little girl.' Somehow that didn't sound very complimentary either.

She sighed. 'Don't worry. I know exactly what you mean. Some people are born looking old. I know, I'm one of them. You see I've always lived with my mother. That's why I've grown to look like her. It wasn't so noticeable when she was active, but now that I have to see to the shop and look after

12

her as well, it does get a bit wearing at times. I suppose that's why I look older than I am.'

I glanced round the pin-neat little shop with its old hand bacon slicer on a marble slab and huge tea-canisters arranged on the top shelf. There wouldn't be any tea in them nowadays, but there had been in Mrs Nugent's time because I'd seen her climb up on a rickety ladder to get them down, and the names on them had seemed like glances into other worlds to me then – Orange Pekoe, Darjeeling and Gunpowder.

'I don't know how you manage,' I said, contritely, 'the shop looks so clean. Not a speck of dust anywhere.'

She shrugged. 'Oh I muddle through somehow. Mother doesn't get up very early nowadays, so when I've given her breakfast in bed, all I have to do is nip up now and then to make sure she hasn't swallowed her false teeth. She will insist on keeping them in, you see, and I wish she wouldn't. Anyway, I don't suppose you want to hear my troubles, I expect you have plenty of your own down at April Cottage, what with the garden and all to see to?'

'Oh, you know who I am then?' I smiled at her over the cards of babies' dummies and hard-skin ointment.

She raised her eyebrows in two arcs over her glasses, rather like a small snowy owl. 'Everyone knows everything in this village,' she said drily, 'or think they do, and what they don't know for sure they make up. I've heard tell that you brought a typewriter with you, and that you came to stay with Amelia Beatty when you were getting over scarlet-fever.'

'Mumps,' I murmured.

'There you are, then. That's exactly what I meant. What they don't know they make up. Now I'll be able to tell them that it wasn't scarlet-fever, but it won't make the slightest difference. They'll have you recuperating from everything under the sun before they've finished. Housemaid's knees, hammer toes, the lot!'

She chuckled. 'As a matter of fact there's a strong rumour floating around that you are Amelia Beatty's daughter by old Farmer Appleby.' Her eyes twinkled. 'Are you?'

'That would be letting the cat out of the bag, wouldn't it?' I liked Miss Nugent enormously. 'Let's keep them guessing, shall we?'

She seemed to like me too, for she said in that dry crackly

way of hers, 'Perhaps you'd like to have tea with Mother and me on Sunday afternoon?'

'Yes, I'd like that very much.'

'You might change your mind when you've met her,' she said, reaching for a duster. 'Likely as not she'll ask you a lot of rude questions.'

'Rude questions? Well, why not?'

'Good. Now then, what can I get you? I'm afraid I haven't got one of those deep-freeze units. Suppose I should have, but I ask you, where would I find room for it?' She looked round helplessly. 'So all the food I sell is more inconvenience than convenience. Fortunately I have a good cellar, deep-delved like the wine in that poem by Keats. Oh, what on earth am I chattering on about?'

'I know what you mean,' I said. 'It's from Keats' *Ode to a Nightingale*, isn't it? "Oh for a draught of vintage, that hath been cool'd a long age in the deep delved earth"!'

'Yes, that's it! I'd half forgotten. I once took an Open University degree course, not that it did me much good. The fact is I should have sold up years ago, but Mother wouldn't hear of it. If someone new took over, they'd find room for a freezer right enough. They'd whip out all these little bitty counters and put in self-service units in two minutes flat.'

'I don't particularly like convenience foods,' I said, 'although I suppose one couldn't have anything more convenient than eggs, and that's what I've come for. Half-a-dozen eggs and a bottle of Jeyes fluid.'

She seemed vaguely worried and upset, and I guessed why. Everything was getting on top of her – the hard-to-cope-with old lady upstairs, the shop that her mother wouldn't let her part with, even the niggling anxiety about the old woman's false teeth which sounded funny but wasn't. It must have been the last straw when I called her 'Mrs Nugent', and that had triggered off a train of thought about having been born old. I realised that it was only the unfashionable 1940s hairstyle, her glasses and pinny that gave the impression of age. Her skin was pink and unlined, and her blue eyes betrayed a twinkling sense of fun when she smiled.

'If it's any comfort to you, Miss Nugent,' I said, 'I adore this shop. It's one of the things I've remembered, with joy, since I was a child. I was so afraid it might have changed;

14

become just like every other corner shop, full of iced lollies and things on special offer – the windows full of those ghastly posters advertising 2p a packet off cornflakes, and you wouldn't believe how often I've wondered if Gunpowder tea actually exploded in the cups.'

The worried frown left her forehead. 'Talking to you has done me good,' she admitted. 'Truth to tell, I thought you might be a bit high-hat being a writer.'

'A – *writer?*'

'Aren't you? Bert Rumbold said you were.'

'Then Bert Rumbold has got hold of the wrong end of the stick!'

'Trust him for that,' Miss Nugent shook her head, 'I might have known. But Bert couldn't wait to tell me that you'd brought a typewriter with you.'

'Owning a typewriter is nothing to go by.' I sighed. 'I now own Amelia Beatty's piano and I can't play a note. Which reminds me, I'd better be going. Some of my own furniture is arriving this afternoon.'

As I paid for the eggs and Jeyes fluid she said wistfully, 'You won't forget that you're coming to tea on Sunday?'

Getting more furniture into April Cottage was like putting a quart into a pint pot, but I knew that Amelia wouldn't mind if I got rid of the horsehair sofa and feather bed when I'd found good homes for them. She was the most practical body I'd ever known and I could almost hear her saying, 'Make yourself comfortable, child, April Cottage is your home now'.

Apparently Amelia was far more practical than I would ever be. In my shoes she'd have rung out the old before bringing in the new.

When the removal men had struggled over the bridge with my settee and armchairs one of them mopped his brow and said, 'Blooming heck, Missis, you'll never get round this lot. How many sofas do you need in one sitting room? Come to that, how many beds do you need in one bedroom?'

I could see his point of view. April Cottage was beginning to look like a saleroom on viewing day. Now that I had almost two of everything each room was stuffed to overflowing.

I had felt strangely excited at the prospect of seeing my own things again. Following the break up of my marriage, and during the painful business of the divorce, I'd lived with my sister and her husband for a while until the trauma was over, but always at the back of my mind was a sense of fragmentation, as if I would never be a whole person until all my bits and pieces stored away in dusty repositories were brought together again under one roof.

Now it seemed that I needed a roof and a half to accommodate all my belongings. When the removal men had departed, puffing and blowing and mopping their foreheads, the cottage looked like a tip.

I was climbing over the horsehair sofa to get to the stairs when Bert poked his head round the door. He gave a deep gurgling laugh when he saw the mess I was in.

'It's no laughing matter,' I said severely, 'I had no idea it would look like this.'

'You should've got rid of that old pianner and the hosshair sofa first.' He nodded sagely. 'I said to my Missis, Ruby should have got shot of what she didn't want before this lot arrived.'

'I realise that now,' I said, getting my leg caught between the sofa and the wall, 'but what on earth am I going to do?'

'Why don't you shift what you don't need into the greenhouse?' He weighed up the situation in a jiffy. 'Stack it up in there for the time being then send it to the saleroom. If you'd had your head screwed on right, you could've got those furniture blokes to tek it away for you.'

'I suppose you're right.' But I hated the thought of stacking Amelia's furniture and relegating it to a saleroom. She'd set great store by her horsehair sofa and piano, and my mind boggled at what she'd have said if she'd heard Bert refer to her loggia as a greenhouse.

'The missis an' me'ull give you a hand,' he went on. 'Well, what are neighbours for? Darr,' he yelled, 'come on out an' help with the humping.'

There was no reply. When I'd got my leg out from behind the sofa I followed him on to the garden path where he cupped his hands round his mouth and gave another yell. 'Darr! Where in tarnation have you got to?'

An ample-bosomed woman with rosy cheeks and iron-grey hair peeped round the porch of the next-door cottage, showered a few hairpins on the path, and promptly disappeared again, like one of those figures in a weather-vane that pop out when it's going to rain.

'Darr's shy, that's her trouble,' Bert said with a wink and a nod. 'She'll come out when she's plucked up enough courage. When she does, pretend not to notice her. Don't say nothing or she'll shoot off like a bullet from a gun. She's a funny 'un, Darr is, though I'll say this for her, she's a fair humper when she does get going.'

What I needed most at that moment was a fair humper, so when Darr appeared, leaving a trail of hairpins all over my sitting-room carpet, I simply ignored her, though it took a bit of doing, considering the size of her, and a near impossibility when she mistook my posterior for the lumpy end of the sofa and began to hump me from behind.

'Darr's always had a fancy for this here sofa,' Bert puffed as we struggled with it through the dining room into the greenhouse.

I leaned against the door and wiped the perspiration from my forehead. 'Why didn't you say so before? Take it and welcome if you want it.'

'Darr's always had a fancy for that square table an' all,' Bert said quickly, 'an' we could do with a feather bed for the spare room, the situation being what it is.'

'Oh?' I was listening with half an ear to what Bert was saying and staring in fascination at Darr's bun, wondering how long it would remain in position seeing that she'd lost all but three of her hairpins.

'An' I know for a fact the vicar would be glad of a new pianner for the village hall. The old 'un sounds like peas rattling in a tin jerry.'

I swivelled my eyes away from Darr who stood there as hefty and solid as a baby hippo. 'You can have the table and the bed, if you like.' I said recklessly, still smarting from the strength of her fingers digging into my rear end. 'I'm sure Amelia would have wanted you to have them, and I'll ring the vicar about the piano later on.'

Bert beamed. 'What about that then, Darr? Ruby's giving us the sofa, the table and the bed.'

Darr made no reply, merely blushed and bent to retrieve a couple of fallen hairpins, jammed them into her bun, and nodded her head so hard that they promptly fell out again.

17

'Now all we have to do,' said Bert, 'is to lump this lot over the back fence and into our house.'

This time I kept my bottom well out of the way as the new humping session began. The last I saw of them that day, they had got the sofa wedged endways near their back door.

Talk about round and round the mulberry bush, I thought, as I collapsed on my own sprawly settee. Then I wondered what Bert meant by 'the situation being what it is'. Were my neighbours going to take in visitors?

Chapter Three

'I saw the furniture van arrive,' Miss Nugent said when I popped up to the shop to buy a slice of ham, 'and so did every other body in this part of the village come to that. *I* couldn't help seeing what was going on, of course, but Mrs Pudney at The Spotted Dog looped back her curtains to get a better view, and Mrs Pickles over the way had her lunch on a tray so as not to miss anything. The nosey parkering lot!' She blushed at me over her glasses. 'How does it feel to be the centre of attraction?'

'A bit of a novelty,' I confessed, 'seeing that I usually become invisible whenever I wait in a cafe to be served. The waitresses dash round serving everybody else, and leave me sitting there like a lemon.' I sighed, 'My husband said I lacked Presence – with a capital P. He always made me wear high heels to add to my height. But then, he was so tall that I suppose I seemed like a fair-haired pygmy to him.'

'You're too modest, that's your trouble.' She began hacking away at the ham with a carving knife because, she explained, her bacon-slicer wouldn't cut ham, 'Though I can't think why you should be. I think you are very nice looking. As a matter of fact, I thought, the first time I saw you, how confident you were.'

'Whatever gave you that idea?' I watched in fascination as the knife slid deeper into the ham the wrong way. 'Anyway, I'm far from being confident at the moment. If I don't soon find myself a job, I'll end up going from door to door with a tin cup and a begging letter. The trouble is, I'm not qualified now for anything except cooking and washing up.'

Miss Nugent paused to wipe her forehead with her handkerchief as the ham slid across the marble slab.

'I say, shall I hang on to that ham for you?' I asked. 'It'll end up on the floor in a minute!'

'Would you mind? Perhaps you'd better come round this side of the counter. Oh my giddy aunt, just look at it! It's a good job Mother can't see what a mess I'm making of it, she'd have a fit if she did. Mind your fingers!' She began sawing again. After a while, her mind went back to our conversation. 'But you must have done something besides cooking and washing-up before you were married,' she said.

'Oh that. Yes, as a matter of fact I trained as a hairdresser. Not that I wanted to, it was more a question of having to. My father was a hairdresser you see, in those days when hairdressing was a Profession – with another capital P. You know, when hot perms were on the go, and women paid half-a-crown a time to have their hair singed.'

'Really? That sounds interesting.'

'Interesting? It was hair-raising!' I thought back to the first-ever time I stood trembling with a lighted taper in my hand, behind a woman with hair a foot long. Come to think of it, she'd started trembling too when I dashed out of the cubicle and came back with a bucket of water in case I set fire to her head.

'It was a family business,' I went on, clinging to the ham like a shipwrecked sailor to a lifeboat. 'Dad and his three sisters were all hairdressers, and I was next in line for the "chop" – seeing my sister had more guts than I had when it came to saying no. She went into one of those lovely Art shops and did barbola-work, and painted violets on wooden boxes.'

I said dewily. 'When it came to my turn to leave school, my Mother had a go at me; said that it would kill Father if I didn't go into hairdressing. I had a terrible mental picture of him laid out on his Death Bed – rather like the "Death of Nelson" you know, so I said Yes.'

'I know exactly what you mean.' Miss Nugent sighed, pushing back her hair with her wrist. 'The same thing happened to me. I wanted to take up nursing when I left school, but Mother wouldn't hear of it. I loved her – so . . . It's a kind of emotional blackmail, isn't it? That's why I'm here, making a bloody mess of this ham! But couldn't you go back to doing hair? It pays very well these days.'

'I don't think so. I'm old hat now. Whoops!' as the ham

slithered to the edge of the slab. 'Not that I didn't enjoy it in a funny kind of way. Sounds daft, I know, but Dad was my whole world to me, though I used to write out my notice every other Friday, and stick it in his overall pocket. Then I'd worry myself sick over the weekend and sneak downstairs and take it out again the first thing on Monday morning.'

'Right,' Miss Nugent said, 'You can let go now. Oh Lord, I have made a mess of it haven't I? Will it be all right do you think?'

I stared at the hacked off slice doubtfully. It was half an inch thick at one end, and four inches at the other. 'I suppose it will be all right if I can get in into my frying pan,' I said.

That conversation came back to me when I was waiting for the ham to cook. Money was a headache as far as I was concerned. Hugo had done all the whizz-kid stuff with bills simply because I had never got past the stage of adding up on my fingers, and that hadn't exactly pleased a man of his intellect. Now I was going to have to tackle my own finances, and I dreaded the thought.

Miss Nugent thought of me as a confident person, but I was far from confident deep down. Possessing a cheerful Cheshire Cat face was nothing to go by. Amelia's small legacy wouldn't last very long in these days of high inflation, so just how was I going to earn a living?

Since the break-up of my marriage I had jibbed at the thought of going back to a nine-to-five job. While marriage had its drawbacks, it did provide an umbrella on rainy days. How was I to know that my umbrella would blow inside out and spring a few nasty leaks into the bargain? But now that I had ventured from under it, I felt the urge to go it alone, get good and wet if necessary, but in my own way as a kind of freelance, doing a variety of jobs.

Propping up the ham in the frying pan for the thick end to cook, I wondered if I could possibly take in washing, address envelopes, or bake little mutton pies and peddle them round the village. Or perhaps I should get down to writing short stories.

All those things sounded fine in theory, but who wanted washerwomen these days – and anyway, I couldn't iron for nuts. Come to that, who wanted little mutton pies, even if I

21

knew how to set about making them. And the thought of all those rejection slips made my blood run cold.

The Tootington to Carnelian Bay bus was packed on Saturday morning with riotous kids on their way to the picture show at the Roxy Cinema in the town square, and with anxious looking young mums who appeared to need at least six arms to cope with their babies, pushchairs and shopping trolleys.

I found a seat at the back of the bus and spent the entire journey gazing into the solemn face of a little girl who was kneeling up on the seat in front – a disconcerting experience, seeing that her round saucer eyes were only about six inches away from mine. She reminded me of a miniature Svengali, and I felt I should probably burst into a quick snatch of 'Ben Bolt' if she didn't look somewhere else. When I tried smiling at her she burst into tears and wailed, 'The lady made a face at me'.

'Then make one back at her,' snapped her mother.

The child obliged by sticking her tongue out as far as it would go, and I returned the compliment. Then I had the feeling that two other eyes were boring into me and turned my head to see the woman from the cottage next door sitting in the aisle seat opposite.

My tongue was still protruding a little way between my teeth as I gazed into her hostile face. Whatever must she think of me I thought. I pretended to spit out a couple of grape pips, returned my tongue to where it belonged and attempted a smile, but she wasn't having any truck with me. She gave an almighty sniff and turned to stare out of the window.

An angular woman with shoulders like wire coathangers, she wore a fawn coat and a brown felt hat. What I could see of her mouse-brown hair was wound up on a couple of pipe-cleaners and skewered with two ferocious-looking kirby grips. Her face was angular with high cheekbones and a bony forehead. Her long thin nose was the quivery type, flushed at the tip with flared nostrils.

The last thing I wanted was an unfriendly next-door neighbour, and I couldn't figure out why she was so hostile. What had I done apart from cutting Amelia's clothes line in two and sticking out my tongue playfully at the miniature

Svengali in front? There must be more to it than that, and I intended to find out what it was.

I decided to collar her as soon as she got off the bus, but the moment it stopped she was off like a runner in the Grand National and fairly cantered down the aisle, her string shopping bag bumping against her stockinged legs. By the time I had managed to get myself and my own shopping basket on to the pavement she had disappeared. I was looking for her when 'Svengali' clambered down from the bus, gave me a gap-toothed smile and said, 'Ta-ta'.

Corporation gardeners were busy planting flowers at the base of a central statue of the man in a tight frock-coat, and pigeons strutted to peck at the crumbs thrown to them by people sitting on a bench close by.

A little girl, bouncing a red rubber ball, uttered a shrill cry of delight as one of the pigeons waddled close to her feet flapping its brownish-grey wings.

I walked quickly down a side street to the promenade, and saw the pantiled roofs of the fishermen's cottages; nets spread out to dry on the jetty, and a brightly-painted coble thrusting against the sea-swell to the fishing grounds.

Summertime would bring its seasonal crop of visitors to Carnelian Bay, but people who wanted amusement arcades and monorails would gravitate towards seaside towns with plenty of bingo halls and discos.

I gazed at the sand extending in a smooth crescent from the harbour to a peninsula below the cliff gardens – a natural promontory lapped by the changing colours of the sea. Perched on the promontory was Carnelian Bay's pride and joy – the Victoria Hall, splendidly grey, shabby and seemingly invulnerable, scene of summertime concerts and flowershows.

Staring out at the blue horizon, I felt tears prickling behind my eye-lids, and I knew that Amelia Beatty had given me much more than a cottage, she had handed me a whole new way of life.

When I had finished my shopping I wandered round the square. Next to Mr Farmer, the chemist's, was an antique shop with a Georgian wine table, a Rockingham jug, two carriage-clocks and a Noritake bowl in the window.

The green velvet curtain threaded on a brass rail behind the window was obviously there to stop busy-bodies like me pressing their noses against the glass trying to see inside the shop. Then I noticed an oblong of white cardboard: 'Mature lady assistant required part-time. Must be refined. Some knowledge of antiques preferred. Inquire within'.

A spur of the moment impulse made me push open the door and walk in. Of course I might have looked more refined if I hadn't been wearing my fur-trimmed boots and lugging a shopping basket, and I'd have certainly smelled more refined if I hadn't just bought a wedge of Brie from a market stall. Still, the advert didn't say anything about smelling refined.

The man who came forward to meet me would be sixtyish with longish grey hair, glasses and a pointed beard. No moustache, just the beard, which gave him a strangely unfinished look. The waistband of his trousers creaked slightly as he bowed obsequiously and rubbed his hands together.

'May I show Modom something?' His voice was like grey velvet with the nap wearing thin.

'Not *ac*-tually,' I replied, unable to tear my eyes away from his top lip, and worrying about what he had done with his moustache. Perhaps he'd meant to trim it one morning and the razor had slipped. '*Ac*-tually I've come about the job.'

I spoke the way I used to when Hugo's boss was coming to dinner.

'Oh,' the antique dealer had thought I was after his Georgian wine table, 'you'd better come into the office.'

I could tell he didn't want me among his Noritaki bowls in my boots and headscarf. His nostrils twitched as he got wind of the Brie.

As I followed him into a cubbyhole behind a Welsh dresser I noticed with horror that the cheese had started to run, and that the piece of lamb I'd bought was oozing pink juice through the brown paper.

'Sit down,' he said. 'No, not on *that* chair. That's mine, this is yours.'

'Sorry.' His was a swivel chair in front of a knee-hole desk, mine a bentwood about six inches higher. If I'd sat on the wrong chair, I might have ended up interviewing him.

He swivelled round suddenly to find a pen, and I kicked my shopping basket under the knee-hole of his desk when he

24

wasn't looking. Anything to get it out of sight. I hadn't expected to feel nervous, but as he found the pen and swivelled back to face me, I felt like a sixth former caught cheating at exams.

'Now then,' he said, 'I'd better take down a few particulars. What is you name?'

My mind went blank. Perhaps it was the hypnotic gaze of his gimlet eyes behind his frameless glasses that unnerved me, or possibly I was worrying about what would happen if he decided to put his legs under the desk. Whatever the reason, my voice sounded strangulated and reasonably refined when it did emerge, and I was terribly glad that my name wasn't Gladys Smogg or Rose Ada Butch. Sally Shelton did have a certain high-toned ring about it.

'I take it that you know something about antiques?' he went on.

'Oh yes. My cottage is fairly stuffed with them.' I wondered what to do with my hands, as the catechism continued.

'What period?' he snapped.

'Well, it's difficult to say precisely,' I hedged, stuffing one hand into my pocket and sitting on the other. 'Mainly Georgian,' thinking it best not to let on that most of it was George the Fifthian. 'Some Victoriana too, of course,' I said remembering Amelia's marble-topped wash stand and the chamber pot with blue roses clambering up its sides.

'I take it, then, that you have a proper appreciation of antique furniture?' He appraised me carefully, tapping together his fingernails.

'Yes, I think it would be fair to say that.' I watched his knees skim the edge of his desk as he gave a half turn on his chair.

'What I need at this moment in time,' he said, tapping his finger ends together more fiercely, 'is a mature person capable of keeping an eye on things when I'm out conducting my business.'

I flinched at 'this moment in time' but gave him a bright smile, hoping to God he'd hire me before he hacked his shins on my shopping basket, and praying he wouldn't pass out from the smell of the cheese before he decided that I was refined enough to work for him. I drew up my eyebrows, and nodded. 'Yes, quite so,' I murmured.

25

'Yes, quite so,' I'd found through those interminable dinners with Hugo's boss, had filled the bill when I didn't know what else to say. That, plus two coats of mascara and a good squirt of 'Elle' had usually seen me through the worst moments.

He reappraised me cunningly as I rearranged my hands. I hardly liked to bother him with such trifles as how long and how much?

'Very well, Mrs Shelton,' he said, possibly thinking no one who looked so daft could be dishonest, 'I'm prepared to give you a trial.' He coughed discreetly, 'Mondays, Wednesdays and Fridays, ten to one, and twenty pounds a week.'

I watched with horrid fascination as he swing his legs under his desk and his shins encountered my shopping basket.

'God strewth! What the hell . . .?' He stopped being refined.

'Oh dear, it's my shopping basket.'

He'd knocked it so far under the desk that I was obliged to get down on all fours to retrieve it.

He looked much less dignified with his legs in the air like a man whose wife has told him to shift because she wants to vacuum under his chair.

'I'm really terribly sorry,' I said, coming up with my Brie in one hand, clutching my headscarf which had fallen off in the skirmish with the other, then diving back to recover the lamb which had made a little pink puddle on his linoleum, and beating a hasty retreat before he had time to change his mind about employing me. He still had his legs in the air when I left him, plus a bewildered expression on his face.

Chapter Four

I popped into the corner shop when I got off the bus at Bagdad Corner.

Miss Nugent was serving two children with sweets, scruffy urchins in jeans and T-shirts. Funny how kids have changed, I thought, as the pair of them hung over the goodies like a couple of old men over a game of dominoes.

'You must make up your minds quickly,' said Miss Nugent sharply. 'Which do you want, the liquorice or the acid drops?'

'Naw,' said the little one, his nose guttering like a candle.

'What do you mean, gnaw?' Miss Nugent was fast losing her patience. 'Only rats and mice gnaw.'

'Naw, I don't want liquorice or acid drops,' the child wiped its nose on the sleeve of its anorak, 'I wanna walnut whip'.

'Well you can't have a walnut whip, can you? You've only got 2p.'

'He hasn't,' said the older boy indignantly, 'he's got fifty pence. Show her, Jason.'

'I do not wish to see his fifty pence.'

'He cannave a walnut whip, if he wants!'

'No, he can't because I haven't got any in stock.'

'Silly old trout,' said the lad. 'Come on, Jason.'

When they had clattered out of the shop, Miss Nugent sighed. 'Oh dear, I don't know what's the matter with me nowadays,' she said 'I get so irritable what with one thing and another. You don't know how I long for the old times when nice little children used to come in to spend their penny a week pocket money. But there I go again. Every time you show your face round the door I start grumbling.'

I grinned. 'Don't worry. I've come to cheer you up. I've got some good news for you.'

27

'Good news?' She sounded as if she'd forgotten there was such a thing.

'I've got a part-time job!'

Her face crinkled with pleasure. 'You *haven't*! Where?'

'At that posh antique shop in the square. You know, the one with the brass rail and green velvet curtain. Why, what's wrong?' My brain conjured up the ghastly possibilities. 'It isn't a porn shop, is it?'

'Oh no, it isn't a *pawn* shop. I mean to say he'd be obliged to hang out three brass balls if it were.'

'Huh?'

She fluttered her hands. 'It's that man – Waldorf Winninger. He – he,' she dropped her voice to a whisper, 'he's a bottom pincher!'

'Is he now? Thanks for warning me, but here's one bottom he won't pinch. I'll wear a tea-tray under my skirt on Monday morning.'

'You don't mean you're actually going?' She flopped onto the stool behind the counter.

'I haven't any option, I've already taken the job. But don't worry about me, I can take care of myself. Mr Winninger won't know if he's on his head or his heels if he tries pinching my bottom.'

She burst out laughing. 'That card goes in the window every other week without fail. No one ever stays longer than a few days. Perhaps you'll be the exception.'

'I doubt it. But even if it doesn't last long it will be psychologically good for me to get out into the hard world of commerce. Know what, Miss Nugent, I'm quite looking forward to my encounter with Waldorf Winninger.'

'I wish you'd stop calling me Miss Nugent,' she said. 'My name is Lizzie.'

We were laughing together when my next-door neighbour hurried past the shop. Hmmm, so she didn't fall at Becher's Brook after all, I thought unkindly, still thinking of her as a Grand National runner. Then I asked Lizzie who she was.

'Oh, that's Miss Cox. You haven't met her, then?' There was obviously no love lost between them.

'Let me put it this way, she didn't exactly rush round with a bunch of flowers and cups of hot sweet tea the day I arrived.

In fact she seems to have it in for me for some reason. Perhaps she doesn't like the cut of my jib.'

Lizzie looked guilty.

'You know why she has it in for me, don't you?' I said, 'come on, spill the beans.'

'I don't think I should tell you. It's all so – petty.'

'What, for heavens sake?'

'Sure you won't think me a gossip? I know I am at times, but not an unkind gossip, I hope. The fact is I can't stand Frances Cox, and what she said about living next door to a – a – made my blood boil.'

'Living next door to a – *what?*' My eyebrows shot up in alarm.

'Next door to a – divorced woman.'

'You're kidding. Is that all?' I breathed a sigh of relief.

'She's a pillar of the church, you see, and she's dead set against divorce,' Lizzie explained. 'But if you ask me she's just hopping mad because you've had a husband and she has never managed to catch one at all.'

'I see.'

'She thinks that divorced women are not quite – respectable.' Lizzie blushed. 'There, I've said quite enough.'

'What else did Miss Cox say about me?'

'She called you a "fancy pants" and said that you dye your hair.'

'Honestly?' I felt quite pleased about that because I had never dyed my hair in my life. My mother had kept the colour of her hair all her days, and I was obviously taking after her. As for being a fancy pants, I wondered if Miss Cox meant the baggy fawn trousers I was wearing when I sawed Amelia's clothes-line in half, or the saggy grey trews Darr had mistaken for the back end of a horsehair sofa. I tenderly massaged my behind at the memory.

Lizzie's face puckered. 'I shouldn't have told you. I hate this shop at times – all the gossip and the fiddle-faddle. I try not to become involved, but people use this place as a confessional . . .'

I knew what she meant. I'd gone through the same thing in hairdressing cubicles. What I didn't know about my clients' nearest and dearest wasn't worth knowing, not to mention their enemies. Apart from incarcerating one's self in an ivory tower and having one's food sent up in a bucket there seemed to be no answer to this gossip lark.

'. . . and I've been through the mill myself,' Lizzie continued. 'It stands to reason that if people gossip about one person they'll gossip about everyone. I went through hell over Leo.'

'Leo?'

Her eyes filled with tears. 'My young man. He was killed during the war – at Dunkirk – at least I suppose he was killed. He was posted as missing, but he never came back.'

'I'm sorry.'

'We weren't engaged, we just had an understanding, but Mother didn't like the idea of him so we had to meet in out of the way places. We were spotted, of course, and somebody', she hung on the word 'somebody', 'felt it her duty to tell my mother. Things might have been different if he had lived.'

The doorbell pinged and a customer came in. Lizzie at once assumed her prim shopkeeper role, but I had noticed how tender her voice was when she spoke about Leo. What a rotten shame she had never married him. She should have done it on the QT. That way people would have had something to gossip about.

Mrs Nugent's arms were like twigs, her hands like claws. She looked as brittle as a battle-honour in some ancient cathedral, and yet she clung tenaciously to life. Her old eyes snapped, crackled and popped like a well-known breakfast cereal as she peered up at me. I braced myself for the rude questions. Mrs Nugent was all mind and no matter.

'Humph, so you are Wilfred Appleby's daughter, are you?' she croaked.

Lizzie threw me a desperate look over the cucumber sandwiches. I did warn you, that look seemed to say.

The little sitting room behind the shop was pin-neat and spotless. A bright coal fire crackled in the hearth, Mrs Nugent's legs were covered with a hand-crocheted shawl and her feet rested on the steel fender. A kettle steamed on the hob, and the bay window was filled with flowering daffodils and hyacinths. The high mantelshelf contained among other things, a pair of Staffordshire dogs, two Spode plates and a Westminster chiming clock.

30

'And you are Mrs Nugent,' I said, ignoring her remark about my parentage and taking her withered hand in mine, 'I remember you well.'

'And I remember you. A podgy little thing you were, with your socks always hanging down. Your mother should have made you wear garters.'

'She did,' I said, 'but my legs turned blue, so I took them off.'

'Ha,' Mrs Nugent snorted, 'I remember you used to stare up at those tea-canisters as if you expected something to pop out of them. Always seemed to have your head in the clouds. Well you haven't changed much, you're still podgy.'

I shot an amused glance at Lizzie.

'You take after your father,' Mrs Nugent nodded. 'He was a big man if ever there was one.' She chuckled, and the sound was like dry leaves chasing before a November wind. 'But then he should have been big and healthy with all that pork to go at.'

'*Mother*,' Lizzie interrupted, acutely embarrassed. 'you're talking nonsense and you know it.'

'Hoity-toity! Remember who you're talking to, my girl! Don't you tell me I'm talking nonsense. I know what I know.'

'Why don't you have a cucumber sandwich?' Lizzie said in desperation.

'Don't want a cucumber sandwich,' Mrs Nugent grumbled. 'They rift up on me something shocking. Nasty slimy things. I can never keep the cucumber between the bread. It always ends up in my lap, and even if I got it as far as my mouth I couldn't chew it with these teeth. Isn't there any cake? I like cake. I want a piece of chocolate cake.'

I handed her a slice covered with hundreds and thousands. 'There you are,' I said, 'get that down you.'

The old woman cracked out laughing. 'I like you,' she said. 'Everyone else treats me like an imbecile. "My, doesn't that cake look lovely," they say, "my word you will enjoy it." Make me sick and tired, they do. But you said, "get it down you". You're a girl after my own heart. I like people who get down to the essentials.'

'Then perhaps we'd better get down to one more essential,' I laughed, tucking the serviette under her chin. 'I'm not Farmer Appleby's daughter. But you never really thought that anyway did you?'

'Don't mind me,' she chuckled, biting into the chocolate

cake, 'life gets tedious at my age. Got to put the cat among the pigeons now and then or nobody would take any notice of me. Do you know what I do? I hide my false teeth in the bedclothes to make Lizzie think I've swallowed 'em.'

She fixed her sharp beady glance on her daughter. 'Well, stop goggling, Lizzie. Where are your manners? Pour me a cup of tea to wash this cake down. You know dry cake sticks in my gullet.'

Lizzie's face was a study as she obeyed her autocratic parent, but I noticed that her shoulders were shaking with laughter.

We nibbled the cucumber sandwiches while Mrs Nugent crumbled her chocolate cake and managed to drop half of it on her shawl. When she'd finished and her daughter had wiped the crumbs from her lips, she sighed. 'Don't know that I want to go on living much longer. Life's no fun when you get to my age. My advice to you, Miss, is not to hang about after you're seventy-five.'

'I'll try not to,' I promised.

'As soon as they start sending for doctors and parsons, that's the time to be off. Especially parsons. I should've gone when my fingers got too stiff to fold the currant bags.'

She stared into the fire. 'It's not so bad until your old friends begin to pop off. Now there's only Rebecca left.'

Her old head began to nod. 'I miss Amelia,' she said. 'We had many a good crack together. Humph! I daresay she would have taken Wilfred Appleby if he'd asked her. He didn't, though. He took up with that lass from the dairy. Her name was Agnes, but we called her Mary. "Mary from the Dairy". A soft thing she was. Hadn't the sense God gave her. Ha, I remember the day she left the dairy door wide open and old Billy Grimble's sheep wandered in. They knocked all the churns for six, and there was Mary trying to get the milk up with a shovel.'

Mrs Nugent chuckled. 'She kept the door tight shut after that, I can tell you. But do you know what she said to me? She said, "Now I'm very wary since I've had sheep in my dairy". And I said to her, "You're a poet and don't know it."'

Lizzie and I exchanged glances.

'Well, that's it for today,' she said quietly. 'Mother's been up since one o'clock, now it's back to bed for her.'

32

She glanced compassionately at the old woman. 'Do you suppose, Sally . . .?'

'Do I suppose what?'

'That there are corner shops in heaven?'

'Well, yes. I suppose there must be. Where else would they buy their Ambrosia?'

It was a fatuous remark, but it made Lizzie laugh, and what I intended, at that moment, was to make Lizzie laugh.

Chapter Five

I edged into Mr Waldorf Winninger's shop crabwise on Monday morning. This time I was wearing my ultra refined get up – a beige two-piece with a white blouse, and a pair of high-heeled shoes that were killing me. I had brushed my riotous fair hair into an upstanding quiff, and had left off my lipstick as a repellent to bottom pinching. All considered, my employer might derive more satisfaction from pinching a draylon-covered Victorian sofa than me. I looked the acme of respectability, furthermore I was wearing my thermal underwear.

'Oh,' he said, when he saw me, 'there you are.'

I couldn't deny it, I was there right enough.

Somehow I hadn't figured the dapper Mr Winninger as one of the bottom-pinching fraternity. It was on the cards that he might pinch the odd widow's mite, given the opportunity, but perhaps I was wrong – I was so often wrong.

He seemed a cold fish to me, creaking round in his knife-edged trousers and stroking his beard as if he was afraid he might lose it. Well, why not? After all, he'd lost his moustache.

'You'd better put your things in the office,' he said in a reproving tone of voice, and I knew he was thinking about that puddle on his linoleum.

When I'd hung my coat in the cubbyhole behind the Welsh dresser, and wondered what he'd do for an office if anyone bought the dresser, he bustled up to me and began reeling off my duties in a voice as dry as original manuscript vellum.

'You must dust and polish all the furniture thoroughly,' he said, 'and keep your eyes skinned at all times. You wouldn't believe how many carriage clocks I've lost over the past six months. If you notice anyone hovering over them, you must hover just behind them. I will not have people meddling with my carriage clocks.'

'Yes, Mr Winninger.' I fixed my face in a suitably intelligent expression and imagined myself floating on light silent wings over his carriage clock thieving customers. And what on earth should I do if I caught one of them in the act – give them a good ticking off?

'Coffee's at eleven,' he continued.

'The hillside's dew-pearled. Lunchtime then hometime, all's right with the world', I thought. Somehow I wished it was going hometime already, and I hadn't even started polishing yet.

'It's your job to make the coffee,' he said. 'I take mine black, without sugar.'

That figured. A couple of spoonfuls of sugar and he wouldn't be able to sit down in his trousers. Personally I'd always considered that drinking black coffee without sugar was so unsatisfactory like talking to oneself. Why didn't he just drink a cup of hot water and have done with it?

'The kettle and cups are in the office,' he went on. That figured too. They would scarcely be standing on his serpentine-fronted sideboard in full view of his carriage clock thieving customers.

I wondered, *en passant*, if I should offer all clients, enterprising enough to make off with a timepiece, a cup of black coffee without sugar on their way to the police station, as a sort of taste of what they were in for at Wormwood Scrubs.

He handed me a couple of dusters and a tin of polish, then creaked away to the office, stroking his bare top lip. I applied myself and a layer of sticky white polish to the serpentine-fronted sideboard without further delay.

Might as well make a good job of it, I thought, lathering on the polish. The trouble was, I couldn't get it off. I rubbed away at it until I was obliged to remove the jacket of my beige suit, and it seemed likely that the blouse would follow in due course. Swiping at nettles with my Father Time scythe was nothing compared to this. My quiff dropped into a straight fringe as perspiration began to trickle down my forehead.

'How are you getting on?'

'Oh fine,' I said in a strangled voice.

'Remember,' he craned his neck to see behind me, 'just the merest trace of polish.'

35

Now he tells me, I thought.

The door opened and a couple of County-looking folk in sheepskin jackets appeared, wanting to look at Waldorf's longcase clocks. I watched, fascinated, as he opened the doors and showed them the internal workings. I had no idea that grandfather clocks contained all those ropes and pulleys and bits of chain and dangling pine-cones. Winding them up would be rather like milking a cow.

Another couple entered and made a beeline for the carriage clocks. Right, Sally, I thought, forward hover!

I had them mentally manacled and on their way to jail before they'd had time to examine the wretched things. I fairly clung to the man's coat sleeve and almost smacked his fingers in my fervent desire to keep him from pinching one of them. They must have figured me for some kind of carriage clock nut as they mumbled something about them being too pricey anyway, and fled to the safety of the street.

Waldorf glared at me, then his eyes fell on the sideboard I'd been polishing. His hair appeared to lift a quarter of an inch from his scalp before it settled back into place, but he was too busy dealing with the sheepskin jackets to give me a ticking off just then. Ah well, it was only a matter of time.

I began polishing again as if my life depended on it, and haa'ed when he wasn't looking. I'd often haa-ed on my own furniture when I hadn't any polish, and it had worked far better than this clarty white stuff in a tin. I began to sing, 'The Voice that Breathed O'er Eden' under my breath.

Sheepskin jackets were now arguing about which bank card to use to pay for their grandfather clock, and whether or not it would fit into their hall. Female sheepskin, with straight blonde hair, wearing boots, didn't think it would. Male sheepskin said they'd better go home and measure. Why, I wondered, did boots look all right on every other woman except me?

Waldorf fixed me with his gimlet eyes and mouthed the word 'coffee' as they got into a refined row about whom should have measured what. I suspected that is was all a ploy, that they didn't want the clock anyway but they daren't say so.

Male sheepskin said testily, 'Well you wanted the bloody thing in the first place, darling.'

Wanted, I thought, looking round the office for the plug.

Past tense. Bet they'll say they'll go home and measure up first and come back another day. And that tetchy 'darling' of his was tantamount to a swear word. Hugo had always called me 'darling' in that same patronising way, when he was really angry with me.

I was scrambling around on my hands and knees, trying to find the plug for the kettle, when the doorbell pinged. That'll be them going out, I thought.

The next thing I knew, Waldorf's naked top lip was two inches from my ear. 'Boo!' he bellowed into it.

I came up smartly, banging my head on his desk lid.

'What the hell do you think you're playing at?' I demanded as I scrambled to my feet.

'So you heard that, did you?' he snarled, 'But where were you when the bell pinged?'

His question smacked to me of that old party game, where was Moses when the light went out?

'For all you knew, a crowd of people might have surged into the shop when that bell pinged. Thieves, Muggers!'

'All I can say to that, Mr Winninger,' I said with dignity 'is that any silly mugger who walks into this shop deserves all he gets! And don't you dare boo in my ear again! You scared the living daylights out of me!'

'Come now, Mrs Shelton,' he said suavely, 'I was merely demonstrating that one cannot be too careful.'

'So it would appear!' I felt like a hen with its feathers growing the wrong way. Ruffled, to put it mildly. 'Now do you want your coffee or not?'

We eyed each other belligerently over coffee-flavoured cups of hot water.

'I have to go out for an hour or so,' he said eventually. 'I have an appointment.'

'Very well, Mr Winninger, I shan't run off with the till, if that's what is worrying you.'

I felt like a limp rag as I watched him go. My head was still smarting from the blow it had suffered when it met his desk lid. There was something about Mr Waldorf Winninger that made my flesh creep. Even so I wanted to do something to impress him, like selling a longcase clock or a Noritake bowl, or even that wretched serpentine-fronted sideboard that looked as if it had been coated with white candy-floss.

37

My arms were fairly dropping off at the roots with polishing when a charming old lady appeared wanting to look at bureaux.

'I just love this one,' she said, 'but I wouldn't want one without a secret drawer. Has this one got a secret drawer?'

'Well, I'm not quite sure. I mean to say, that's the thing about secret drawers, isn't it? You never know whether you've got one or not until you touch a hidden spring.' I gave her an engaging smile.

'How much is it?'

I fiddled around for the price-tag. 'Seven hundred and fifty pounds.'

'How old is it?'

'Positively ancient,' I said.

'Then it must have a secret drawer, mayn't it?' She stroked the Pekinese dog under her arm. 'Would you be awfully clever and find it for me?'

For seven hundred and fifty pounds I was prepared to find the Kohinoor Diamond.

'There! That loose panel! I'm sure that's it,' she said quickly. 'Oh, how exciting! Do pull just a little harder!'

The loose panel came off in my hands.

'Oh, what a pity,' she sighed. 'I did so want a bureau with a secret drawer. I like to hide my gas bills, you see.'

'Your – gas bills?'

'And my electricity bills! Hiding one's bills is so much fun, isn't it?' She brightened a little. 'Never mind, you might have a bureau with a secret drawer in stock next week. I'll call again, my dear. Mr Waldorf knows me quite well. I pop in four of five times a week, you see. He gets quite short with me at times, but it has been so nice to meet an obliging lady like you. Well, bye-bye for now. Say good-bye to the nice lady, Ming.'

I spent the next ten minutes looking round the office for a tube of Evostick.

The next customer was a man who marched into the shop, cast an experienced eye over a set of copper jelly moulds and two Leeds pottery plates on a crummy-looking fitment, asked, 'How much?' presented a tradecard, and demanded discount.

'I'm very sorry,' I said, 'but I have no power to . . .'

'You're new here, aren't you?'

'Yes,' I admitted.

'Wally's gone out, has he?'

'Yes, but . . .'

'Don't worry!' He gave me the benefit of a hundred-watt smile, unhooked his sunglasses and brought out his wallet. 'He knows me! You have my card. Can't wait. Tell you what.'

'What?' I asked suspiciously.

'I'll give you the marked price for the jelly-moulds and the plates. Just you throw in the shelves and we'll make a deal, eh?'

'Well, I'm not sure . . .'

He began counting fivers into my hand. 'Seventy, seventy-five, eighty, eighty-five. Now what do you say?'

'I'm still not sure.' I counted up on my fingers.

'Not good enough, eh? Right, eighty-five, ninety, ninety-five, one hundred.'

'All right. Fair enough!' Tickled pink because I'd got fifteen pounds over the odds for the crummy shelves, I began flustering to find paper to wrap up his purchases.

'Don't bother wrapping them up,' he said briskly, 'I have my car outside. Got to get going! Nice to have done business with you. Here, let me unhook those shelves for you.'

What a nice man, I thought, as he revved up his Mercedes and disappeared like a bat out of hell.

I was happily polishing the serpentine-fronted sideboard when Waldorf Winninger reappeared.

'Anything happened?' he inquired.

I faced him confidently. 'Yes, Mr Winninger. As a matter of fact I've taken a hundred pounds!'

'You've done *what*?'

I noticed that he'd had his hair cut and his beard trimmed. His eyes flicked round the shop. 'What the hell have you done with my Georgian hanging-shelves?' he snapped.

'That's what I was going to tell you. Here's the man's card.'

He studied it briefly, then went up in smoke. 'You mean to say that you let that shark have my Georgian hanging- shelves for fifteen quid? You – you – *imbecile*!'

I figured, on my way home, that that was probably the dearest haircut Waldorf Winninger would ever have, and I wouldn't be going back to work there again.

Lunchtime, then homeward, all's right with the world! Well at least I hadn't had my bottom pinched.

Chapter Six

Lizzie called to me excitedly as I passed the shop. 'Well, how did it go?'

'Very quickly,' I said, 'In fact it's gone for good.'

'What has?'

'The job. I got the bullet!'

'Come in and tell me about it.' She put the Closed sign in position. 'Let me make you a cup of tea, you look all in.'

'No, thanks. You have quite enough to do as it is.'

'He didn't . . .?'

'Pinch my bottom? No. He gave me the sack because I sold a set of Georgian shelves for fifteen pounds,' I said mournfully. 'Not only that, I made a mess of his serpentine-fronted sideboard, and found a secret drawer in a bureau where there wasn't supposed to be one . . .'

Lizzie's face puckered, her shoulders began to shake.

Suddenly I saw the funny side of things myself and I burst out laughing too.

'You should have seen his face when I asked for my wages,' I gasped. 'He said I was lucky he hadn't sent for the police: that I owed *him* money. He was dancing up and down with rage when I left him.'

I mopped my streaming eyes, 'Well how was I to know those worm-eaten old shelves were worth a bomb? He should have told me.'

'Serves him right,' Lizzie gurgled. 'No wonder he can't keep a shop assistant.'

'I wouldn't care, but he'd only been out for a haircut.'

'You should never have gone there in the first place. I knew it wouldn't work out right.'

'I know, but I really needed that job. Now I'll have to

/9j/4AA

40

find another, and jobs are not all that easily come by these days.'

'Hmmm. Well I know of one that's going, but that wouldn't be your cup of tea either.'

'I don't know what is my cup of tea any longer. Tell me what is the job?'

'Well, Mrs Billy Watson's daughter came in the shop this morning. Her mother broke her legs some time ago . . .'

'What, both of them? Good grief.'

'Yes, unfortunate isn't it? The point is the proprietress of the Red Lion Hotel where she works, is desperate for a temporary dog'sbody until Mrs Billy's legs get better.'

'The Red Lion? You mean that hotel in the town square? The one with the archway and the cobbles?'

'Yes, that's the place. But honestly, Sally, the job wouldn't suit you at all. You're not the dog's body type.'

'My dear Lizzie, what I need right now is to earn an honest penny. Anyway what makes you think I'm not the dog'sbody type? I've been one all my life. What's the name of the proprietress? I'll ring her as soon as I get home.'

Lizzie started to flutter. 'Her name is Mrs Amor, but I'm not at all sure . . .'

I giggled. 'I just hope she doesn't ask for references from my previous employer.'

'Mrs Amor?'

Amelia's telephone was one of those old black models with a twisted flex, the kind that knotted itself into short sheepshanks during every conversation.

'Yes?' Mrs Amor sounded snappish.

'I understand that you are in need of help.'

'Who the hell is this? The Samaritans?'

That took the oil out of my diesel engine for a start. 'No. My name is Sally Shelton, and Mrs Billy Watson-with-the-bad-leg's daughter told a friend of mine that you need a dog's-body.'

The line began to crackle, the flex to knot up, and I wished I had never made the call in the first place. Perhaps I'd better start peddling pies after all. 'I'm sorry to have bothered you,' I said.

'Hang on a minute.' I heard a throaty chuckle at the other

end of the line. 'Sorry I bit your head off. The truth is, I'm fraught and getting fraughter by the minute. You're ringing about the general assistant's job, are you?'

'Well, yes.' General assistant sounded better than dog's-body, I reasoned.

'When can you start?' Mrs Amor said. 'What about tomorrow morning at eight?'

'I suppose I could start then,' I said doubtfully, 'but isn't that a bit sudden? What I mean is shouldn't we meet to discuss it first?' I wasn't sure that I liked the idea of working for someone I'd never even met.

'You're right. Call and see me tomorrow about nine thirty. 'Bye.'

I didn't like the sound of her at all.

The man who received me was in his middle thirties, fair-haired, with fingernails bitten down to the quicks. He walked with his head thrust forward as if he was about to break into a run. His name was Gabriel, he told me, and he was officially the barman. I longed to ask him what he was unofficially but decided I'd better not.

I learned later that he very often did break into a run when dire emergencies were imminent at the Red Lion, and that dire emergencies occurred there at least twenty times a day. No wonder he had no quicks left to speak of.

'Mrs Amor will see you in her private apartment,' he said, rushing me at breakneck speed under the archway and through a cobbled yard full of beer barrels and budding aubrietia in ornamental wheelbarrows. 'Mind that bottom step as you go up, and the third from the top is a bit wonky too.'

'Thanks for telling me.' I was facing a flight of sagging stone steps leading to what looked like a hayloft.

'Give the door a good thump,' Gabriel advised, 'or she won't hear you. No use ringing the bell, it's bust.'

'Oh, I see.'

'And don't lean on that iron rail,' he warned me, 'it wants seeing to.' He hurried away through a side door leading into the hotel.

I had the feeling that I needed seeing to as well as I picked my way up the steps to a nail-studded door which looked like something out of one of those filibustering Burt Lancaster films of the 1940s, and banged on it with my fist.

'Come in,' said the tart voice I recognised from our telephone conversation. 'Sit down. I shan't be a minute, I'm in the bath!'

Mrs Amor's apartment looked as if hurricane Freda had hit it. She'd told me to sit down, but there wasn't anywhere I could sit without a major clearing up operation. Newspapers and magazines were scattered everywhere. The long settee in front of the empty fireplace was littered with books and bills. Ashtrays were full of stubbed out cigarettes. The mantelpiece was crowded with photographs set at odd angles, the lamp-shades were all lopsided with bobble fringes like soft green grapes, even the curtains weren't hanging straight, and the pot-plants in the hearth were drooping for a good drink of water.

Ancient oak beams arched to an infinity of cobwebs, and yet the room possessed a musty kind of charm and homeliness, and sunlight streamed through the windows lighting up pieces of dusty antique furniture that Waldorf Winninger would have given his eye-teeth to possess: a pretty escritoire, a canterbury, a Queen Anne chair, and a Victorian screen pasted with cut-outs of the Death of Nelson and Bonny Mary of Argyll, amongst others, which had a depressing effect on me.

I was studying the screen intently when a door opened and a wide-eyed woman wearing a white bath robe confronted me. 'So you are Mrs Sam, are you?' she said.

'Mrs – Sam?' I asked cagily.

'Well, yes. The Samaritan woman! The one who is going to help me out of a jam! Have a gin and tonic! Now, start asking questions. That's why you came, isn't it, to ask questions?'

She reminded me of Bette Davis in '*The Letter*', as she jerked across to the drinks cabinet, running her fingers through her wet cropped hair. 'Well, what do you want to know?'

I swallowed hard.

'What's the matter?' she demanded, shoving a drink into my hand. 'You wanted to discuss things, so hadn't you better start discussing?' She stared at me with her dark, frantic-looking eyes. 'Have you got a black dress? A black jumper and skirt would do. All dog'sbodies wear black jumpers and skirts – and black stockings. You have rather fat legs so you shouldn't mind that too much. Black's slimming! Cheers!'

I stood open mouthed, clutching my gin and tonic. What a pity, I thought, that Vivien Leigh landed the part of Scarlett O'Hara in *Gone With the Wind*. This woman would have been a cinch for it thirty years ago.

'So you want to be my general assistant, do you?' she said dramatically.

'Not particularly,' I replied, a trifle tartly. 'I simply need to earn some money.'

'Come to work here and you'll earn every penny,' she said. 'I'm surrounded by incompetent fools.'

I couldn't help it. 'Hire me,' I replied, 'and you'll be surrounded by one more.'

She stared at me, round eyed, then burst out laughing. 'I quite like you,' she said. 'You have a sense of humour, and God knows you'll need it. But I don't quite understand. You're not the dog'sbody type at all, and I should know. I've hired six of them in as many months, all of them were as dim as Naafi candles, but you're different. Why the hell do you want to be a general assistant, here of all places?'

'I thought I'd explained that,' I said, 'I need to earn some money.'

'It's only temporary, you know.' She frowned. 'When that wretched Mrs Billy Watson comes back, you'll be out of a job again.'

'Yes, I realise that.'

She shrugged. 'OK. Fine. Report for duty at eight o'clock tomorrow morning, but you won't stick it if I'm any judge. Have another drink?'

'No, I won't if you don't mind.' I wasn't used to drinking gin and tonic first thing in the morning and my head felt as if it was stuffed with feathers, but there was something about Mrs Amor I couldn't resist.

I found myself outside the nail-studded door not knowing what had hit me. Hiccuping, I almost did a nose dive down the stone steps as I leaned too heavily on the iron railing.

I stood for a minute or two under the wide archway before venturing out into the sqaure thinking how dreadful it would be if I were arrested for being drunk and disorderly at ten fifteen in the morning.

Chapter Seven

The Red Lion, I thought, had been designed to cause as much work and inconvenience as possible. The dining room was upstairs, and the still room was two steps down along a meandering passage.

Many a hot dinner, I imagined, must have landed on the carpet outside the dining-room door if the hapless waitress was unfortunate enough to catch her toe on the top step going up, and many an empty plate must have smashed to smithereens if she had been luckless enough to catch her heel in the frayed carpet going down.

There were two bars, a fancy cocktail lounge with plush seats and copper ornaments adjoining a snug where the locals played dominoes. These were on the ground floor where one might reasonably expect to find them.

The snug was known as 'Dirty Dick's Parlour' which seemed a good excuse not to get rid of the cobwebs. The kitchen was on the ground floor too, and connected to the upstairs still room by a dumb waiter – a sinister shaft with thick hairy ropes – down which one shouted orders to the cook, and occasionally had surprising things shouted back at one, the most common being, 'Bloody hell, give us a chance, can't you?'

The first time I stuck my head into the aperture and gazed down its murky depths, my startled gaze met what appeared to be stalactites of blood and guts hanging from the sides.

Possibly, I thought, someone had murdered a cook after an unsatisfactory luncheon, had chucked her body down the shaft, and left her bits and pieces dangling there as a grim warning to others.

Cook was called Marguerite Burns, a prophetic name in her

case, a daisy of a woman, one that Amelia would have dubbed 'too slow to go last'. She plodded heavily round the kitchen wearing fur-trimmed boots and a white overall which hung down over the top of them. Her face was as pasty as an underboiled suet pudding, and her hair was the colour of marmalade sauce.

I discovered later that she had six children under ten and that, I figured, was enough to slow anyone down.

Her running mate in the kitchen was a wiry little body called Polly Flounders whose job it was 'ter foller' Marguerite, mop up the messes she made, rush any burnt offerings out to the dustbin before Mrs Amor saw them, make sure that the chicken portions were thawed out in time for lunch, peel potatoes when the frozen chips ran out – which they did with monotonous regularity, and remove traces of mould from the tops of the trifles.

'You needn't look so pleased with yourself,' she told me severely on my first morning. 'You'll have awl this to see to on my days awf. An' mop the floor, an' mek the sangwidges for the suppers, an' a thousand an' one other jobs into the bargain, so just keep your eyes open.' She sniffed disapprovingly. 'I'll be glad when Mrs Billy Watson's legs gets better, so I will. How are her legs getting on anyway?'

I admitted that I had never seen Mrs Billy Watson's legs in my life.

Daisy Burns didn't come to work on Sundays because her husband turned nasty if she had to work on his day off. That's when Mrs Amor took over in the kitchen and saw to the Sunday lunches. Daisy did the grills and the Chicken Maryland, which consisted of fried chicken and chips with tinned sweetcorn and slices of banana.

There were phantoms, what Polly called 'shift-relievers', who drifted into the kitchen when we went off duty, but I never got to know any of them. They simply appeared, like zombies, with their sandals in plastic bags, and promptly disappeared into the staff toilet to comb their hair and put on fresh lipstick.

'Those dozy ducks should mek the supper sangwidges by right!' Polly complained, 'but like as not they'd forget to put the meat in 'em!'

I had to admit that Mrs Amor put the rest of us to shame.

Possessed of a restless burning energy, she would be shouting up the dumb waiter one minute and standing beside one looking down it the next. The minute after that she would be serving drinks in the cocktail lounge, and the minute after the minute after she would be playing dominoes in Dirty Dick's Parlour.

But the anchor-man was 'The Archangel Gabriel' – the loping barman who had obviously figured out that walking bent double would increase his wind resistance. That way he could lope all the faster to the butcher's when we ran out of chops, to the baker's when we ran out of sliced bread, and to the supermarket when we ran out of everything else. He told me with modest pride, that he had once run the four-minute mile in three minutes 59 seconds, that time he dashed down to the White Horse on the seafront to borrow a jar of French mustard.

The menus fascinated me. Printed on thick white card emblazoned with a Red Lion rampant on what looked like a field of bangers and mash, they lulled expectant diners into a false sense of security, and whetted their appetites for such delicacies as mock turtle soup with sherry, prawn cocktail, egg mayonnaise, and smoked salmon for starters, with iced gâteau and peach melba for afters.

The trouble was we didn't have any mock turtle soup, prawns or smoked salmon, and the iced gâteau was a myth in the mind of Mrs Amor, who worked on the principle that if you put enough sherry into oxtail soup and dolloped a good scoop of ice cream on to a slice of Swiss roll, nobody would know the difference, and wouldn't care all that much anyway.

She was, on the other hand, almost fanatical about her cheeseboard – a wooden trolley with a domed plastic lid, under which reposed a choice selection of smellies, which had to be taken out, exorcised, the jagged edges trimmed off, and the remains embellished with fresh lettuce every morning.

I felt like a prison wardress in my black get-up when I marched up to the still room on my first morning, and began rolling butter – which promptly unrolled and went limp the minute I'd done it.

Gabriel, who was keeping an eye on me, stared doubtfully at the mess I was making. 'You're supposed to plop 'em into cold water,' he said at last. 'And don't dig down so deep with the curler. Haven't you ever rolled butter before?' – which seemed a superfluous question in the circumstances.

He loped onto the landing to read the newspaper requirements of the guests chalked up on a blackboard, and lolloped off to the shop round the corner, muttering 'Two *Times*, one *Guardian*, four *Daily Mirrors*, and three *Suns*.'

A few minutes later he reappeared with one *Times*, two *Guardians*, five *Daily Mirrors* and sporting a pink *Financial Times*.

I wondered, as I gouged into a second half pound of butter, why he hadn't just taken the blackboard round to the newsagents with him. His forehead was creased into so many furrows that he could easily have screwed his hat on. Poor Gabriel, he was ageing prematurely. Then it was my turn to go out on the landing and scrutinise the blackboard for the guests' morning tea requirements, and I started ageing prematurely too.

It was my job, Gabriel told me, to set the trays, make the tea, rattle upstairs with it, knock on doors, wait a few seconds to give folk time to get their false teeth in, then waltz it into them.

'Do I have to open the curtains and give them a weather forecast as well?' I inquired anxiously.

'No, just stick it on the bedside table,' he said, vainly trying to sort out the morning papers, 'and watch out for that chap in Number Five.'

'Why? What's the matter with him?'

'He's got a red beard,' said Gabriel.

'Is that – bad?' I murmured faintly.

'And one earring,' Gabriel supplied, adding to my distress.

'I – I suppose you wouldn't care to . . .'

'No fear!' Gabriel shook his head emphatically. 'He called me "dear" when I showed him up to his room last night.'

I wondered what he would call me when he saw me, as I plodded heavily upstairs carrying his tea-tray, knocked and waited, my heart thumping like a sledge hammer.

'Come.'

I came with a rush, caught my toe on the edge of the carpet, and tipped the tray and its contents over the red-bearded man, naked to the waist, who was sitting up in bed as expectantly as a bride on her wedding night.

'Christ almighty! What the hell . . .'

That was enough for me. I fled downstairs to the still room and stood panting with my back to the door.

Gabriel gave me a worried look. 'That didn't take long. Did you give him his tea?'

'Y-yes, in a manner of speaking.'

'What did he say?'

'I'd rather not repeat it, if you don't mind.'

Any minute now, I thought, he'll poke his soaking wet beard round this door and demand to speak to the management. But he didn't. He simply disappeared, gold earring and all, without paying his bill.

It was the talk of the hotel, of course. Polly Flounders waxed indignantly when she went up to change his bed.

'Soaked through, it was,' she cried scornfully, 'an' him a grown man! Well, I mean to say!'

It's all in the life of a dog'sbody, I thought as I climbed wearily from the bus and made my way down the lane towards April Cottage after that first traumatic morning at the Red Lion. I knew I'd have to confess the truth to Mrs Amor sooner or later, and stump up what the red-bearded bloke owed her for his overnight stay out of my own money. Perhaps I'd soon be picking oakum, or whatever women did in prison.

I was lying supine on my sprawly settee when a knock came to the door. That'll be the police, I thought, lifting my throbbing head, come to arrest me for assault and battery. But it wasn't. It was the vicar of Tootington, a mild little man with greying hair and a nervous tic under his right eye.

'Mrs Shelton?' he murmured, somewhat overcome by my appearance – ruffled hair, unrelieved black garments, and red carpet slippers. 'My name is Arthur Abercromby. I – that is – you telephoned me about a piano.'

'Oh, Mr Abercromby! You don't know how relieved I am to see you. I thought you might be the police!'

'The – police?' he blinked nervously. 'Why? Have you committed some kind of felony?'

'That's just it. I'm not quite sure. You see, he left without paying his bill, and it was all my fault because I tipped the tea-tray over him. But I didn't say it was my fault at the time because I was afraid of getting the sack on my first morning, and I'd already had the sack on my first morning, just the

49

other day when I let a shark have a set of hanging shelves for fifteen pounds. I simply felt that someone might put two and two together and come up with the wrong answer. Do you see what I mean?'

'Not entirely.' He blinked unhappily, 'I simply called about your piano.'

'My piano?' I pulled myself together with an effort. 'Oh, you mean Miss Beatty's piano? Yes, of course, it's in the greenhouse. I mean the loggia. Do come and look at it. I'll be happy to give it to you if you really want it.'

'But I thought you said that it was Miss Beatty's piano. Forgive me, but have you her permission to – er – give it away?'

We stared at each other uncertainly. Mr Abercromby eased his clerical collar as if it was about to choke him. 'You must forgive me,' he said, 'if I seem a little – inadequate. The fact is, I've never been a vicar before. This is my first parish.'

'And I'm not helping much, am I? I'm terribly sorry, I was half asleep when you knocked,' I said apologetically, 'the truth is, I've had a terrible morning, and my head is spinning. Perhaps I watch too many television serials, but you see, I tipped a tray of tea over a man in bed and he left without paying his bill . . .'

The vicar raised his eyebrows. 'It's quite all right, Mrs Shelton,' he said faintly. 'You don't look like a felon to me.'

'I thought that the long arm of the law might be round to arrest me for assault and battery,' I sighed, 'though spilling the tea over that man wasn't really my fault, I tripped over the edge of the carpet and the tray simply sailed through the air. And in case you're worried about the piano, it *is* mine to give away. Not that I want to part with it, for Miss Beatty's sake. But I am rather inundated with furniture at the moment as you can see, and I can't play the piano anyway.'

The vicar looked slightly more relaxed as he perched on the edge of the settee although the nerve under his right eye continued to twitch occasionally, and he seemed poised for flight. I longed to ask him what he did before he became the Vicar of Tootington, but felt that he might think me a busybody if I did. The poor man, I thought, must have plenty of those to deal with without me.

'The piano's in the – er greenhouse – at the moment,' I

50

said. 'Perhaps you'd like to look at it before I make you a cup of tea.'

'It's a splendid instrument,' said Mr Abercromby admiringly when he saw it, 'in tip-top condition. Rather too good for the village hall. Are you sure you wouldn't rather sell it privately?'

I ran my fingers over the shining wood, thinking how many hours of loving work had gone into producing that deep patina, and how many tins of Brasso it must have taken to make the candle-holders glint so.

'No, Mr Abercromby,' I said softly, 'I wouldn't sell it for the world, but I'll gladly give it to you if you want it. You see, Amelia Beatty loved this village, and I know she'd want you to have her piano.' Then, as my eyes encountered the velvet-covered music stool, I smiled and added, 'But I won't part with her piano-stool and its contents if you don't mind. I couldn't bear to part with "The Red Shadow".'

The vicar smiled. He really was a very nice man, I thought, feeling a sudden kinship with him. He was having a tough time too apparently. The difference between us lay in the fact that the only person I had to worry about was myself, while he, poor soul, was responsible for the welfare of an entire community.

The bane of my life at the Red Lion was that someone would ask for boiled eggs for breakfast, because we hadn't got any egg-cups.

When I mentioned this to Mrs Amor she shrugged it off with, 'My dear Mrs Sam, nobody ever asks for boiled eggs'.

The day somebody did, I served them in the lids of hot-water jugs, and prayed to goodness that they wouldn't topple over before they'd dug their spoons into them. They did of course, and I had to scrape the yolks off the tablecloth.

Holidaymakers, I discovered, like to wander down to breakfast two seconds before the dining room closed and then pore over the menu. Most of the men wanted bacon and egg with sausages and fried bread, whilst their diet-conscious wives preferred poached or scrambled eggs and black coffee.

When they'd made up their minds, it was my duty to stick my head down the dumb-waiter and holler to Daisy such cryptic messages as 'three fulls, two floaters and a couple of how's your fathers'.

51

Apart from that I was ever conscious of the need to keep my head as far away as possible from the red and yellow stalactites dangling down the shaft.

It was all very confusing, especially when the floaters appeared before the fulls, and I had to squeeze the whey from the how's your fathers, and Daisy kept shouting, 'have you told 'em what bloody time it is? It's all right for them, but I have my living to earn.'

Every Monday at one o'clock, the Red Lion was invaded by a jolly upstanding bunch of middle-aged Carnelian Bay businessmen – bank managers, butchers, bakers and candlestick makers – all of them florid and overweight, suave and immaculate in grey suits, blazers or sports jackets, possessing a certain air of having plenty of money in the bank. In short, Rotarians.

When they appeared, Bette Davis Amor blossomed like Scarlett O'Hara beneath the cottonwoods of Tara.

It was a set menu; tomato soup, roast, apple tart and custard, and Monday mornings were taken up with shoving the dining-room tables together and covering them with long white cloths. Gabriel did most of the ho-ing, whilst I did the heaving, then Mrs Amor would appear and say, things like, 'Hang on, you haven't got that cloth on straight,' or 'You'll have to move the president's table further away from the fireplace. He'll hit his head on the mantelpiece when he stands up if you don't.'

Meanwhile, Gabriel kept nipping down to the kitchen to see what they'd run short of, and I'd watch him from the window overlooking the archway, running like a deer to the shops. He'd be a cinch, I thought, as a British entrant in the next Olympic games. No one would ever catch him in the final leg of a sprint relay.

While Gabriel was dashing hither and thither, Mrs Amor would rush downstairs to baste the joint, turn the roast potatoes, and rescue the apple tarts before Polly Flounders had time to whip them out to the dustbin.

On my second Monday, I had just finished polishing the cruets and plonking breadrolls on the side plates, when I realised that we were six short, and hurried into the kitchen to find a first-class row brewing. Mrs Amor, her eyelids weighed down with blue eyeshadow was having a go at Daisy for leaving the apple tarts in the oven too long, while Polly was scraping away diligently at the burnt bits.

'I wouldn't care,' said Mrs Amor dramatically, ' if I had asked you to do anything more than to see to things whilst I was changing my dress. That and make the tomato soup and the custard! It isn't as if you had any grills to see to on Mondays, Mrs Burns! Oh *do* stop flopping around in those blasted boots of yours! After all, it *is* May! Why don't you give your feet a treat and put them into sandals?'

I backed out of the kitchen and flew back upstairs to the still room before anyone caught sight of me. Daisy and Polly had never forgiven me for taking Mrs Billy Watson-with-the-bad-legs' place, and obviously considered me an unsuitable stand-in for her. They'd probably have gone on strike if I had told them that the milk was about to boil over.

At one o'clock, when the Rotarians were seated in the dining room, I hovered anxiously over the lift-shaft as a brimming tureen of tomato soup was placed, like a sacrificial offering, in the dumb-waiter.

'Right, it's on,' cried a disembodied voice from the kitchen. 'Haul away.'

I hauled obediently.

'Careful now. My gentlemen are all ready and waiting.' I jumped nervously as Mrs Amor appeared at my side – she'd been down in the kitchen ten seconds previously.

Her gentlemen were destined to wait a bit longer. The lift jammed for some reason, but I kept on hauling away at the rope, wishing that someone would give me a quick burst of 'Shenandoah' on a mouth-organ. It was like trying to pull up an anchor embedded in a coral reef.

Suddenly the obstruction cleared, the lift shot up, the tureen tipped over, and the soup rained like blood down the shaft.

Unfortunately, Polly who had had her head in the shaft when the soup went up, still had it in there when the soup went down.

'Oh my gawd, I'm scawlded,' she yelled. 'It's all your fault, Daisy Burns. You left the bloody ladle in again!'

Muffled curses floated up from the kitchen as Daisy and Polly skidded round the kitchen ankle deep in tomato soup.

With a hoarse cry, Mrs Amor rushed from the still room.

Seconds later she had joined the other two in an involuntary skaters waltz past the sinks and gas-cooker.

I stood with my elbows on the ledge, staring in horror down the shaft. It was then I realised that those stalactites weren't blood and guts after all, but congealed tomato soup and custard.

Gabriel who had been in the dining room while all this was going on, loped into the still room with a serviette draped over his arm.

'Where's the soup?' he demanded. 'They're getting restless in there.'

'The soups gone for a Burton,' I told him. 'And if you think those Rotarians are getting restless, you should nip down to the kitchen and get a load of what's happening down there. Only mind where you put your feet if you do.'

'I wouldn't go down there for a thousand quid,' he said tautly.

'Neither would I.'

'What the hell are we going to do?' He mopped his forehead with the serviette.

'What did you do all the other times?'

'Where's the Missis?'

I pointed down the shaft. 'I think she just went round for the third time.'

'Well don't just stand there. *Do* something!'

'What do you suggest I do?'

'How the hell should I know? *Anything!*'

I considered the problem. 'I suppose I could go in and give them a soft-shoe shuffle.'

Gabriel withered me with a look.

'Why don't *you* do something?' I asked.

'Like what?'

'Well, there's only one sensible thing we could do.'

'What's that?'

'We'd better go and remove the soup spoons and bread rolls, hadn't we? After all, they won't be needing them now – and we were six short anyway.'

Chapter Eight

My goodbye present to Amelia, when I'd recuperated from the mumps, was a tiny shoot in a plantpot which we'd bought from the town square on market day.

The trouble was, I didn't know what to buy for Amelia. It had to be something she'd really like. I'd seen a watch-shaped bottle of 4711 eau-de-cologne in the chemist's shop window. On the other hand, she might prefer one of those lace-edged hankies in the haberdasher's across the road, or a box of chocolates with a picture of kittens on the lid.

It was Amelia who made up my mind for me. 'What I'd really like,' she said, 'is a clematis plant. You see, child, it will keep on growing and reminding me of you.' She didn't mind a bit that it cost only one and sixpence, and when we got back to April Cottage, we'd had a little planting ceremony. 'I know,' she said in that dry, humorous way of hers, 'we'll plant it near that awful telegraph pole they've stuck up inside my back gate. It won't look nearly so ugly when it's covered with pretty purple flowers.'

Now Amelia's clematis had not only covered the telegraph pole, but seemed likely to make a take-over bid for the country's telephone system, and I knew I'd have to do something about it, although it seemed a pity to chop away at all that trailing greenery clustered thickly with buds.

The telephone wires sagged and groaned as I shook them free of clinging tentacles. Nettles were one thing, I thought as I stood there in my Bjorn Borg get-up, clematis quite another. Nettles stayed on the ground where they were supposed to be, while clematis had a runner-bean propensity for ending up in the darndest places. This particular one had even got a stranglehold on the shed.

55

All that, I thought, for one and a tanner.

Perspiration had sneaked past my sweat-band. I was puffing and blowing with exertion, when a face appeared over the back gate, and a voice said, 'M – Mrs Shelton?'

'Yes.' I wiped my forehead with the back of my hand and looked at the owner of the voice, a fair-haired woman, fiftyish, wearing a blue dress.

'I'm the vicar's wife,' she said.

'Strewth! I mean, won't you come in?'

Why the hell is it, I thought, that nobody ever calls to see me when I'm wearing a nice summer dress? Not that I had any nice summer dresses anyway. I wasn't a nice summer dress type of person.

'Perhaps I'd better come back when you're not so busy.' She sounded wistful.

'No, don't go away!' The wistful note in her voice got through to me. I divested myself of my clematis beard and curls, hastily brushed the palms of my hands across the seat of my old grey trousers, and unbolted the gate. 'Do come in. I'll make some coffee.'

We smiled at each other uncertainly when we were seated together on my sprawly settee, and I couldn't help wondering why she seemed so ill-at-ease. After all, she was the vicar's wife, and I was the miserable sinner who had not, so far, crossed the threshold of her husband's church.

'It was kind of you to let us have your piano,' she said, 'the old one sounded like that honky-tonk thing Winifred Attwell used to play.' Then she coloured to the roots of her hair. 'What I mean is, the old one was rather out of tune.'

But why the note of apology? Perhaps she thought that vicar's wives shouldn't mention honky-tonk pianos.

'I saw Winifred Attwell and her honky-tonk piano once at the Palladium,' I said, pouring the coffee. 'She was great! Of course that was in my pre-Hugo days.'

'Hugo?'

'My ex-husband.' I thought I'd better get that cleared up first. 'I'm "Mizz" Shelton nowadays. Neither flesh, fowl, nor good red herring.'

'I'd heard that you were divorced,' she said. 'I'm very sorry. That must have been a heartbreaking experience for you.'

'Yes it was.' I warmed to her immediately.

'I know what marital problems are like.' She stirred her coffee. 'You see – our son married a – a coloured girl, a very charming girl, but, well, things are not working out very well for them either.'

'Oh, how sad.'

'Yes, it is, especially as she has just had a baby.' Her eyes filled with tears. 'He's a lovely little thing; our only grandchild, but I don't think we'll be seeing much more of him. Stephanie – she's our daughter-in-law – is talking of going back to Jamaica and taking the baby with her.'

And I thought I had problems. I offered her a plate of biscuits. 'Here, have a chocolate finger,' I said.

'T-thank you.' She gave me the ghost of a smile. 'It's funny, but I've never told anyone here about my troubles before.'

'Come to that, neither have I.'

'Not only that, but my husband is going through the mill, too . . .'

'He mentioned that this was his first parish.'

'Yes, and it hasn't been easy changing our life-style at our age, believe me. But Arthur had always felt the urge to go into the ministry – to help people, and I couldn't stand in his way, could I?'

'No, of course you couldn't.'

'The trouble is that Arthur is so unsure of himself at present; terribly aware of his own shortcomings. I'm afraid he hasn't learned how to cope with those people who know far more about church matters that he does. Some of the gentry folk are very dogmatic, you know, and so very knowledgeable. Oh dear, I shouldn't be telling you this, but I'm afraid my husband is very depressed about it, and so am I. He's developed a nervous tic recently, and I'm sure that's because he is so afraid of doing and saying the wrong things.'

Like me with Hugo's boss, I thought, and all too often with Hugo himself. I'd had all on, at times, to arrange my features into an expression to please Hugo, and I had never understood why people, well endowed with human failings themselves, should appoint themselves the stern judge of other folk's failings. Now it seemed a pity that poor Mr Abercromby should be made to develop a nervous tic in a Christian community.

'Are there many gentry folk in Tootington?' I placed a slight emphasis on the word gentry, which meant, as I recalled, people of high birth, politeness and good breeding.

Mrs Abercromby hesitated. 'Well, there are the Nettlefolds at the Hall. Lady Nettlefold is in her eighties. She's a massive woman, if you know what I mean. Then there's her nephew, Alfred, who is one of our churchwardens, and her grand-daughter, Natalie, who rides a lot . . .'

I could just imagine that the Nettlefolds might be prickly people to deal with, and that it was they and other people like them who had brought on the vicar's nervous tic.

' . . . and the Brassingtons who live at the Grange. They're an odd, unhappy couple, but his family goes back to the Crusades. Several of his ancestors are in the church with their legs crossed.'

I tried hard to keep a straight face.

'Mrs Brassington is quite nice in a vague kind of way, but George Brassington has never understood Arthur. You see, all the previous vicars came from families which put one son into the Army, the second into the Navy, and the third into the Church.'

I nodded sympathetically.

'Oh, please forgive me,' Mrs Abercromby said, 'I didn't come here to carp. I really came to ask if you would be interested in joining the Mother's Union or the Young Wives.'

'Actually,' I said, after a short silence, 'I don't think I'm qualified to join either.'

'Oh, how tactless, how stupid of me!' The vicar's wife upset her coffee in her distress. 'There! Now you see what a blundering fool I am! I seem to have this propensity for saying and doing the wrong thing just like Arthur.'

She clattered her cup onto the low table beside her, and looked at me appealingly. 'Imagine if I'd said that to Lady Nettlefold! You see, she's made us both so nervous that I'm almost afraid to open my mouth whenever we meet, so I either sit mumchance, like a tailor's dummy, or blurt out the most awful things. Lady Nettlefold's so *big* and imposing. She doesn't walk – she *sweeps* into a room, like a Spanish galleon.'

'I know exactly what you mean. Large ladies who sweep into rooms put the fear of God into me too.'

'Do they really?'

'Mrs Abercromby,' I said earnestly, 'you are looking at the world's Number One coward. I've never learned how to cope with Spanish galleons either.'

She laughed, and I saw what a pretty person she was, with her finely grained skin and blue eyes.

'My husband told me I'd get on all right with you,' she said. 'He told me you were – human.'

'Aren't we all?'

'I'd like to think so, but sometimes I'm not so sure.'

'Have some more coffee?'

'No, thank you, I really must be going.' Mrs Abercromby got to her feet, but I knew that she was still on edge; still unsure of her ground.

I wanted so much to help her. 'I'm sorry I'm not eligible for Young Wives or the Mother's Union,' I said anxiously. 'Haven't you anything else I could join?'

'Well, there's the Women's Institute, but I'm not in charge of that. Your next-door neighbour, Miss Cox, runs the whole bang-shoot, but I don't think she likes me very much.'

That makes two of us, I thought.

Mrs Abercromby brightened. 'What about the church choir?'

'I'm afraid I can't read music.'

'Neither can I,' she admitted. 'Neither can anyone else except Lady Nettlefold, and Alfred. But no, I'm being unfair. That television chappie, Dominic Douglas, can read music, but he's not really a choir-member. He simply turns up if and when he feels like it.'

She sighed. 'He's another bone of contention between my husband and Lady Nettlefold. She can't bear the thought of the village being invaded by what she terms "the intelligencer" – people who don't belong here, whilst we, Arthur and I, that is, feel that folk have a right to choose where they live . . .'

Her eyebrows drew together in a delicate frown. ' . . . I mean to say, it isn't as if Tootington was divorced from the world. It's a beautiful village. Lots of new people have moved in recently, but Lady Nettlefold won't tolerate them, and that upsets Arthur.'

She gathered up her handbag and gloves, and I knew that she was angry deep down inside. 'Nor can Lady Nettlefold come to terms with a man like my husband, just because he gave up a well-paid job in industry to train for the priesthood. Not for prestige, but simply because he listened to the voice of his conscience.'

'I see.'

'I'm sorry to have been so outspoken,' she apologised. 'On the credit side, there's Commander Bruce. He lives in that lovely Georgian house near the bridge. You know the one I mean?'

I nodded.

'He's one of the nicest people one could wish to meet.' She took out a handkerchief and blew her nose hard. 'A perfect gentleman. The only one amongst the so-called landed gentry who has taken the trouble to get to know us.'

We were standing together at the front door of April Cottage. 'Oh, dear,' she said, 'whatever must you think of me?'

I smiled. 'I think that you are very human, too.'

'Afraid I've made an awful fool of myself.'

'No you haven't, Mrs Abercromby.'

'My name's Avril,' she said.

'Mine's Sally.'

Avril, I thought, as I watched her hurry down the garden path and cross the creaking bridge over the beck, wasn't that French for April?

Chapter Nine

I was still mulling over our conversation when my next-door neighbour hammered peremptorily on my front door and informed me that her telephone was out of order.

'It's all your fault,' she snapped, flaring her nostrils. 'I saw you dragging at the telephone wires earlier on, and I knew what would happen as a result. Well, it *has* happened! My telephone won't work, and I have come to tell you that I think your behaviour is disgraceful! *Quite* disgraceful! To think I lived in harmony with Amelia Beatty for so many years. Now you've come along to vandalise all the things she cared for – her tiles, her clothes-line, her clematis!'

'I-I'm terribly sorry, but . . .'

Miss Cox did not give me time to finish my sentence. 'I knew the kind of person you were the minute I saw you hacking away at her clothes-line and tearing up those tiles. Have you any idea what Victorian tiles are worth nowadays? No, of course you haven't, because you are a person who cares nothing for the past.'

She fixed me with her codfish eyes and settled her coat-hanger shoulders disapprovingly. 'You are a disgrace to the community. But if you think I intend to let the matter of the telephone wires rest here, you are very much mistaken.' Her nose twitched alarmingly. 'I shall inform the powers that be – the telephone people . . .'

'The Post Office,' I interposed.

'The Post Office,' she corrected herself unthinkingly, 'of your action in tearing down their lines of communication.'

'But I haven't, have I?'

'Haven't *what*?'

'Torn down their lines of communication. What I mean to

say is, the wires all zinged back into place once I'd got rid of the clematis. At least I thought they did. Perhaps you'd better come in. I'll check with the exchange.'

'I have no intention of setting foot over this threshold,' Miss Cox said, dilating her nostrils. 'Ring the exchange if you wish, but you'll get no reply.' She folded her arms aggressively across her skinny bosom. 'Ring anyone you like! You'll get no answer!'

'I wish you'd change your mind,' I said. 'It is rather difficult to carry on a row – I mean a conversation – on the doorstep.' But Miss Cox remained as immovable as the Rock of Gibraltar.

Aware of her eyes boring into the back of my neck, I walked to the telephone, consulted the book lying beside it, and dialled a number. What if she's right, I thought, what if I have wrecked the village communication system?

The Reverend Arthur Abercromby answered my call.

'Oh, hello,' I said breathlessly, 'has your wife come in yet? She has? May I speak to her? This is Sally Shelton.'

'Hello, Sally?' Avril sounded breathless, too.

'I – I'm just ringing to say that I shall be delighted to join the church-choir,' I said.

'You will? Oh, that's marvellous. I didn't think you were all that keen. Why did you change your mind?'

I glanced over my shoulder at Miss Cox. 'Let's just say circumstances beyond my control.'

I extended the receiver to Miss Cox. 'Would you care to speak to the vicar's wife?' I asked.

'No I would not! Well, of all things!' Miss Cox cantered away snorting steam from both nostrils.

'Sally, what on earth's going on?' Avril demanded.

'I'll tell you later.'

I was trembling from head to foot when I sank down on my settee. Now I have made an enemy, I thought. Miss Cox might just possibly have forgiven me for being in the wrong, but she would never forgive me for being in the right.

As my mother would have put it, 'There's one born every minute Sally. A fool, that is.'

I popped into the corner shop to speak to Lizzie on my way to work the following morning.

'For heaven's sake, tell me how Mrs Billy Watson's legs are doing.'

'Mrs Billy Watson's legs?' Lizzie frowned. 'She's had the plasters removed, so far as I know. Why?'

But I hadn't time to tell her as I sprinted up the lane to catch the bus.

I needed to earn money, but the Red Lion was beginning to wear me down. Daisy and Polly hadn't cottoned on to me since the day I arrived, that much was clear. Obviously they didn't want anyone else muscling in on Mrs Billy's job, but was it my fault that the woman had managed to break both her legs at the same time? One break I could understand and condone, but two breaks smacked of gross carelessness. What had the wretched woman done anyway? Skidded on two banana skins at the same time?

Life's rails seemed to me to be slightly buckled as I marched up to the still room and began rolling butter. I hadn't quite got over Miss Cox's verbal assault of the day before, and I knew that my strained relations with her were hardly likely to improve from now on.

It was unnerving to slash away at Amelia's nettles, to pull up her Victorian tiles, and tug away at her creeping clematis, knowing that Frances Cox was watching my every move from her kitchen window.

Perhaps it wasn't such a good idea to have come to live in April Cottage, after all. Perhaps I should have sold it to the highest bidder, and lost myself among the thousands of other divorcées in some big city or other.

Then I gave myself a swift mental kick in the pants. The world was full of Frances Coxes. I'd have met her ilk in any town or city the length and breadth of the British Isles. One did not just fold up and give in at the first setback. I loved April Cottage. It was my home now and, like me or lump me, Frances Cox would have to put up with me, and I with her.

If only the blasted butter wouldn't keep on uncurling. If only Polly and Daisy weren't so hostile. If only I didn't have to carry up the morning tea-trays. If only I didn't have to tell Mrs Amor about that man in Room Five. If only somebody *loved* me!

At that moment, Polly floundered into the still room. She evidently hadn't got over having her head 'scawlded' because

63

she was wearing a close-fitting white turban which gave her the appearance of an ancient Egyptian priest. I had gathered that she and Daisy weren't on very good terms at the moment because Daisy had left the ladle in the soup tureen, and that I was in even worse odour because I'd kept on hauling at the ropes when I should have let go.

I never knew what to say to Polly, who was one of those sharp-eyed sharp-tempered little bodies who appear to be scowling even when they're reasonably happy. Her mouth drooped down at the corners because she invariably had a fag end dangling from one side or the other.

It crossed my mind, as she bustled into the still room carrying a bucket and mop, that the only way Polly could possibly appear good-humoured was if she stood on her head.

She gave me a sharp aggressive look and started scrubbing away at the floor like a sailor swabbing the deck of a battle-cruiser. I lifted first one leg and then the other as the tide began to lap round my shoes; sat on the kitchen table momentarily to stop myself sinking in the flood, and then blurted out, to ease the tension, 'Mrs Billy Watson's had her plasters removed!'

'Ayow!' She stopped swabbing, leaned on her mop, rolled her fag end across her bottom lip before it had time to raise a blister, and continued, 'Is that a fact? Poor thing! Legs like pipe-cleaners she's got! Snapped like twigs, they did. Just like twigs. Cawse,' she nodded her bandaged head like a mandarin, 'she's claiming cawmpensation. Well, I mean to say, wouldn't you?'

'Claiming cawmpensation?' I asked warily. 'Who from?'

'Why from 'er, of cawse. Mrs Lah-di-dah down yonder.'

I gathered that she meant Mrs Amor.

'I mean to say, it *was* her fawlt!' Polly dug a packet of cigarettes from her overall pocket, lit a fresh cork-tip from the glowing embers of the old, then plopped the dog-end into the bucket of water. 'She should've had that carpet seen to ages ago.'

I eased my feet on to the floor and felt the water seeping through the soles of my shoes as I asked, 'Carpet? Which carpet?'

'That carpet in Room Number Five.'

'Did you say Room Number Five?'

Polly regarded me suspiciously. 'What's up? You a bit mutt and jeff?' she asked.

'Pardon?'

'That carpet in Room Number Five,' she bawled. 'The one with the frayed edges! The one Mrs Billy Watson tripped up on! Pore soul! Hadn't a dawg's chance, she hadn't. Not with her legs! Two tibias gawn in a matter of seconds! Don't seem right, do it?'

'No, I suppose not.' Suitably chastened, I glanced down at my own legs with renewed respect. If I'd had legs like pipe-cleaners, my tibias might have 'gawn' too when I tripped over that same carpet. Thank the lord I had underpinnings like oak trees!

Polly seemed more kindly disposed towards me now. She applied her mop to the flood area round my feet, sopped up most of the moisture, rolled her fag across her bottom lip, and bellowed at me as she went out through the door, 'You should go to the hawspital with your ears!'

At half-past ten, Mrs Amor rushed into the still room like a whirlwind. I was standing at the sink at the time, drying the breakfast pots. Now was the moment to tell her about the red-bearded ripper in Room Five.

I cleared my throat. 'Mrs Amor,' I began, 'I have something to say to you . . .'

'Not *now*, Mrs Sam!' She waved her arms dramatically. 'I'm late for an appointment as it is! Just look after things until I get back. Don't suppose we'll be all that busy, but don't let Daisy Burns fall asleep with her head in the oven will you? And what about that cheeseboard and the chicken? They must be seen to before lunchtime. The lettuce is beginning to wilt.'

The lettuce, I thought, was not the only thing that was beginning to wilt. As for that roasted chicken on the side-board, perched on a china stand, I actually felt sorry for it, sitting there on its parson's nose, waiting for someone to come along and fancy a slice or two from its wrinkled breast, its only companions a couple of wire racks full of vins – rouge et blanc – and nobody ever seemed to fancy them either. Not that I minded. If someone wanted wine with their Chicken Maryland, I'd be the one to remove the cork, and I didn't

65

fancy the idea of standing in the dining room with a bottle clenched between my knees.

I wandered down to the kitchen later on to find Daisy, lolling on a stool near the dumb-waiter, reading a paperback romance.

'Everything all right down here?' I inquired brightly.

'Get lost,' she said, turning over a page.

I got lost without further ado; wandered back to the still room; remembered the cheeseboard, started trimming the rough edges from the Danish Blue; dusted the chicken, and attempted to resuscitate the lettuce without actually giving it the kiss of life.

Time was hanging as heavily as those ropes and pulleys in Waldorf Winninger's grandfather clocks, when suddenly Gabriel appeared – a kind of running commentary of dire information.

'Customers,' he muttered, running on the spot. 'Cocktail lounge. Get down there at the double!'

As soon as he'd gone, I started running on the spot, too, tying on my frilly apron, and looking round for the order pad.

When I'd discovered the wretched thing lurking under a pile of tea-towels, I raced down to the cocktail lounge to find a group of bright young things poring over a menu.

A frightfully jolly young chap with a public-school hair-do and wearing a hacking jacket over well-cut cord trousers, appointed himself their spokesman.

'Oh, good-oh, here's the waitress,' he chortled, as I licked the end of my pencil. 'We'll have smoked salmon for starters.'

His face puckered into a pained expression when I explained, in my most refined accent, that the smoked salmon was 'orf'.

'Oh blarst,' he said, 'suppose we'll have to settle for the prawn cocktails, then, eh, what?'

'Sorry,' I murmured, feeling as if I'd just had a dentist's injection in my upper gum, 'I'm afraid the prawn cocktails are orf, too.'

'What about the mock turtle soup with sherry?'

'I'm afraid not.'

He regarded me coldly. 'It might be simpler,' he said, 'if you told us what is orn.'

'Excuse me,' I muttered, making a dash for the kitchen, 'I'll find out for you.'

Daisy was still sitting on her stool by the dumb-waiter,

flicking over the pages of her novelette. She glanced up at me coolly as I rushed in and asked, 'What have we got for starters?'

'Tomato soup,' she said.

'What about egg mayonnaise?'

'Ain't had time to boil no eggs.'

I felt like Charles the First on his way to execution as I walked back to the cocktail lounge, but the bright young things had obviously got the message.

'Come on,' I heard hacking jacket say to the others, 'we're wasting our time here. Let's go to that new place at Little Blewitt. I've heard they do the most marvellous cold lunches – crab, lobster mayonnaise, chicken in aspic – the lot!'

I caught a glimpse of well-upholstered backsides and tossing blonde hair as the two girls followed their escorts.

I had never felt so inadequate in all my life.

It hadn't been a very satisfactory morning, I thought, sitting on the bus. I hadn't had the opportunity of telling Mrs Amor about the man in Room Five, and I'd had 'words' with Daisy Burns into the bargain.

'I don't know what you're going on about,' she'd said truculently when I'd told her that hacking jacket and his party had walked out, 't'ain't no skin off your nose, is it? And it ain't my fault that we haven't got no shrimps nor nothing.'

'I'm not saying it is, but we might have been able to offer them egg mayonnaise if you'd taken the trouble to boil a few eggs.'

'I like that,' she shouted, not liking it one little bit. 'Who are you to tell me what to do?' Her suety complexion flushed the colour of beetroot as she jumped up from her stool and flung down the book she was reading. 'Well, I won't stand for it! I'll tell Mrs Amor.'

'I don't think you will,' I replied hotly.

'Oh, I see. You'll make it your business to go tittle-tattling.'

'Not I! I'm not the keeper of your conscience, Mrs Burns! I just happen to think that if you accept money for doing a job, you should do it to the best of your ability.'

'I know your sort,' she yelled, 'creeping about the place as if butter wouldn't melt in your bleedin' mouth! Getting in with the management! Shouting orders at me down that bloody

67

dumb-waiter! Well I know what you're after, Mrs Clever Clogs. You're after Mrs Billy Watson's job, aren't you? Think if you get in with Mrs Lah-di-dah Amor you'll smarm your way in here permanent. I had that figured out the minute you walked in! You and your skin-tight skirt an' short blonde curls!'

'Wrong again,' I said, trying to control my temper. 'I came here as a stop-gap, and if Mrs Billy Watson hobbled in this very minute, I'd welcome her with open arms!'

Skin-tight skirt and short blonde curls indeed! If my skirt was skin tight it was because I couldn't afford to buy a new one, and I was sick and tired of references to my hair.

I left her chuntering under her breath and slamming a pan of water on the stove to boil. Seemingly we were going to get some hard-boiled eggs after all. But the incident had upset me, and I was shaking when I caught the bus home to April Cottage.

As soon as I opened the door the charm of the place enfolded me. I kicked off my shoes, sank down on the settee and tried to get things into perspective.

Did it really matter that Daisy Burns disliked me so much or that I'd made an enemy of Frances Cox? A few weeks ago I was unaware of their existence, and what were a couple of flare-ups with people who scarcely mattered to me at all compared to the hurt I'd experienced when I'd found out that Hugo was having an affair and wanted a divorce. But deep down inside I knew that it did matter: every human relationship was valuable.

Getting things into perspective meant taking a long clear look at my life, asking myself where I was going, what I wanted.

All I wanted at that moment was to shave my head and go into a convent.

Then I thought about the tea-chests Bert and Darr had helped me to lump into the loggia the day my furniture arrived. I'd packed them even before Hugo and I moved into that brand new bungalow with the carriage-lamps and the tinsel Christmas tree, and I had forgotten what was in them.

Hugo and I had lived together in that bungalow less than a year when the other woman trauma started, and the way the wind was blowing then it seemed pointless unpacking anything more. And so the chests had gone into storage with the rest of my things.

Suddenly this seemed the right moment to open them.

The first thing I unwrapped was my mother's old vegetable knife – the only one I'd ever possessed that was any good at peeling potatoes and getting rid of the eyes.

'Hmmm, so there you are,' I said to it severely. 'I thought I'd lost you ages ago.'

Forgotten treasures appeared one by one; cookery books, ornaments and photograph albums.

There was Gran's earthenware jug, the one my sister Holly and I had once given her for a birthday present filled with sweet-peas. That jug had cost us half-a-crown and had skint us of pocket-money for a week.

Memories came flooding back. Memories of that tall Victorian house where I'd been so happy as a child, with the front room carved up into cubicles, and my mother busy in the kitchen making cups of tea for the 'perms'.

Looking back down the years, it seemed to me that the most precious thing of all was security. All I had ever really wanted was home – and love, the greatest security of all.

Love had spilled over into our days – like bright ribbons on special birthday presents, and my sister and I were products of an age when children were taught that it is better to give than to receive; to fight our own battles; eat our crusts to make our hair curl, and never to let the sun go down on our anger. Not that we'd had anything to be angry about.

Thinking back to Hugo, I realised that I had offered no resistance to that 'other woman' because Mother taught me that love is either given freely and unreservedly – or it is not 'given' at all.

When I was crying my eyes out over some lost puppy-love, she would say in that forthright way of hers, 'Listen Sally, hold your head up whatever happens. Laugh and the world laughs with you, cry and you cry alone. Always remember that, my love.'

At the bottom of the second chest was a case filled with hairdressing equipment; things I'd kept when I married Hugo. Neck-brushes, clippers, scissors, metal wave-grips, nets, curl-clips, a hand-dryer, and a hand-stitched cotton cape.

69

I felt glad that Hugo wasn't standing behind me to make some remark about 'pulling myself together' or 'acting my age'. He wouldn't have understood why my eyes were full of tears.

And I could never have explained to him the look on Gran's face when my sister and I gave her that jug full of sweet peas, or my mother's look of sweet concentration as her sturdy fingers stitched the hem of that cotton hairdressing cape.

Chapter Ten

Thank God for Sunday, I thought, burrowing sleepily under the bedclothes. Thank goodness for one beautiful, lovely peaceful day in the heart of the country. No noise, no hassle, no one to bother me. No Red Lion Hotel, no Daisy Burns, no Polly Flounders. Just me yanking up Amelia's rhubarb. Ah bliss! Even the tax-collectors would be off duty!

'Praise my sowl the King of Hea-*ven*! G'arn there! To His feet thy tri-hib-utes bring! Ransomed, healed, *re*-stored, for-hor-hor-given! Nay, not that way, tha' silly bugger! Gerrof me foot tha' big soft gobbin! Who like me His pr-haise should sing . . .'

I sat bolt upright and looked at the clock. Half-past six! What the hell was going on? I almost fell into my dressing gown, drew back the curtains, and looked out.

Great lumbering cows, their rear ends caked with mud, were plothering through the meadow behind April Cottage, urged on by an old chap in baggy trousers and a flat cap who was thwacking away at their rumps good-naturedly with a branch wrested from a burgeoning hedgerow.

When all his beast were safely through the gate, he opened his toothless gums in another paeon of praise to his Maker, and shambled away still singing, 'Praise my sowl, the King of Hea-*ven*.'

'Ye gods,' I said aloud, stumbling back to bed. But the pillows had taken umbrage at my absence, and refused to get comfortable again.

I lay on my back and stared at the ceiling for a while, then the sheets turned nasty, the eiderdown started to creep away from me, and what had been a snug nest minutes before, became a sea of heaving bedlinen.

71

At seven-thirty I gave up the battle of the sheets, got up again, thrust my arms into my dressing-gown, and stumbled downstairs to the kitchen to make myself a cup of tea and a slice of toast.

The cows were now mooing round the meadow, calling to the calves which were bottled up somewhere in Farmer Appleby's byres. Not that old Farmer Appleby who had married 'Mary from the Dairy' lived there any more. He had gone, long ago, to that great haystack in the sky. His eldest son, Andy, Lizzie had told me, was in charge of the farm nowadays.

I almost choked on my toast when the other row started. I thought at first that someone was strangling a cow. But surely cows, even when they were being strangled, didn't go oom-pah-pah with enigma variations.

The new noise was coming from Bert's back garden. I rushed through the loggia in my dressing-gown to find out what was going on, and hung over the fence to see Bert sitting at the door of his garden shed, wearing his usual clobber – dungarees, striped flannel shirt, and studs – but instead of his usual flat cap, his head was adorned with a peaked hat liberally trimmed with gold braid.

His lips were puckered to the mouthpiece of a tuba which he held in his arms like an outsized infant. His eyes were closed, and his red-veined cheeks puffed out like a couple of russet apples.

The sound that emerged from the business end of the tuba was an unmusical burping. At that moment Darr came out of the cottage, showered a few hairpins, caught sight of me in my dressing-gown, uttered a strangled cry, and promptly skedaddled back indoors.

Bert's eyes shot open, he unpuckered his lips, let the air out of his cheeks, pushed back his hat with one hand, and said, 'Nah then, Ruby. Been having a bit of a lay-in, have yer?'

'What on earth are you doing?' I asked.

He gave me a pitying look. 'Well, I ain't planting tatties.'

'I know that. But why are you sitting in the garden playing a tuba?'

'I'm getting tuned up before the lads arrive.'

'The – lads?'

He frowned. 'Aye, we've got a fête next Saturday, an' it'll be

72

a fête worse than death if we don't get to grips with Colonel Bogey.'

'You mean that you're going to get to grips with Colonel Bogey out here in the garden?'

'Why not? It ain't raining. We'd go into the shed if it was.'

He was explaining things slowly to make sure I took it in. It occurred to me that Polly Flounders thought I was deaf, now Bert Rumbold thought I was daft, leaning over the fence in my dressing gown, asking soft questions. Well, I thought, if daft questions needed to be asked, the fence between Bert's cottage and mine seemed the right place to ask them.

'How many?' I ventured.

'How many what?'

'Lads,' I said.

He screwed up his eyes. 'Dunno. Never thowt to count 'em. There's Ted and Tucker on't trombones, ould Gabby on't cymbals, and the lad who stands by to steady him . . .'

'That's four.'

'No, it ain't. That's three and a half,' Bert reasoned. 'Well, I mean to say, you can't count the lad as one, he's only eight.'

'Oh, I see. Three and a half, then. How many more?'

Bert continued his mental arithmetic – a painful process by his look of concentration. 'Why, there's Pickleses lads, Durking and Wilkins, and Ambrose Lanfeard. He's young Farmer Appleby's cowman, and a fair hummer on the euphonium.'

'How many Pickleses lads?' I inquired.

'I've already told you – Durking and Wilkins.' Bert was getting impatient.

'Oh, sorry. I didn't realise that Durking and Wilkins were Pickles, I thought they were surnames.'

'Damn all,' Bert roared, 'tha's got me in a pickle now. What's tha want to know for anyway? Tekkin a census, are yer?'

'No, I was just wondering how many of you could get into that shed if it happened to be raining. Isn't it a bit of a squeeze?'

'Not if we stands shoulder to shoulder wi' the trombones at the front and the door open.' His face clouded. 'There was a time when the trombones stood at the back, but I copped so many clouts on the back of me neck that we had to make an alteration. Course, we wheel the handcart out first.'

73

'That's all right then.' I felt vaguely relieved for some reason.
'Is it?' Bert scratched his head. 'Danged if I can see why.
What was wrong with it in't first place?'

As the whole conversation appeared to be taking an Alice in
Wonderland turn, I backed away from the fence. 'Well,' I said
airily, 'I'd better get ready for the fray.'

Bert closed one eye. 'Which fray?' he demanded.

'The pulling up the rhubarb fray.'

'Pullin' up the rhubarb! Tha's niver going to pull up Miss
Beatty's rhubarb?'

'Yes. It isn't a punishable offence, is it?'

'That rhubarb's been flourishing since I were a lad,' Bert
scowled, 'Why in tarnation do you want to pull it up?'

'Because I don't like rhubarb. I never have. Even my mother
couldn't get me to eat it. It sets my teeth on edge.'

I thought Bert's broken capillaries would break out in
broken capillaries. 'What about custard? If you smothered it
wi' custard you wouldn't taste the rhubarb.'

'But I'm not struck on custard either.'

'By heck. Don't like rhubarb an' custard! I've niver heard tell
of such a thing!'

The conversation was leading to a bust up between Bert and
me, and the last thing I wanted was to fall out with him. One
hostile neighbour was bad enough. Two would be impossible.

'All right. I won't pull up Amelia's rhubarb if it's going to
upset you. If you like rhubarb, feel free to come over and gather
as much of it as you want.'

His scowl disappeared. He smiled benignly, 'Well, that's real
nice of you. As a matter of fact Darr an' me have had the
pleasure of that rhubarb for the past thirty years. Miss Beatty
couldn't abide the stuff neither.'

Sally Shelton, I thought, as I changed into my gardening gear,
was no name for the inhabitant of April Cottage. 'Solomon'
Shelton would be a more suitable appellation, and I wondered
what the penalties might be if I attempted to come to grips with
the inmates of those concrete pools abutting the rockery. I still
hadn't discovered what swam beneath the clouded water, but if
it proved to be a shoal of herring, would I be in danger of
infringing someone's fishing rights?

All appeared to be quiet under the scummy surface – but

was it? What was hatching down there? That's what I had to find out, but what would I do with whatever it was?

I'd always had a horror of things that darted about in dirty water. When I was little and all the other kids went fishing for tadpoles, I didn't want to know. All that quivering black jelly destined to evolve as fat slippery frogs put the fear of God into me, and I knew that if anything jumped or plopped, or if a fin cut the water at that minute, my yells would drown Colonel Bogey.

What I needed was a ladle, or possibly a dragnet. But, I told myself firmly, whatever was lurking there couldn't be all that big, and there was I, a grown woman, afraid of a few baby Brontosaurus.

I peered cautiously over the fence, and saw eleven heads wearing gold-braided hats. Sunlight glinted on oom-pah-pahing tubas and trombones, and they were actually in tune.

Scrambling up a bit higher for a better look, I saw that the hats were all the band had in common. From the head downwards they were dressed, Bert fashion, in dungarees, with a smattering of cord bags, Fair-isle sweaters, holier-than-thou waistcoats and stout farm boots.

I recognised the ancient chorister who had thwacked the cows through the gate earlier on as Ambrose Lanfeard – that 'fair hummer' on the euphonium, and the old chap who stood sagging at the knees with his cymbals at the ready could be none other than Ould Gabby. Behind him stood a cherubic boy with fair curly hair, counting 'three, two, one . . .'

'*Now*, Gabby!' Bert roared, whereupon the old fellow clapped his cymbals together with such force that he tottered backwards and would have landed on his backside among Bert's spring onions if the little lad hadn't been there to stop him.

'Bravo,' I called as the band juddered to a halt and began wiping its united foreheads on handkerchiefs plucked from the top weskit pockets, 'that was splendid!'

Eleven and a half pair of eyes swung in my direction.

'All right, were it?' Bert smiled complacently.

'Great!' I leaned my elbows on the fence. 'By the way, you haven't got a shrimping net, have you?'

'A *shrimping net*? Why in tarnation do you want a shrimping net?' Bert's eyebrows shot up into his gold-trimmed hat.

I swallowed hard. 'I want to go fishing.'

'You'll have all on to do that, Missis,' said one of the trombones, 'the tides in.'

'Oh, that doesn't matter. I'm only going fishing in the garden.'

'Now what the heck are you up to?' Bert demanded.

'Up to?' I gave him an innocent look. 'Nothing much. I just want to clean out the rock pools. You don't mind, do you?'

'I don't mind what you do, just as long as you don't start hefting up that rhubarb,' Bert said.

'I've got a shrimping net, Missis.' The little lad who had saved Ould Gabby from the spring onions stepped forward. 'I could run home an' get it for you if you like.'

Fifteen minutes later, when the lads were having another go at Colonel Bogey, 'Half-Pint', as I'd secretly named the little lad, had fished seven newts from Amelia's concrete pudding basins and had them safely encapsulated in a jam-jar.

'Aren't they beauties?' he said with an ecstatic smile.

'Hmmm.' I repressed a shudder at the sight of seven amphibians, like miniature salamanders, darting hither and thither in their jam-jar prison.

'Are you sure you don't want to keep 'em?'

'No, that I don't! They're yours if you want them.'

'Cor,' he murmured, clutching the jam-jar to his skinny chest. 'Seven newts! That's five more than Herbie Parrott's got.'

He beamed up at me. 'I'll look after 'em you see if I don't. I'll get me mum to buy me a proper bowl. Well, I'd best be off to see to me great-grandad. He's getting a bit tottery nowadays,' he confided. 'Me mum plays hell-up wi' him, but he wain't give up his cymbals for no one.'

Why should he, I thought, as Half-Pint launched himself and his jam-jar over the fence to be in at the big finale to Colonel Bogey. Wasn't that what life was all about? Clanging one's cymbals with all one's might and not caring tuppence about landing on one's backside as a result.

Chapter Eleven

'Ruby! Are you there, Ruby?'

I got up stiffly from my sprawly settee when I heard Bert calling to me over the back fence.

'Coming,' I sang out, not that I felt much like singing. I was bushed, whacked, jiggered, as I shambled out to see what Bert wanted.

'Darr's dishing up the steak and kidney pie,' he said. 'Why don't you come over an' have a bit? Darr's mashed pertaters will stick to your ribs a treat.'

The thought of pertaters sticking to my ribs was a pleasant one. My stomach felt like a torn skull and crossbones flapping against a broken flagpole.

'Thank you very much,' I said gratefully, 'if you're sure it won't be too much trouble for – er – Darr.'

'Wain't be no trouble to Darr,' he said. 'Only don't say nothing to her or she'll come over all unnecessary.'

'I'd better wash my hands and face first, and change into something more suitable.'

'No need for that. Just hoist the'sen over the fence.'

I just hoped that Miss Cox wasn't watching as I clambered over Bert's fence and dropped down among his spring cabbages.

Darr was busy in the kitchen, wreathed in steam from the bubbling pots and pans on the cooker. It seemed odd not to greet my hostess, but I dare not take the risk of her coming over all unnecessary, so I simply smiled and nodded, and she, all of a fluster, returned the compliment.

Didn't she ever speak, I wondered, and what on earth was Darr short for?

'For what we are about to receive, may the Lord mek us truly thankful,' Bert said when the three of us were seated at

Amelia's square table. 'Now get stuck in, Ruby. I know you modern lasses. Think you can live on a couple of lettuce leaves an' a stick of celery, but I knows better.'

The notion of being a 'modern lass' lifted my spirits enormously as Darr heaped a generous portion of steak and kidney pie onto my plate, shoved a dish of carrots under my nose, another full of peas topped with a lump of melting dairy butter, a third of steaming mashed potatoes, and finally a jug of onion gravy.

'This tastes marvellous,' I said to Bert. 'Your wife is a very good cook.'

'Did you hear that, Darr?' Bert hollered across the table, 'Ruby says you're a very good cook.'

Darr blushed, ducked her head, and showered a few hairpins into the mashed potatoes.

'She were pleased about the rhubarb,' Bert explained, 'that's why she told me to ask you over. You were pleased about the rhubarb, weren't you, Darr?'

I wondered, as I munched happily on my steak and kidney pie, what Bert and Darr talked about when they were alone. It was an odd experience sitting there not daring to look at my hostess, with Bert acting as an interpreter.

'That was delicious,' I said when I'd finished. 'I've never tasted such lovely pastry before.'

'Ruby says she's never tasted such lovely pastry before,' Bert relayed to his wife, who flushed crimson and shot out to the kitchen.

'About Darr,' I said hesitantly when she was out of earshot, 'I feel a bit awkward about not speaking to her.'

'No need,' Bert said. 'She likes you all right. She wouldn't have given you a second helping of gravy if she didn't. The best way to get round Darr is to tek no notice of her, no notice whatever. That's the way I courted her. Just took no notice of her . . .'

'But how? I mean – how did you get to the point?'

'How did I ask her to marry me, you mean? Well, I didn't exactly *ask* her. I spoke to her dad first, then I slipped the engagement ring round the spout of a teapot – an' gave her the teapot.'

'Oh, I see,' I murmured, bewildered by the complexity of their courtship. 'Then what?'

'Why then, in two shakes of a lamb's tail, there we was in front of the parson.'

'But surely she must have said something at that stage,' I ventured. 'What I mean is, you can't very well get married without saying *something*.'

Bert chuckled. 'No, she didn't. At least no more than she was obliged to. She just kind of nodded her head and mumbled, but the reverend took it as a sign of ass-ass . . .'

'Assent,' I prompted.

'Yeah, that's it! A sign of assention. She kind of rose to the occasion in a manner of speakin'. Didn't exactly say "I do", but she didn't say "I don't" neither.'

He snapped his braces with the air of a man well contented with his lot. 'Don't know that I could stand a gabby woman,' he said. 'Most women talks too much for my liking. Darr an' me gets on just fine together.'

'I'm sure you do.'

'But we're up against a bit of a problem at the moment. A serious problem. It's my old Dad, you see . . .'

'Your old – Dad?' I tried not to sound too surprised.

Bert sighed. 'Yes, he's coming to live with us. That's why we wus glad of your feather bed. He ain't never slept on nothing but feathers afore, an' he wouldn't have tekken kindly to springs at his time of life. Likes to sink into slumber, does my old dad. Can't bear being sprung up atop of a mattress.' He sighed more deeply than before. 'I'm not looking forward to it, I can tell you. Him an' Darr don't hit it off together. He will interfere with her arrangements, and she don't like that, Darr don't.'

'I see. But couldn't you have got him into a home?'

'We have got him into a home,' Bert said tartly, 'we've got him into our home, more's the pity. He'll be here next week.'

'That's not what I meant. Couldn't you have got him into an old folk's home?'

Bert shook his head. 'Naw, we tried but it weren't no use. There was no place he could go an' tek his feather bed with him – nor that confounded cat of his. The homes we tried would've tekken Dad, but no way would they tek his feather bed and his cat, so we're landed with him – and *it*!'

'Oh dear, I am sorry.'

'It's bound to cause upsets, isn't it, when he starts interfering with Darr's arrangements?'

'Yes, I suppose so. But I can't see why people in charge of old people's homes shouldn't bend a little about cats and feather beds.'

'Neither can I, but they wain't. All they'll allow old folk is a cubicle, a locker, a strip of carpet an' a sprung mattress. So if we wants the old chap to die happy, we've got to tek him, his cat an' his feathers under our own roof. But I ain't lookin' forward to it.'

Darr came back at that minute bearing a steaming dish of Spotted Dick smothered in custard.

'I were telling Ruby about my old Dad,' Bert informed her as she plonked the pudding on the table. 'A reet gaffer he is an' all. He'll have your garden sorted out in a couple of flicks of a donkey's lugholes.'

'Really?' I perked up a bit at that. 'I could do with a hand now and then.'

'Oh, he wain't exactly give you a hand,' Bert said, 'he'll climb up on a couple of boxes – seeing as how he's a bit on the short side – lean on the fence and tell *you* what to do.'

'I see.' If there was anything I needed it was a 'reet gaffer' leaning on the fence telling me what to do. I started on my portion of pudding, trying hard to ignore the custard.

'Ruby was saying we should've got him into an old folks' home,' Bert told Darr through a mouthful of steamed suet and currants.

'No I didn't mean that. I happen to think that old people are better off living with their relatives, as long as they hit it off together.'

'Which Darr an' Dad don't,' Bert said gloomily.

'And I certainly don't think that old people should be put into homes where they can't have their own belongings around them.'

'There ain't no homes like that in this area.' Bert swallowed his last spoonful of Spotted Dick. 'They're all as cold as charity.'

'Then it's high time somebody started one.'

'Aye, I agree with you. But – who?'

I offered to help with the washing up, but Bert said that Darr wouldn't like that at all.

'You will thank your wife for me, won't you?' I murmured, feeling foolish, seeing that Bert's wife was standing two feet from my left elbow. 'It was a lovely meal.'

Darr shuffled her feet in her carpet slippers, seemed about to say something, changed her mind, and headed back to the kitchen.

'By gum,' he said, 'I thowt she were gonna say summat that time.' He pushed back his hat with the gold braid which had remained firmly on his head throughout the meal. 'She likes you, Ruby, an' no mistake.'

As Bert and I stood together on the front path, an old lady on a sit-up-and-beg bicycle wobbled along the main street.

'How do?' Bert hollered, seeing nothing unusual in the strange apparition.

Her long voluminous skirts were almost catching in the back wheel as she pedalled towards the corner shop. Her head was covered with a black velvet tam-o-shanter, and there was something decidedly Victorian about the cut and design of her tightly-fitting waistcoat with leg-o-mutton sleeves.

'You'll come a cropper one of these days if you're not careful,' Bert yelled to her as she dismounted on the slight incline.

'You mind your manners, Bert Rumbold,' she retorted, 'I've been riding this bicycle for the past forty years, and I haven't come a cropper yet!'

Bert grinned. 'She'll be on her way for a bit of a crack to old Mrs Nugent.' Then his smile faded. 'It's a damn shame! I was one of her best babbies!'

'One of her – babbies?' Could the old lady on the bicycle, by some quirk of fate, possibly be Bert's mother, estranged from 'the gaffer', his cat and his feather bed?

'Aye,' Bert sighed, 'Nurse Pintuck brought me into the world. The biggest babby she ever had! Twelve pounds two ounces, an' screaming fit to bust!'

Visions of a red-faced infant wearing a flat cap crossed my mind; a kind of miniature present-day Bert Rumbold entering this world in a striped flannel shirt and dungarees, bringing his tuba with him.

I shook my head vigorously to clear my mind. 'Why is it a damned shame?' I asked.

'Because that damned Lady Nettlefold down at the Hall

81

wants her out of her cottage, and she wain't rest until she's got rid of her.'

'But how can she, if the cottage belongs to Nurse Pintuck?'

'Ah, that's the snag. It don't belong to her. It belongs to her ladyship. Her *ladyship*,' he repeated bitterly 'I'd cry shame on myself if I was her *ladyship*!'

'Why? What on earth do you mean?'

'What do I mean? I'll tell you what I mean! Lady Nettlefold wants shot of Nurse Pintuck so she can modernise her cottage an' put her gardener an' his family into it, that's what!'

'But surely, she can't turn her out without offering her alternative accommodation, can she?'

'Oh, she's found her that right enough,' Bert said, 'in one of those homes we wus talking about at dinner time. She's going into the Anchorage in Carnelian Bay, with a strip of carpet between the beds an' all her worldly goods in a locker. But it ain't good enough, if you ask me! That old woman deserves summat better than that in my opinion.'

I watched Nurse Pintuck wheel her bicycle to the side door of the corner shop, liking the indomitable tilt of her head in its black velvet tam-o-shanter.

What kind of person was Lady Nettlefold anyway, I wondered, as I walked back to April Cottage, to give Mr Abercromby a nervous tic, and to turn a character like Nurse Pintuck out of doors?

Someone should start a real home for old people, I thought as I marched up my front path. A place where they could take all their personal belongings – cats, feather beds and all – and live out their lives with dignity and independence.

Perhaps someone would, one day. Someone with a lot of money and their heart in the right place.

Chapter Twelve

Lizzie was nearly in tears when I called in at the shop on my way home. I knew she tried hard to keep calm and unemotional to be able to cope with all the demands on her time. Now she blinked her eyes rapidly behind her glasses.

'Has – has anything happened to your mother?' I scarcely dare ask, my mind was filled with visions of swallowed teeth and ambulances.

'She went up in smoke, that's all,' Lizzie sniffed.

'My God! You don't mean she set fire to her bedclothes?'

'I didn't mean that literally,' poor Lizzie said, 'I mean she went up in smoke when that letter from Miss Marshall arrived. I've never seen her so mad, but I had to leave her and come down at eight o'clock to serve Mrs Pickles. She was standing on the doorstep waiting for the shop to open, though why anyone should want a toilet roll at that hour in the morning beats me.'

'Perhaps she ate something that disagreed with her last night.'

The ghost of a smile touched Lizzie's mouth. 'Anyway, you can imagine what I felt like. I served her with the toilet paper, but she seemed in the mood for a gossip, and I daren't ask her to leave or push her out of the shop. Word would have gone round the village in ten minutes flat that Lizzie Nugent was having another tussle with her mother.' Lizzie gave an almighty sigh. 'They seem to have some sort of a bush telegraph system in this village.'

I was beginning to realise that, but she still hadn't told me who Miss Marshall was and what she had written to make Mrs Nugent so angry.

Lizzie started dusting automatically as she explained that

Miss Marshall was a peripatetic hairdresser who used to come once a month to trim her mother's hair. The letter was to say that she had decided to retire. 'Not that I blame her for that,' Lizzie said, 'I wish I could retire and that's a fact, but I think she might have told Mother the last time she came instead of letting her mark the calendar as usual.'

'Perhaps she didn't know then that she was going to retire,' I said, trying to find a crumb of comfort.

'Thinking back I'm sure she did. I wondered at the time why she looked so relieved when she went out.' Suddenly Lizzie saw the funny side of things. 'I offered to cut Mum's hair for her,' she said, 'and that made her madder than ever. She said if I cut her hair the way I slice ham she'd look a right clip and no mistake.'

'Oh Lord.'

'But it wasn't just having her hair done that Mother enjoyed, it was putting a ring round the next date on the calendar – that and being the centre of attention for once in a way. You see Miss Marshall always stopped for a chat and a cup of tea afterwards.'

I couldn't bear to see Lizzie in such a jam, then I thought of the case of hairdressing equipment I'd come across the other day.

'Don't worry, Lizzie,' I said, 'I'll cut your mother's hair if she'll let me.'

Lizzie's nose turned pink and I thought she was going to cry again. 'Would you really? But no, I wouldn't dream of asking you – I know how much you dislike hairdressing,' she said.

'Ah but you didn't ask. I offered.'

'I – I don't know what to say.'

'It's what your mother says that matters. She might go up in smoke again at the very idea. Why don't you go and ask her, while I stand by with the fire-extinguisher.'

Lizzie hurried off upstairs, and returned beaming like a lighthouse.

'You needn't bother with the fire-extinguisher,' she said. 'Mother's as happy as a sandboy. Oh Sally, you don't know what a good turn you've done me.'

It was starting to rain when I hurried down to the letter-box near the bridge and saw Avril coming towards me.

'Hello. I was just on my way to see you,' she said, 'to tell you about choir-practice. It's tonight at half-past seven.'

'Tonight?'

Her face puckered. 'You can make it, can't you? Oh I know you're not all that keen, but I'd like you to come if only for a bit of moral support.'

'All right then, I'll be there.' Why, I wondered, did one make such hasty decisions only to regret them later on? But a promise was a promise.

'Why don't you walk back to the vicarage with me?' she suggested brightly, 'We could have a cup of tea and a natter.'

'Thanks, I'd like that.'

'Just a sec. Do you mind if we stand under this tree for a minute until I find my rain hood?' She fiddled in her handbag. 'Aren't these concertina-shaped things the bitter end? But at least they keep one's hair dry.' She glanced sympathetically in my direction. 'Wish I had a spare one for you. You're getting soaked. Haven't you got an umbrella or a headscarf?'

'I've got one of those collapsible umbrellas in my shoulder-bag,' I said.

'Why don't you put it up then?'

'It won't *go* up, that's why. Well, the woman in the shop said it was collapsible when I bought it, so I haven't any come back under the Trade Description Act. First the end fell off, then the chain, and now the spokes have packed up as well.'

'Even so . . .' Avril giggled.

'Oh, all right!' I dug out my collapsible umbrella, opened it as far as it would go, and stood there peering at her through a palisade of dangling aluminium spokes. 'Satisfied?'

'You *are* a nut, Sally,' she laughed, 'but at least it will keep your head dry.'

'I know it sounds odd,' I said dreamily, 'but I rather like getting wet in the rain.' I sniffed the air rapturously as we stood together under the tree. 'Everything smells so fresh, as if the world had just been re-born. If there's a nicer smell than lilac in the rain, I can't think what it is. Can you smell lilac?'

'Hmmmm.' Avril sniffed the air too. 'It's coming from Nurse Pintuck's garden down the lane there. She has the most glorious little garden, just like one of those pictures on a Birthday card.'

'Is it really true that Lady Nettlefold wants her out of her cottage?' I asked as we walked on.

'I'm afraid so. It's a crying shame, isn't it? Arthur has spoken to her ladyship on Nurse Pintuck's behalf, but she wouldn't listen to him. And would you believe it, that old lady hasn't even got an indoor loo! The poor old soul has to dash out of doors every time she wants to spend a penny. She hasn't got any running hot water either.' Avril jerked angrily the strings of her rain-bonnet. 'But you can bet your bottom dollar that as soon as Nurse moves out of her cottage, Lady Nettlefold will have it modernised fast enough to make your head spin!'

Anger bubbled up inside me. 'I'd like to meet Lady Nettlefold one of these days,' I said darkly.

'You will,' Avril said apologetically, 'tonight at choir practice.'

'Oh Lord!'

'Do you know,' Avril sighed, 'that her ladyship won't even let Arthur choose the hymns? She sends him a typewritten list the first thing every Monday morning.'

'No wonder he's developed a nervous tic!'

'Not to mention Mr Plunkett, the organist.'

I stopped dead in my tracks. 'You mean to say that Mr Plunkett has developed a nervous tic as well?'

'No,' Avril said, 'I mean that Lady Nettlefold sends him a typewritten list too.'

As we stopped near the bridge to post my letter, I looked over the parapet at the rain plopping into the water, and stared at the lovely Georgian house with its lawns sloping down to the river. 'Isn't that absolutely marvellous?' I said mistily through the spokes of my collapsed umbrella. 'It's so utterly English and "Is there honey, still, for tea?" that makes me want to cry.'

Memory wafted me back to the days when I would skip along beside Amelia clutching a bag of crusts to feed the birds on the village duckpond. I said involuntarily, 'My husband couldn't bear walking in the rain. He much preferred sitting over the fire – especially on Sunday afternoons – doing *The Times* cross-word. So I'd mend his socks, or make a trifle for tea in absolute silence, when all the time I was longing to be outdoors.'

I leaned my arms on the parapet. 'It was marvellous last Sunday afternoon. I went for a walk all by myself, down the lane to the beach, and I crunched there along the shingle, feeling for all the world like a little girl who has been let out of school before the bell rang. Do you know what I mean?'

Avril nodded. 'Yes,' she said softly, 'and I can't tell you how much I envy you, Sally, seeing the world through rose-coloured glasses.'

She leaned her arms on the bridge too, smiling through a haze of memories. 'I often wish that I could go back to the first time Arthur and I walked across this bridge together. I thought that Tootington was the prettiest village I'd ever seen in my life, with the church and the river, the road curving away under those trees to the village green, and those lovely cottages with white fences and windowboxes.' She sighed. 'Now I hardly notice it at all. What I mean is, I don't *see* it any more the way I used to. All I can see is that big house over there. Lady Nettlefold's house!' She huddled into her coat as if she had gooseflesh. 'Ridiculous, isn't it? I loathe and detest that house. If only she'd let her bushes straggle a bit, or allow a weed or two to sprout up in the gravel. And have you noticed the blinds? I suppose she keeps them lowered to stop the sun fading the carpets.'

I admitted that the house did look a bit grim; out of character with the rest of the village, and I realised that Avril had become obsessive about Lady Nettlefold.

'I suppose she must have had a very good voice in her younger days,' Avril went on as we passed a row of cottages with pantiled roofs, flower-filled gardens and window-boxes, 'now she insists on singing descants even though she can't hit top C any longer.' She smiled shame-facedly. 'I'm sorry, I shouldn't have said that, but it's true, and now I come over hot and cold every time there's a descant. The tension is almost unbearable at times.'

'Sounds like a ball of fun,' I said dolefully. 'If there's anything I need right now it's a bit of extra tension to add spice to life. As if I hadn't got enough on my plate with that wretched next-door neighbour of mine.'

Avril shot me a startled glance. 'You mean – Miss Cox? Why, what's going on?'

'Oh, nothing much, except that we're into a vendetta that makes the Corsican Brothers look like two old ladies arguing over a card of elastic at a jumble sale.'

'Oh dear.'

'What do you mean – oh dear? Why are you looking at me in that strange way?'

'I suppose I'd better tell you now as later. Miss Cox is a member of the choir too!'

We walked in dejected silence past Lady Nettlefold's wrought-iron gates. The rain hadn't seemed all that wet before, but it did now.

'Cheer up.' Avril smiled uncertainly. 'We all have a cross to bear. I have Lady N and you have Miss Cox. Actually I wouldn't mind swapping crosses seeing that her ladyship weighs all of seventeen stone.'

She giggled suddenly. 'You know, Sally, it's lovely to have someone to be miserable with.'

As we turned the corner into Vicarage Lane, I stopped to look at a house with a For Sale notice in the garden. Set back from the road, with wide lawns, tall chimneys, and a conservatory, it seemed vaguely familiar to me.

Then suddenly I remembered why. Amelia had once taken me there to see an old lady she knew. Oh what on earth was her name? Miss Bell – was that it? No, but I felt certain that her name began with a B. Then I caught sight of the name plate on the gate: 'The Hollies' – and I remembered that old lady's name. Miss Berry! Yes, that was it!

Memories flooded back to me. I remembered how excited I'd been because the Hollies belonged to a Miss Berry.

Avril tugged anxiously at my arm. 'Is anything the matter?' she asked. 'You're getting terribly wet, you know.'

'Am I? Never mind. It's just that I remember this house. A very old woman answered the door to us, and showed us through to Miss Berry's drawing room.

'She was sitting in a chair with a rug round her knees – Miss Berry, I mean – and I gave her a bunch of flowers.' I glanced at Avril apologetically. 'Oh, I'm sorry, but I know every nook and cranny of that house. You see, when I'd given Miss Berry the flowers, she told me to go through to the kitchen for a mug of milk and a hot buttered scone.'

'And then?' Avril prompted with a smile.

'Well, then the housekeeper took me upstairs and showed me all the rooms, even the attics. I was absolutely spellbound. I'd never seen anything like it before except at the cinema. The skirting boards were at least a foot deep, and there was lots of stained glass and moulded cornices. It was all a bit dark and sombre, of course, and the furniture was mahogany; huge sideboards with silver dishes, and heavy oil-paintings in gilded frames, but I adored it – especially Miss Berry's bedroom. She actually had a four-poster bed with hangings, and a white lace valance.' I sighed. 'I suppose Miss Berry must have died years ago. I wonder who the house belonged to after that.'

'The last owner was Lady Nettlefold's sister,' Avril said. 'That much I do know for certain. I remember her quite well as a matter of fact.'

'What was she like?' I asked.

'As different from her sister as chalk from cheese,' Avril commented, re-tying the strings of her rain-hood. 'Meg Nettlefold was a lovely person; a lavender-and-lace type of lady, all sweetness and smiles. Apparently she and her sister never really saw eye to eye over anything, and I can understand why. What puzzles me is how they ever came to be sisters in the first place. Anyway, when Meg died, Lady N couldn't wait to put the property on the market, but the sad thing is that nobody seems to want it now.'

She tucked her hand into the crook of my arm. 'I suppose it's far too big and inconvenient for a family house these days, and too far off the beaten track for a hotel, so there it stands. Poor old house. I can't think what use anyone could make of it nowadays.'

'It would make a marvellous old people's home,' I said wistfully.

Chapter Thirteen

St Chad's was a charming little Norman church with a fine Jacobean oak reredos, glowing stained-glass windows, and a Saxon font.

I knew all that because I'd popped in there on my way back from the vicarage and treated myself to a booklet on its history. Apart from that, I'd decided to have a good look at the scene of the forthcoming choir-practice to find out if there was any way of nipping in without Miss Cox seeing me. There wasn't.

As the church clock struck half-past seven I slunk, like a Disney cat, down the aisle.

Avril hurried forward to greet me, and I had never been so glad to see anyone in all my life.

Apparently neither had she. 'I thought you'd chickened out,' she said, *sotto-voce*, clasping my frozen hand.

'I very nearly did,' I muttered, 'in fact I think I'll go home now, if you don't mind.'

'No, of course you're not late,' she said in a psuedo-cheerful voice, 'Lady Nettleford hasn't arrived yet, and as we can't begin without her, I'll have time to introduce you.'

A small worried-looking man with thinning hair and a Kitchener moustache bustled up to me, mopping his eyes with a large white handkerchief.

'I'm Algernon Plunkett, the choir-master,' he said.

'How do you do?' I asked uncertainly, wondering what I had done to engender such an outburst of emotion.

'I have a bad cold,' he informed me, 'a very bad cold!'

'I'm sorry to hear that.' I hoped he realised that I couldn't possibly have passed it on to him.

'Thanks. Well, now that you are here, can you sing?' He stared at me through streaming tear-ducts.

'Not very well, I'm afraid, although I did once take the lead in "The Merry Widow".'

He seemed impressed. 'Really? How did you get on with "Vilia"?'

'I don't really know, Mr Plunkett, except that everyone breathed a sigh of relief when I vanished away in the woods. Looking back, I don't suppose I'd have got the part at all except that the leading lady lost her voice at the last minute.'

Avril tugged at my hand and led me across to the male section of the choir, facing the ladies across a strip of blue carpet.

'This is Commander Bruce,' she said, 'who lives in that lovely Georgian house near the bridge. We passed it this afternoon if you remember.'

'How do you do?' I smiled up at him, liking enormously his twinkling blue eyes, tanned face and clipped moustache. Then, because I felt I ought to say something more, 'I – I think your house is beautiful.'

'How kind of you to say so, Mrs . . .'

'Shelton,' I supplied. 'Sally Shelton.'

'And this is Mr George Brassington.'

George Brassington's handshake felt like a bowl of luke-warm rice pudding after Commander Bruce's vice-like grip. He had slate blue eyes, puffy lids, a paunch, and thick sensual lips.

It must be rather odd, I thought, standing in the choir-stalls and seeing one's ancestors lying in the nave with their legs crossed. But the crusader Brassingtons were all lean, aesthetic-looking gentlemen wearing coats of plates, pauldron, vambrace, and gauntlets.

Well, perhaps they didn't get all that much to eat during the Crusades, I reflected, shaking my head to clear my mind of a mental image of George Brassington stretched out near the font in his tight twill trousers and hacking jacket.

'And this is Ambrose Lanfeard.'

I confronted a smiling gargoyle wearing a drooping posy of wild-flowers in his buttonhole.

'How do?' Ambrose's extended hand felt like nail-studded leather. He gave me a long, searching look. 'Ah've seen you afore, 'aven't I? Did you catch owt in that shrimping net young Robbie lent you?'

91

'Yes. As a matter of fact he fished out a jam-jar full of newts.'

'Well I'll be buggered!' Ambrose chuckled deeply. 'By the way, Missis, you've got a reet sod of a garden there if you don't mind my saying so. What's tha goin' to do with all them bushes?'

'I'm going to separate them.'

'Thou'll hev a job on,' he said, shaking his grizzled head. 'Ah've seen some bushes in my time, but ah ain't niver seen none like them afore. Tha' can't tell wheer one begins and t'other finishes.'

'I daresay you're right, but I mean to try just the same.'

I'd forgotten where I was for a moment, and looked up to see George Brassington's stare of contempt. The Commander, on the other hand, appeared to be enjoying the conversation.

Avril sprang nobly to my aid. 'Now I'll introduce you to the ladies,' she said, hauling me across the strip of blue carpet. 'Miss Cox you already know' – she passed that off beautifully, 'and this is Miss Fanshaw.'

Miss Fanshaw resembled a whippet, all sinew and knotted muscle. Her halo of white hair looked as if it had been curried rather than combed. She gave a loud hacking cough as we were introduced, and said in mild irritation, 'Another wretched soprano, I suppose? I can tell by the colour of your hair. Never met a dark-haired soprano yet.'

'And this is Miss Handyside.'

'How do you do?' I looked up into a pair of forget-me-not blue eyes beneath a tip-tilted hat of the 1930s vintage.

'As well as I can under the circumstances,' she murmured. 'You see, my dear, I have heart trouble. Palpitations, if you know what I mean.' She tapped her fingers lightly against her cushiony bosom.

'Oh, I am sorry.'

'But I try hard to be brave.'

'Yes, I'm sure you do.'

Avril had done her vicar's wife stuff admirably. As I stood in the pew directly in front of Miss Handyside, I leafed through a hymn book and felt a distinct sensation of being churned up inside – the sensation that one has at a wedding, wondering if the bridegroom is going to turn up.

Suddenly Avril, who had preceded me into the pew said,

speaking from the side of her mouth like a ventriloquist, 'Oh Lord, here she comes – the Grand Panjandrum!'

I stared at the imposing figure of a woman in an ankle-length purple dress, wearing a hat like a wreath, who moved down the aisle like a battle-cruiser about to blast the enemy. She was escorted by a thin little man who seemed ready to sink to his knees by the sheer weight of the burden he supported.

So that was Lady Nettlefold – all seventeen stone of her, with three chins, pince-nez spectacles on a gold chain, hair like a judge's wig, a mink stole and size ten shoes.

'I do wish you would let go of my arm, Alfred,' she said testily, shaking off the thin man like a fly on a net curtain, 'your weight is insupportable. Go and sit down.'

'Yes, Aunt.' Alfred Nettlefold scuttled away obediently, and I wondered what would happen to him if he said 'No, Aunt' once in a while, but I could guess the answer to that. He'd be cut off without a penny to bless himself.

No wonder the poor little fellow seemed so nervous and dried up. At least a fly on a net curtain would have lived a little; spread its wings in the sunshine once in a while; have known the ecstasy of playing the violin with its back legs before someone swatted it.

'Allow me, your ladyship!' The organist made a sudden swoop from a pile of cushions so arranged on the organ bench that he could reach the manual and the swells at the same time. One of them was embroidered with the legend: 'Thou, God, See'est Me' – which seemed to me a highly unsuitable motif to sit upon.

Once Lady Nettlefold was settled, Mr Plunkett dashed back to his keyboard, re-stacked his cushions and announced that we would sing Psalm One Hundred, 'Jubilate Deo'. Unfortunately his sneezing got in the way.

'Psalm One Hundred! "Oh be joyful in the Lord all ye lands" – A-tishoo!'

I turned my head at that moment to see if he'd managed to stay put on 'Thou, God, Seest Me'; found myself looking into the limpid eyes of Miss Handyside in the row behind, and said foolishly, 'I thought for a minute he was going to say A-men.'

'What did you say, my dear?' Miss Handyside fiddled inside her coat and a loud whistling filled the air. 'Would you mind repeating it? I'm afraid I forgot to switch on my hearing-aid.' The whistling grew louder.

'It doesn't matter,' I muttered, my cheeks scarlet with embarrassment.

'Stop! Stop playing this instant, Mr Plunkett!' Lady Nettlefold thumped on the floor with her walking stick. 'Someone is chattering. I simply will not have it! Who was it, eh?'

'I'm afraid it was me, your ladyship,' I owned up. 'I'm very sorry.'

'Who are you?' she demanded. 'I haven't seen you before. What's your name?'

My mind went a complete blank, the way it did in Waldorf Winninger's antique shop on the day of my interview.

Avril came nobly to my rescue. 'This is Mrs Shelton,' she said, 'a newcomer to the choir.'

'Indeed. Then perhaps Mrs Shelton would have the courtesy to keep quiet while we are trying to sing.' She gave me a long, cold stare. 'Pray continue with the psalm, Mr Plunkett –and do, for goodness sake, stop sneezing.'

I stood stiffly to attention with my mouth shut as the choir battled its way through 'Oh be joyful'. I'd never been any good at psalms, and wasn't even sure that I'd found the right page in the psalter. Why on earth didn't whoever printed the wretched things put all those c's and crosses? What did xciii stand for, anyway?

Avril handed me her own psalter open at the right page, and gave me a sympathetic dig in the ribs. She might just as well have handed me a Pitman shorthand.

Apparently Ambrose Lanfeard hadn't got the hang of psalm-singing either, not that he appeared in the least concerned about the row he was making, or singing long notes when everyone else was going like the clappers on the short ones.

Lady Nettlefold thumped loudly with her walking stick again. Everyone except Ambrose quavered to a halt. 'No, no, no!' she bellowed, punctuating every no with a ferocious jab of her silver-knobbed cane. 'Stop it at once, I say!'

As Mr Plunkett hurried forward, scattering cushions in his wake, her ladyship berated him soundly for allowing what she termed 'this travesty' to continue.

'If Mr Lanfeard cannot sing the psalm properly,' she thundered, 'he must stand down. I will not listen to this caterwauling a minute longer!'

The unhappy choir-master wiped his streaming eyes. 'Please stop, Ambrose,' he murmured, 'you heard what Lady Nettlefold said.'

The old chap took his time complying with the request, and cocked a bushy eyebrow. 'Am I or am I not mekkin' a joyful sound unto the Lord?' he demanded.

'You're making a sound certainly. Whether it could be termed joyful is a matter of opinion.'

Ambrose lowered his psalter and glared at the choir-master. 'Did anyone hear the Lord thumpin' on the ceiling?' he said. 'No, because the Lord has more manners than to interrupt one of his servants mekkin' a joyful sound – which is more than I can say for some fowk.'

The corners of the Commander's lips began to twitch. George Brassington, on the other hand, was not amused.

'Don't be so fatuous, man,' he snapped. 'If you can't sing at least talk sense. Are you drunk?'

'I don't drink,' Ambrose said indignantly, 'leastways not what *you* would call drinking. All I ever do is wet my whistle at the Spotted Dog on a Saturday night. I don't go in for all them fancy wines and sperrits like some fowk I could mention. My sperrit comes from the Lord, not that there fakey wine shop in Carnelian Bay!'

'Enough of this nonsense,' Lady Nettlefold thundered. 'Are you or are you not, Mr Plunkett, going to do your duty by this choir? Mr Lanfeard should be removed at once. Anyone who cannot sing a psalm properly has no business to be in a church choir!'

Ambrose treated her to a baleful stare. 'Neither has anyone who can't hit the top note in a descant,' he said triumphantly.

Lady Nettlefold clutched her mink stole and fairly throttled it. 'Oh,' she roared, 'the crass impertinence of the man! Alfred! Take me home at once! I shall not stay here to be insulted!'

I thought for a moment that Alfred was about to have a seizure. His narrow face turned a sickly shade of grey and his pale blue eyes bulged in his head.

As her ladyship struggled to turn and got wedged sideways

on in the pew, little Miss Handyside, standing behind me, flopped forward like a rag doll and flung her arms round my neck for support.

Nobody except the Commander noticed the minor contretemps. Everyone else's attention was focused on Lady Nettlefold. It was the Commander who strode across the strip of blue carpet to save me from strangulation, and rescued Miss Handyside's hat which had fallen off in the foray.

'We must get her out into the fresh air at once,' he said crisply. 'Will you help me, Mrs Shelton? I suggest that you take one arm while I take the other.' He gave me a brief encouraging smile. 'I think she's coming round now.'

Together we manoeuvred Miss Handyside down the aisle while the other choir-members stood frozen to immobility – rather like that game of statues I used to play at school. Miss Cox's mouth was sagging open, Lady Nettlefold was still wedged sideways in the pew, Miss Fanshaw's hair seemed to be starched into a kind of halo, old Ambrose looked as if he'd been carved out of stone, while George Brassington looked for all the world like a brass-rubbing. Only Avril grasped the fact that Miss Handyside had fainted, and hurried down the aisle after us.

Outside the church, the Commander and I sat Miss Handyside on a flat gravestone under the elms.

'I'll fetch my car,' he said briskly.

'Smelling salts! My handbag,' Miss Handyside murmured. 'Oh dear, I feel so ashamed of myself.'

I found her salts and held the bottle under her nose until a tinge of colour crept back to her ashen cheeks. 'No need to feel ashamed,' I reassured her, 'you couldn't help fainting.'

Avril hurried up to us. 'Would you like me to put your hat back on for you?' she asked.

'My hat? Why, haven't I got it on? I'm sure I had it on when I left home this evening.' All of a fluster, the old lady continued, 'It's my heart, you know. The doctor said I mustn't get upset, but I couldn't help getting upset when Lady Nettlefold starting thumping with her stick . . .'

'No, of course you couldn't.' I gave her another whiff of the smelling salts.

'It seems all wrong, doesn't it,' she sniffed, 'that people

96

should behave so badly in church? But I've seen it coming. Oh yes, I have.'

'Please, Miss Handyside, don't distress yourself . . .'

'It's all because of dear Rebecca Pintuck, you know,' she went on, refusing to be comforted. 'Ambrose Lanfeard has always thought a great deal of Rebecca, that's why he goes out of his way to upset her ladyship. Not that I blame him, I really don't . . .' She glanced down at the gravestone. 'Oh!' she cried. 'I'm sitting on Prudence Smollett! I beg your pardon, Prudence! Oh dear, oh dear . . . I want to go home!'

'Commander Bruce has gone to fetch his car,' Avril assured her. 'You'll soon be home now.'

'All this trouble because Eunice Nettlefold wants to put poor Rebecca into a home. I don't know what the world's coming to, I really don't!' Tears welled up in Miss Handyside's forget-me-not blue eyes, and she dug her fingers into my arm. 'What frightens me most is that what is about to happen to Rebecca could easily happen to me! I can't sleep for worrying about it – being turned out of my home, I mean.'

'Don't worry about it now,' Avril advised gently. 'Ah, here's the car.'

'You've both been very kind to me,' Miss Handyside murmured, dabbing her eyes with a cologne-scented handkerchief. 'Oh, I should so like a cup of tea.'

'I'm sure Mrs Shelton will make you one,' Avril said. 'I'd come with you only . . .' She gave me a desperate glance, 'only I think I should get back to the choir-practice – or what's left of it.'

As Commander Bruce helped Miss Handyside into his car, Avril said, 'To be honest, Sally, I could run away! Can you imagine what I'll have to face back there? I'm only glad that Arthur had a meeting of the Men's Fellowship tonight and couldn't be here to see this shambles. You do see what we're up against, don't you?'

'Yes, I do,' I acknowledged. 'That woman's a menace.'

If anyone thought that all vicars had to do was turn up in church on Sunday mornings, wearing a nice clean surplice, I thought as I got into the car, they had another think coming.

Strangely enough, when the Commander and I had helped Miss Handyside to her front door, her attitude towards us changed completely.

97

'I feel quite well now,' she said firmly. 'Please don't fuss over me any more.'

'But I thought you wanted a cup of tea,' I said.

'So I do, but I'm quite capable of making it for myself.' She sounded quite huffy, and shut the door in our faces.

'What was all that about?' the Commander asked wryly as we made our way back up the path.

'I'm not quite sure, but I think it had to do with being independent.' I smiled ruefully. 'Well, thank you, Commander . . .'

'Get in the car,' he said quietly, 'I'll drive you home.'

'There's really no need. I can walk.'

He smiled. 'I don't doubt it, but I intend to drive you. What is this, anyway – Independence Day?' In the driving seat, he turned to me and said, 'Where do you live, Mrs Shelton?'

'April Cottage. Facing the common.'

'Really?' He raised a quizzical eyebrow. 'That was Amelia Beatty's cottage, wasn't it?'

'You knew her?'

He chuckled. 'That I did. Everyone had a healthy respect for Amelia, even our irascible friend, Lady Nettlefold.'

I wondered what he meant, but felt too shy to ask.

'I'm afraid this has been a traumatic evening for you one way and another,' he said lightly as he stopped the car outside April Cottage.

'Yes it has, but I'm used to things going wrong,' I said, trying to match my tone of voice to his. 'That's the story of my life.'

'I only hope that tonight hasn't put you off joining the choir,' he said.

'Too late for that. I've already joined.'

'And you are obviously a lady who is not easily thrown off course?'

'Well, I was in the Wrens at one stage,' I told him, 'but I'm no heroine for all that. Actually, Commander Bruce, when everything is boiled down to the essentials, I suppose I'm just as scared as Miss Handyside when it comes to coping with life.'

'If I may say so, you coped very well tonight,' he remarked.

'I didn't cope with a thing,' I said. 'You did.'

He slid from the driving seat and opened the passenger door for me just as Frances Cox hove into view.

'Well, goodnight Commander Bruce,' I said, wishing that my eagle-eyed next-door-neighbour had not spotted us.

'Goodnight, Mrs Shelton,' he replied, 'and thank you for . . . Ah, good evening, Miss Cox.'

'Good evening, Commander Bruce,' she replied frostily, turning towards her cottage without another word.

It was written in large, disapproving letters on Frances Cox's forehead, what she thought of Commander Bruce driving me home. I knew, without a shadow of doubt, what she was thinking, and what her wagging tongue would make of an innocent encounter.

After all, Commander Bruce was a very handsome man, and I was nothing but a gay divorcee with dyed hair in her estimation.

Put together those two components – and POW!

Chapter Fourteen

I thought I'd laid aside my scissors and comb for the last time when I married Hugo. Now here I was taking a retrograde step and packing my attaché case with something akin to nervousness. It was such a long time since I'd cut anyone's hair.

Memories came crowding in on me as I folded the cotton hairdressing cape and laid it neatly in the case. I'd had my share of awkward clients in my time; perms that didn't 'take' for some reason or other, women with two hairs and a nit who expected to walk out of my salon looking like Brigitte Bardot; brides who appeared on their wedding day bringing their head-dresses with them so that I could twiddle their hair round them and skewer them firmly in place so they wouldn't come adrift halfway up the aisle, old people who had said wistfully that they couldn't afford the price of a hair-do for a special occasion – but they'd got one just the same.

'All they have to do is tell you a hard-luck story,' my father would say, 'and you fall for it every time.'

'Yes, I know,' I'd retort, 'you taught me the business, remember?'

My father didn't just give the little pathetic-looking old ladies free haircuts, he'd slip them half-a-crown to buy themselves some fish and chips on their way home.

We were both 'sucker bait', that's why we loved each other so much and found such a lot to laugh about.

One day perhaps I'd write a book about hot perms and henna-packs, and about that salon on the ground floor of a Victorian house where we coped with tong-waves and blisters, wigs and pincurls.

Lizzie met me at the side door.

'Is your mother ready?' I asked apprehensively, gripping the handle of my attaché case.

'Ready! Sally, she's been ready since four o'clock this morning.'

'You're kidding!'

'I'm not. I've scarcely had a wink of sleep all night. Talk about a little girl waiting for Father Christmas. First she wanted a drink of water, then a cup of tea, At six o'clock she demanded breakfast and – I don't know how to tell you this, but you've got an audience.' .

'An audience? Who, for Pete's sake?'

'I hope you don't mind, but Mother wanted Nurse Pintuck to come along and watch the proceedings.'

'Nurse Pintuck? Oh, I'd love to meet her!'

'You would? Thank God for that!'

I felt rather like an actress going on stage as I stepped into the back room where the two old ladies awaited me.

Mrs Nugent clawed her walking-stick expectantly. 'Ah,' she croaked, 'so you're not wearing trousers today! I've heard about them, you know. But I don't approve of women dressing like men. They haven't got the right-shaped backsides.'

'I never wear trousers on special occasions,' I said lightly, 'only when I'm gardening, to save my tights.'

'Tights,' she muttered, 'tights! What's wrong with stockings? You'll never catch a man, Miss, if you keep on wearing tights. Men like black stockings and suspenders! You ask 'em if you don't believe me.'

'*Mother!*' Lizzie's eyebrows seemed about to disappear into her hair with embarrassment.

'Don't you "Mother" me. I know what I'm talking about! You think because I'm old and desiccated that I don't know what's what. But I'll tell you this, my girl, Lily Langtry wouldn't have been seen dead in tights and trousers!'

I looked round helplessly, not knowing what to say next, and caught the eye of Rebecca Pintuck.

In a split-second moment, I felt that I had known her all my life, and yet she hadn't said a word. She didn't have to; her eyes said it all. In one glance she excused Mrs Nugent's forthrightness, understood Lizzie's embarrassment, and approved of me.

101

Nurse Pintuck possessed the charm of a Victorian daguerreotype; the sepia beauty of a girl caught, with frills and buttons, on the eve of her twenty-first birthday, when life was all promise and rainbows.

Still amazingly beautiful despite her advanced years, she wore a neatly buttoned to the throat crêpe-de-chine blouse, and smelt of oatmeal and lavender-water. Her snow-white hair was covered with the floppy black velvet beret which reminded me of an outsize mushroom, and her ankles were slim and dainty beneath her capacious skirts. I was even prepared to bet that she was wearing black silk stockings and suspenders.

'I don't think you've met Nurse Pintuck.'

'How do you do, my dear? I've looked forward to meeting you.'

'Never mind all that,' Mrs Nugent broke in. 'Help me up, Lizzie! Where's the chair? Fetch the chair! You don't expect me to have my hair cut standing up, do you? And what about the newspapers? You should have brought some newspapers . . .'

'Gently, Mother. Just sit still for a minute. I'll fetch the chair if you'll be patient.'

'You should have fetched it sooner,' wheezed Mrs Nugent. 'That high-backed one from the other room. Really, Lizzie, you do poke-stick about at times!'

'You forget, Mother, that I have the shop to see to as well.' Lizzie was getting into a tizzy. 'There's the bell! I'll have to go. Oh dear!'

I gave her a look. 'Don't worry,' I said, 'I'll see to everything.'

Things were slipping back into place now. I remembered some of the tetchy clients who needed firm handling and reassurance; nervous old ladies who said that the perming machine was getting too hot before it was even plugged in; recalcitrant children who had behaved far better when I'd sent their mothers out of the cubicle.

As I carried in the chair, and spread newspaper to catch the clippings, I caught Nurse Pintuck's look of quiet amusement, and wondered how many hysterical mothers and crying babies she had soothed in her time.

'Oh Lord,' I prayed inwardly, 'let me not cut Mrs Nugent's hair like a slice of Lizzie's ham.'

When Liz returned from serving her customer, her mother

was peering at herself in a square of looking-glass. 'There,' she said, 'that's what I call a haircut. Both sides dead level. Now where's my tea? I want my tea. Lizzie put the kettle on.'

When Lizzie had fled to the kitchen, Mrs Nugent started hunting under a pile of cushions, and produced a worn leather purse. 'How much do I owe you?' she wanted to know. 'Miss Marshall charged me seventy-five pence.'

'You don't owe me a thing,' I said, acutely embarrassed.

'I think, my dear,' Nurse Pintuck said, quietly, 'that Mrs Nugent would prefer to pay you. You see, if you don't make a charge – even a small one – she couldn't very well ask you to come again, and she does want you to come again, I'm sure.'

'You're quite right, of course. I hadn't thought of it that way.' Once again I experienced the feeling of having known Nurse Pintuck all my life, and suddenly I knew why. She reminded me of 'Gran'. Although they didn't look alike, they had in common a calm, realistic outlook on life which had nothing at all to do with facial resemblance.

Gran had been my refuge throughout the stormy years of childhood; the one who comforted but seldom cosseted – and she had always smelt of lavender and oatmeal soap too.

'Come again? Of course I want her to come again. She didn't tug me once. Not like that stuck up Miss Marshall. She used to tug my hair something dreadful when she was in a hurry.' Mrs Nugent said, counting her money, adding it up wrongly, and starting all over again.

As Lizzie brought in the tea-trolley, Nurse Pintuck said, 'I understand that you singe hair, and I wondered – would you consider singeing mine? Not now, of course, but if I made an appointment. Could you possibly come to my cottage one day?'

'Yes, of course.'

'I shall want another appointment too.' Mrs Nugent was obviously put out because I was paying too much attention to Rebecca Pintuck. 'Hand me that calendar, Lizzie! And while she's about it, she'd better cut yours, too. It looks a dreadful mess, scraped up like that.'

'Darr! Where in tarnation have you hidden my shoes? Tha' doesn't expect me to go to the fête in me carpet slippers, does tha'?'

I was in the front garden snipping lilac with a pair of scissors at the time, and waited with bated breath to hear Darr's reply. None came. I was beginning to think of Darr's voice as 'the Lost Chord'. Perhaps she was making hand signals in there.

Minutes later, Bert hurried down the garden path clutching his tuba, wearing his peaked cap, and a navy blue suit so tight that he had been obliged to leave the buttons of his waistcoat undone. However he'd come to grips with Colonel Bogey in that outfit I had no idea.

My bedroom had two windows, one overlooked the cow-pasture behind April Cottage, the other overlooked the common and things were starting to hot up out there.

The scene reminded me of a Heath Robinson cartoon, with ropes holding things up or holding them down, and boxes of bunting with lengths of string attached; knotted string which nobody had had time to unravel.

The night before, a firm of contractors had appeared with a lorry load of canvas which turned out to be a small marquee and several tents. Putting up deckchairs was nothing compared to the workmen's bewilderment when faced with all those pegs and guy-ropes, and I'd watched in fascination as they attempted to solve the canvas conundrum, lugging and tugging, and finally leaning against the side of the lorry completely exhausted before nipping up to The Spotted Dog for a drop of light liquid refreshment.

When they finally departed, the common looked like the tented field at Agincourt.

Now it was a perfect day. Not a sign of a cloud in the clear blue sky, the trees on the common were in full leaf, birds were skimming; the push-chair and pram brigade was coming up the road from the housing estate. There was a sense of occasion.

I saw, from my bedroom window, Bert and the lads scrambling on to a stationary wagon. Some of them wore suits, the rest of them were arrayed in whatever seemed most fitting. What a pity, I thought, that they didn't have uniforms.

I held my breath as Half-Pint gave his great-grandfather a boost from behind to get him on to the lorry. Apparently he hadn't boosted him hard enough, for Ould Gabby sprawled flat on his face and had to be hauled into a sitting position by the trombones.

Then Ambrose Lanfeard appeared, and scrambled aboard

104

the bandwagon in his cowman's get up, farm boots and all, his outfit rendered even more remarkable by the carnation he wore in his buttonhole, and the peaked, gold-trimmed hat atop his grizzled head.

While all that was going on, I was flitting between my bedroom and Amelia's minuscule bathroom, getting ready for the fray, looking at myself in the mirror, thinking that all the rushing about at the Red Lion and my days in the garden were nicely ironing out the bumps in my waistline.

At two o'clock, a black limousine drew up in the road outside April Cottage. From it emerged Lady Nettlefold, wearing an ankle-length dress of barrage-balloon dimensions, followed by little Alfred, dapper in a topper and pin-stripe morning suit, even though it was afternoon.

The band broke into 'God Save the Queen' which must have inflated her ladyship's ego enormously. Leaning on Alfred's arm, she listened standing to attention, and then sailed forward to a bunting-bedecked platform from which she declared the fête open. Not that anyone was really listening. A baby began to bawl and was hushed by its mother, whilst a contingent of young Tootington tearaways engaged in a savage game of football inches away from the loud-speaker system.

Avril and Arthur, I noticed, were on the platform as well. Neither of them looked entirely at ease.

I ran a comb through my hair and twitched the hem of my skirt to make sure it was level, though why that should worry me I wasn't sure. Hardly likely I'd meet many people I knew, but old habits die hard and I still adhered to my mother's principle of always going out neat and tidy in case I got knocked down and had to be rushed to hospital. I smiled to myself as I ran downstairs to join the crowd on the common, remembering her horrified expression the day she discovered I'd pinned up my petticoat. 'You can just take that off and sew it properly,' she said, 'whatever would the doctor think?'

'Roll up, roll up!' I rolled up obediently, clutching my purse and a plastic carrier bag. Who knew what I might feel tempted to buy? The mushrooming tents were crammed to the flaps with produce, and the rush for the raffle had started already.

I squandered 10p on the coconut shy and felt relieved when

105

I missed. When all was said and done, what on earth should I do with a coconut if I won one? I'd need a hammer and chisel to get it open with.

The tombola was a different matter..I quite fancied the first prize – a set of round raffia table mats – and had three goes at winning them before I gave up. Perhaps I'd better buy a raffle ticket, not that I'd been all that lucky with raffles. The only prizes I'd ever won in my life were forty cigarettes when I was too young to smoke, a baby's hot water bottle when I hadn't a baby and a dress to fit a six foot mannequin, not a five-foot two inch shrimp like me.

What pleased me most was the number of people who nodded and smiled at me – women I'd seen on the bus, some of the women from the cottages near the common, folk I'd met in the corner shop, the village postman, and a couple of farm labourers with their families, which imparted a pleasant sense of belonging.

Lady Nettlefold, who had required the combined efforts of Alfred and the vicar to get her down from the platform, was now having a go at the tombola. One of the helpers spun the drum and out came 419. Pink, the winning number!

Trust her to win those table mats, I thought. I bet she has as much use for them as a hole in the head. Whoever said, 'To him that hath shall be given', had summed things up in a nutshell, and Gran had usually added in her down-to-earth way, 'Hmm, that's true enough, and those that have nothing much shall have even the little they have got taken away from them!'

Lady N thrust the mats at poor Alfred who was already carrying her bouquet and her handbag. Wherever she went, people parted like the Red Sea as the formidable female Moses toured the stalls, using her walking stick like a water diviner's rod – shushing people out of her path with it and swiping imperiously at whatever got in her way.

Unfortunately for her, a Jack Russell got in her way, and received a clout on the nose to serve him right. The dog immediately bared its teeth and began to worry the hem of her ladyship's skirt.

There was a fine old schemozzle as Alfred, making a dive to save his aunt's spotted voile dress, dropped first the bouquet and then the table-mats which bowled away like hoop-la rings. It was getting more like a circus every minute.

Arthur Abercromby eased his clerical collar and hurried to the scene of the debacle, closely followed by Avril who appeared to be advising him to keep out of it. After all, it was Lady Nettlefold's own fault. If she hadn't hit the dog on the nose it wouldn't have started to worry her skirt, Alfred wouldn't have dropped the mats and the bouquet, and several toddlers would not have taken fright and started to cry. Now a row was developing between her ladyship and the owner of the Jack Russell, who objected to its being attacked by a grown woman who, in his opinion, should have known better.

'Do you realise to whom you are speaking?' rumbled the affronted lady.

'Ah divn't gie a cuss to whom ah's speaking! Thoo hed no reet ti thump our Buster!' he retorted.

'Please, sir,' Arthur Abercromby tried to pour oil on troubled water, 'try to take a Christian view . . .'

'Tek a Christian view? Ah'll tek 'er to court if she clouts my dog again!'

This was better than a night at the cinema, I decided. *The Dogs of War* wasn't in it. The band struck up Colonel Bogey, Ould Gabby clashed his cymbals with such force that he tottered backwards off the lorry, had his fall broken by the sloping roof of the beer tent and the heads of several surprised imbibers, landed unhurt, and was helped inside the tent to be revived. So far as I knew, he stayed there being revived for the rest of the afternoon.

Strange, I thought, that Lady Nettlefold possessed this penchant for putting people's backs up. The Red Sea had parted again to let her through. I could see her rosy wreath of a hat moving in the direction of the refreshment tent, so I promptly moved towards the other side of the common to see what was going on over there.

The Women's Institute stall appeared to be doing a roaring trade. As a 'Towny' I'd never come into contact with the W.I. before, and looked admiringly at all the glistening pots of home-made jams and jellies, not to mention the stacks of hand-knitted dish-clothes, toilet-roll holders and babies' bootees.

It seemed nothing short of amazing that a small body of local ladies had been able to produce such a bewildering variety of goods – not only pickles, but hand-crocheted bedspreads and doilies, cakes and quilted tea-cosies, embroidered aprons and handkerchiefs. Tootington, in winter, must be a hive of industry, I thought. In autumn, indeed throughout the year, those small bodies would be busy scouring the hedges for blackberries, orchards for windfall apples, greenhouses for tomatoes, and would set about sugaring and boiling, pulping and straining; plumming, strawberrying, blackcurrant and raspberrying for all they were worth.

I felt weak at the knees at the thought of all that hard work – the washing and sterilisation of jars, making mob-caps from squares of gingham, and sticking on labels. My mother had been a dab hand at jam-making, but she hadn't succeeded in passing on the art to me. My jam always went sugary or didn't jell properly, or turned out so stiff that it wobbled off the bread.

Suddenly I caught sight of a familiar hat – a brown felt hat above a flushed high cheekboned face with a long nose and flaring nostrils.

Miss Cox was in charge of the ladies doing the serving. Her colleagues appeared to be large jolly-looking women in summer dresses and hand-knitted cardigans, but my neighbour wore a no-nonsense tweed skirt, a crêpe-de-chine blouse buttoned well up to the neck, and was directing operations with the military precision of the Duke of Wellington at Waterloo. It wouldn't be her fault, I felt, if a pot of piccalilli was left standing after the fray.

I might have treated myself to a jar or two of jam if I'd felt reasonably certain that Miss Cox would not serve me. As it was, I edged away from the stall and treated myself to an ice-cream cornet instead. Then I got caught up in a jostling throng near a grassy rectangle where a bizarre figure in a green fringed suede tunic faced ten skittles, with a look of deep concentration on his face and a wooden ball grasped firmly in his right hand.

'Go on, Dominic.' Someone yelled as he bent forward to unleash the ball at the skittles, 'Make believe you're Sir Francis Drake an' the Spanish Armada has just sailed into Carnelian Bay!'

So that was Dominic Douglas, the television chappie Avril had told me about. I could see why Lady Nettlefold disapproved of him. He might have been 'the Last of the

Mohicans' with his mane of brown hair, hooked nose and ruddy complexion. All he needed to complete the Red Indian image was a wampum belt and a tomahawk, but the locals seemed to like him judging by the way they egged him on as he sent the ball thundering down the fairway. There was a cheer and then a groan as only one skittle fell.

'Damnation,' he said cheerfully, 'I was looking forward to a rasher or two for breakfast tomorrow.'

'Thoo'll be lucky,' said an old chap smoking a clay pipe. 'Yon pig ain't 'ad time to grow no rashers yet.'

I stared in the direction of his pointing finger, and saw a pink snout snuffling through the bars of wooden crate under a horse-chestnut tree.

Funny things, pigs, I thought, all pink and bald and beady-eyed, but lovable in an off-putting sort of way.

'Don't tell me you're thinking of taking up pig-farming Mr Douglas?' someone quipped.

'Why not?' Dominic grinned. 'It might be more profitable than making television documentaries.'

'I heeard tell tha'd bought a few hens an' a billy goat,' said the old chap with the clay pipe, 'But tha'll need tha' wits about tha' if thoo's thinkin' of tekkin' up pigs.'

'Right, Silas, I'll remember that.'

'Tha' should've veered that last ball to the left,' said the man in charge of the pig.

'If I don't knock down seven skittles with the next ball,' Dominic commented drily, 'I'll veer off home. I've spent two quid bowling for that wretched swine of yours.'

The next ball missed completely, and he waved aside suggestions that he should have just one more go. As he turned aside, I found myself in the path of the first television producer I'd ever encountered.

Dominic Douglas, I thought, as we side-stepped each other, was a larger-than-life personality, and obviously a hero with the locals who treated him deferentially, despite their jocular remarks – and he was playing to his gallery of admiring onlookers for all he was worth.

But Mr Douglas was not a man to drift away without a flourish. He had to do something dramatic to finish the show. He grabbed me by the elbow. 'You, Madam,' he said, 'appear to possess a useful set of muscles. I cede my territorial rights to you!' He dragged me forward. 'This lady will bowl in my stead. May her efforts be crowned with success!'

'Now just a minute! I don't want to bowl for the pig . . .' I protested.

'What? You mean to tell me that you don't wish to bowl for that valuable piece of pork on four legs! That hunk of porcine pulchritude! Impossible! Every man, woman and child in their right senses would admire to possess all that quivering pink flesh; trotters, chitterlings, streaky, oyster and pearl! Think of that pig, Ma'am, grown to maturity. Think of it salted, pickled, brawned and fried. You, your husband, children and grandchildren could live off that pig for the next decade or two, and you have the temerity to tell me that you do not wish to bowl for it? Here, let me hold your carrier-bag and ice- cream cornet while you have a go!'

'You don't understand,' I insisted. 'If I didn't know what to do with a coconut, I certainly wouldn't know what to do with a pig.'

I saw, to my horror, that the Commander was standing on the edge of the crowd, smiling at me.

That did it! If Dominic Douglas thought that I would engage in a wrestling match, he had another think coming. He was using me as a stooge in a comedy act. The only thing I could do was give in gracefully, hand over my carrier-bag and ice-cream cornet without further ado, and let fly!

There was a full-throated roar from the spectators. 'By gow,' said the old chap with the clay pipe, 'she's got four of 'em down!'

Scarlet with embarrassment, I closed my eyes and sent the second ball down the fairway, hoping against hope that I would not fracture anyone's tibias in the process.

Another roar came from the spectators. I opened my eyes to find that I had downed another four skittles.

'I knew you had muscles,' Dominic chuckled, 'but I didn't realise they were bionic!'

'I don't understand. I've never bowled in my life before.'

Dominic burst out laughing. 'Ever heard of beginner's luck?'

'Yes of course, but . . .'

Suddenly the pig stuck its snout between the bars of its wooden prison, and my heart melted. It was such a little pig.

At least, if it belonged to me, I'd make sure that it wasn't salted or fried. I'd love it as tenderly as anyone could love a pig. I felt that I owed it one more honest try to save its life.

I took careful aim and sent down the last ball. It missed by a mile.

'Eight out of ten,' said the man in charge. 'What's your name, Missis?'

'It doesn't matter about my name,' I replied, relinquishing my high-flown notions of delivering the pig from its fate, 'someone's bound to win it outright.'

'You're right there. Some young farmers will bowl till they're cross-eyed to win that pig. But eight out of ten weren't bad for a wumman.'

I took a firm hold of my plastic carrier-bag and the melting remains of my ice-cream cornet and hurried away. I was tired, hot and thirsty. Now, to crown all, I had that pig on my conscience, and I'd made a fool of myself into the bargain. At least Commander Bruce might think so.

I bumped into him on my way to the refreshment tent.

'Two minds with a single thought,' he said easily, raising his light panama hat. 'I expect you're pretty exhausted after all that effort. Would you care to join me in a cup of tea?'

I had half expected his wife to be with him, but he was alone, an immaculate figure in a light-weight grey suit.

As he went off to get the tea, I wondered what his wife was like and why she wasn't with him: imagined her as a slender woman with pale blonde or silver hair, felt sure that she must be very beautiful. Men as handsome as the Commander didn't marry fat unattractive women. I could just see her, tall and graceful, drifting around that lovely Georgian house of theirs, arranging flowers, wearing a silk dress, giving orders to the housekeeper. Some women had all the luck.

I kicked my plastic carrier-bag under the table as he came back with the tea and biscuits.

'Well, how are you enjoying the Tootington village fete?' he asked with a twinkle.

'It's much more ambitious than I thought,' I replied, knowing that my hair was beginning to droop with the heat. 'What is it in aid of?'

'Community funds, broadly speaking, and the upkeep of the village in particular,' he said. 'The money goes into various accounts; the church, the village hall, keeping the common land well tended, that kind of thing, and there's a fund for children whose parents can't afford to take them on holiday.'

'Really? How splendid. But what about the old people? Isn't there a fund for them too?'

'Now that you come to mention it, there isn't.' He frowned. 'But there certainly should be. That's worth looking into, Mrs Shelton. Can't think why nobody has ever put forward that point before.' He gave me a quizzical glance. 'What made you say that?'

'I suppose I was thinking of Nurse Pintuck. It struck me how awful it must be for her having to move away from the village and all her friends at her time of life.'

'Go on,' he said quietly.

'I know that State homes are very efficiently run,' I floundered, 'but I don't think old people care all that much about efficiency. All they need is to feel – wanted. Do you know what my grandmother once told me? That food, given without love, has no nourishment.'

At that moment Miss Cox entered the tent. 'Oh Lord,' I blurted out, 'please excuse me, Commander, but I really must be going.'

'Why? Is anything wrong?' He rose to his feet as I scrabbled under the table for my plastic bag.

'No! That is – I've just remembered something! A – a phone call!' I said the first thing that came into my head. 'Please stay and finish your tea, and thank you.'

I just had to get out of the tent without Miss Cox seeing me, but it was too late, and I knew what she was thinking – a divorced woman setting her cap at a married man. I knew it was ridiculous to feel guilty when I hadn't done anything wrong, but there was something about Miss Cox that would make Saint Peter at the gate of heaven feel guilty about letting in the Archbishop of Canterbury.

Back at April Cottage, I changed into my gardening togs and did a couple of hours' hard labour on the weeds. Whatever must the Commander have thought when I dashed away like that?

Just before I went to bed at ten o'clock, I stood by the bedroom window and looked up at the sky. Everything was calm after the excitement of the afternoon. Most of the tents had been dismantled, and pin-pricks of light were shining from some of the cottages across the common. The sound of laughter drifted down from the Spotted Dog, making me feel lonely and a little vulnerable. It would be rather nice, I thought, to walk into the warm atmosphere of the pub and wet my whistle with Ambrose Lanfeard and the lads, but I was far too shy and tired for that. Bed seemed an inviting prospect after the exigencies of the day.

I'd barely got my head on the pillow when someone hammered at my front door, and hammered a second time before I'd had time to struggle into my dressing-gown.

'All right, I'm coming,' I called out. 'Who is it? What do you want?' I opened the door a crack.

'Are you the lady who bowled for the pig this afternoon?'

'Yes,' I said cautiously.

'Skittled eight, did you?'

'Yes. Why?'

'Didn't leave your name and address?'

'No, I didn't. Oh Lord!' I suddenly remembered that I hadn't paid the 10p. 'I'm terribly sorry, I'll go and get my purse.'

The youth on the doorstep scratched the back of his neck and shuffled his feet awkwardly. 'Nay, there's no need for that. Mick an' me don't want nothing for bringing it.'

'I'm sorry, I'm not with you.' I knew I was tired, but he wasn't making sense. 'You don't want nothing for bringing –what?'

'The pig,' he said patiently. 'You won it!'

Chapter Fifteen

'What did you do at the weekend?' Mrs Amor asked.

'I – I won a pig,' I said modestly.

'I thought for a moment you said you'd won a pig.' She was adding up a column of figures as she spoke, and her question had been of a perfunctory nature.

'Yes, that's what I did say.'

'Eighty-seven, ninety-nine. *Huh*?' She stopped adding, threw down her pen, and stared at me. 'A *pig*? What the hell are you going to do with it?'

'I'm not quite sure.' I shook my hands free of washing-up water. 'I wish you'd get some of that washing-up liquid they advertise on TV,' I said, 'this stuff is bringing my skin off.'

'Never mind about your wretched skin. What about the – *pig*?'

'What about it?'

'Suppose you tell me? Where is it?'

'In my garden shed at the moment. I didn't know where else to put it.'

'I'm surprised you didn't bring it to work with you.'

'I would have done, but I didn't have a collar and lead.'

'Thank God for that! What the hell do you feed it on?'

'Swill,' I said. 'Well, that's what pigs like, isn't it?'

'Oh go on!' She took off her spectacles and started to laugh. 'I don't believe a word of it.'

'No, honestly, it's the gospel truth. You should have seen me yesterday. I spent the whole morning traipsing round the village with a plastic bin-liner. I don't know what I'd have done without Half-Pint's bogie.'

'Half-Pint's bogie,' she repeated tonelessly.

'Yes, Half-Pint and his pal, Herbie Parrott were absolutely

114

marvellous. You see, they organised a "Miss Piggy" campaign. I had no idea that there was so much cold rice pudding in the world until they tipped out the contents of that dustbin-liner.'

'How would your pig like a couple of burnt apple tarts and a dish of mouldy trifle?' Mrs Amor asked.

Kidding about Miss Piggy was fun, but I knew I couldn't keep her indefinitely. Then it occurred to me that as Dominic Douglas had spent a couple of quid bowling for her, he might be prepared to give her a home. My life seemed to revolve around my pig at the moment. As soon as I got indoors I swapped my black skirt for grey trews and dashed down to the shed to look at her.

Bert was hanging over the fence. 'Nah then, Ruby,' he said, 'going to have a get together with yer Christmas dinner? I allus say there's now't to beat a lump of roast pork at Christmas.'

Bert Rumbold had had Amelia's sofa, her table, feather bed, and rhubarb, but he wasn't having a hunk of Miss Piggy.

'I'm not going to eat that pig,' I said firmly. 'I've grown fond of her, and I think she likes me too.'

'Grown fond of a *pig*?' I'd flummoxed Bert completely this time. 'Well, if that don't beat all! A right mess we'd be in if young Farmer Appleby blubbed his eyes out every time his porkers went to the bacon factory.'

'That's as may be, but my mind's made up. Miss Piggy isn't going to end up with Tootington stamped right through her.'

'You're the daftest lass I've ever met in all my born days,' he snapped. 'Well, if you're not going to eat that pig, what are you goin' to do with it?'

'I'm going to ask Dominic Douglas to take her.'

'What? That television bloke? Why, he's dafter than you are!' Bert climbed down from the fence and went indoors calling, 'Darr, where in tarnation have you got to? I wants a cup of tea, an' I wants it bad!'

Dominic was sitting with his feet up listening to Brahms on the radio.

'I'm sorry to disturb you,' I said, peering round the back door of his cottage.

'Nobody ever disturbs me. Clear a space and sit down. Do you like Brahms?'

'Well, yes,' I said, a little nonplussed by his airy disregard of formalities, 'but I prefer Elgar.'

'You do?' He regarded me coolly. 'Why?'

I'd never really considered the matter before. 'Because he's so – English, I suppose.'

'Oh, so you go in for all that imperialistic gob-stopper stuff do you?' he said without rancour. 'Good old England, and all that. But it isn't what it used to be in Elgar's day, is it?'

'No I suppose not, but it's still a good place to be so far as I'm concerned.'

He grinned amiably. 'I suppose you're right, especially here in the heart of the countryside. Julienne and I stuck London as long as we could before we moved up here. She kept telling me that London was no place to bring up children.' He got up, stretched his arms and announced his intention of making coffee.

'I didn't realise that you had any children,' I said. 'How old are they?'

'Not they – it!' He looked a bit sheepish. 'I have one very bald daughter aged two days.'

'How marvellous. What's her name?'

'Fern. Though Jule will probably change her mind fifty times before we get her to the font.' He started measuring coffee beans into a grinder. 'Hope you don't mind waiting,' he said, 'I'm a purist when it comes to food and coffee.'

'So was my ex-husband,' I told him, 'only he preferred Delius to Brahms and Kenya to Continental.' I looked round at Dominic's kitchen with its white-painted dresser, littered wooden table and farmhouse type doors with iron snecks. 'I once had a kitchen that smelt like this one – vaguely Continental, I mean, with a coffee grinder and lots of copper pans and herb-racks. Now I use instant coffee and live mainly out of tins.'

I got up and looked out of the window at the Douglas's 'spread' – a rough field with a tethered billy goat, and two long wooden sheds. Hens sprayed everywhere, pursued by a couple of determined looking roosters.

'I really came to see you about my pig,' I said, 'the one I won at the fête. You see, I can't look after her properly, and I

116

wondered if you'd like to keep her. I couldn't bear her to be made into sausages.'

'Well, I'll be damned! So you won her after all, did you?' He plugged in the percolator. 'Sure I'll take her. She can live in the far shed.' He laughed. 'God knows what Lady Nettlefold will say when she finds out, seeing that she's made my life hell over that pasture which she claims belongs to her. Not that I care all that much what she says. Here's one serf who will not bend the knee to the feudal system.'

'So you've come up against her ladyship too?'

'Who in this charming but benighted village has not?' He cocked an eyebrow. 'The woman's a gauliêter. It's time something was done about her.'

'I know. But what?'

'Damned if I know,' he said, as the coffee 'perked', 'though I did toy with the idea of making a film pointing the differences between town and country life, and I guess I did have Lady N all set to play the role of the "Big Bad Wolf". The trouble is, the television company I freelance for won't give me the go ahead.'

'Why not? It sounds like a good idea to me.'

He shrugged. 'They think it hasn't enough bite. What I need is an angle, a gimmick.'

'You mean a controversial figure of some kind?'

He frowned. 'My God, I think you've got something there. A controversial figure, but who?'

I warmed to the subject. 'What about a punk rock star?'

'Hell,' he said, 'you've hit it bang on target. Go-Go Shingles! The naughty boy of the swinging eighties. Twelve appearances in court on alleged drug offences; three times married, a cult figure with the teenagers. I wonder what Go-Go would make of Tootington and Lady Nettlefold. Might be well worth finding out.'

'You mean – you'd bring him here?'

'Sure as hell I would. It's a brilliant idea. Can you imagine it? Go-Go Shingles singing in the church choir; talking to the villagers, taking tea with the vicar?'

'No, quite frankly I can't.' I wished I'd kept my mouth shut.

'Look, would you excuse me for a few minutes? I want to telephone the studio. Help yourself to coffee, and bring that pig of yours any time you feel like it.'

117

Half-an-hour later he was still on the phone and had obviously forgotten my existence.

Apparently he was still phoning someone when, at tea-time, Half-Pint and Herbie Parrott loaded Miss Piggy on to Herbie's bogie and wheeled her in state to her new home.

'We had to knock till our knuckles ached,' Half-Pint told me later, 'then he came to the door with his hair sort of standing on end, an' told us to put Miss Piggy in the shed. I just hope he doesn't forget she's there, that's all.'

Chapter Sixteen

I was nodding off into the butter when Mrs Amor rushed into the still room a few days later. Was it my imagination, or was something wrong with her? Her eyelids were red and puffy as if she'd been crying. I felt tempted to ask if anything was troubling her, but decided not to. Despite her brittle air of sophistication, she was an intensely lonely, private person, I felt. One word out of place and she might tell me to go to the devil.

'I have to go out on urgent business this morning,' she rasped in her smoker's voice. 'Can you cope?'

'I think so. But isn't this Rotarian Monday?'

She lit a cigarette with shaking fingers. 'They're not coming today,' she said, 'nor any other day. You see, they've cancelled for good and all. Now the rot's really set in!'

'The rot?' I continued rolling butter as if my life depended on it.

'Oh, for God's sake, Mrs Sam, you know what I mean, don't you? The face is,' she rummaged through her handbag to find a letter and perched her glasses on the end of her nose to read it, 'they're terribly sorry but they feel that our standard of service has fallen short recently, and they have had no alternative but to take heed of members' complaints and to find other accommodation for their weekly meetings.'

'I'm terribly sorry,' I said.

'So am I. That's why I'm putting the Red Lion up for sale. It's going downhill fast, and I know it. Oh, I've tried to make a success of it, but I can't cope any more. Things were different when Charlie, my husband, was alive, but when he died and the licence was transferred to me, I went to pieces.'

'Seems a pity,' I said, choosing my words with care, 'it could be a little gold mine if only . . .'

'If only what?' She stubbed out her cigarette in the lid of a hot-water jug. 'Well, go on, Mrs Sam. Tell me how you think this goddam hotel could be made into a gold mine. I'm all ears!'

'Well, the dining room's in the wrong place for a start.' I murmured unhappily.

'Go on.'

'If the dining room was downstairs, you could do away with the dumb-waiter. Have you stopped to consider how much muscle power is required to hoist up meals from the kitchen? Not only that, but the food's half cold before it reaches the customers.'

'I'm listening,' she said coolly.

'If you had a downstair dining room,' I ploughed on, 'the food could be served through a hatch.'

'Got it all worked out, haven't you? And if I did that, where would I put the cocktail lounge? And what about the hotel residents? Where would they have breakfast?'

'Downstairs of course. And Dirty Dick's Parlour could be easily divided, couldn't it?'

'It could,' she conceded, 'if I had the money to do it with, but I haven't. If you want the truth, I'm flat broke.'

'I don't see any real problem there,' I said. 'After all, the Red Lion isn't a tuppeny-ha'penny hotel stuck away in a side street. It's possibly the best known hotel in Carnelian Bay. If it belonged to me, I'd play up its history for all I was worth; starting advertising Dickensian game pies and venison . . .'

'Oh great,' she snapped. 'Marvellous! Can you imagine Daisy Burns roasting a haunch of venison?'

'No, of course not. You'd need a chef for that. But Daisy could do bar-snacks, couldn't she?'

'And just where would I get the financial backing for these pipe-dreams of yours?'

'Why not try the bank?'

'What? Land myself up to the ears in a loan when I could simply sell out and be rid of the whole thing? No, my mind's made up. This shambles over the Rotarians has decided me. Thanks for trying to help, but no! In any case it's not your worry, is it?'

120

When she had gone, I pondered the state of affairs at the Red Lion. No use Mrs Amor telling me that the hotel wasn't my worry, I was the sort who worried about everything, especially things that were none of my business, the way I worried about the plight of the old district nurse the Nettlefolds wanted to put into a home.

I sighed as I finished rolling the butter. It was all very well re-organising things in my mind, but I knew that people who are down on their luck, short of ready cash, and a bit defeated into the bargain, don't think all that clearly. So why didn't I just stop worrying, tidy up the cheeseboard, and dust the chicken?

While Polly Flounders was inclined to favour me a little more because I had told her the state of Mrs Billy Watson's legs, Daisy Burns still wasn't having any truck with me when I went down to the kitchen to find some fresh lettuce for the cheeseboard.

'We ain't got no fresh lettuce,' she said belligerently. 'What do you expect me to do – knit you some?'

'Not at all, Mrs Burns,' I said coolly. 'You'd probably drop all the stitches if you did.'

'Now you look here,' she blustered. But I didn't wait to 'look here'. I found my purse, walked out of the hotel, went round to the greengrocer's and bought a couple of healthy-looking heads of lettuce, a couple of pounds of tomatoes, and a cucumber the size of a baby marrow.

Daisy was sitting with her head in *Doctor Tim Takes Charge* when I plonked the produce on the draining-board, and shot me a filthy look when I started washing the lettuce.

'Has Polly thawed out the chicken portions?' I asked her.

'You'd better ask Polly about that, hadn't you?' she snapped.

'Polly isn't here. I'm asking you, Mrs Burns.'

She threw down her book in a temper. 'It ain't my job to thaw out the chicken portions,' she burst forth, 'and it ain't your bloody job to ask. Why the hell don't you get back upstairs where you belong? *I'm* in charge down here. Just clear that lettuce off my draining-board, and wash it in the still room.'

Ignoring the tirade, I asked her if she had hard-boiled any eggs.

'Whaffor?' she demanded, taken aback by my persistence.

'For the egg mayonnaise, of course.'

She threw back her head and laughed. 'Egg blooming mayonnaise! And just how many folk are going to want that? If you want hard-boiled eggs, my lady, you can hard-boil them yourself.'

'Right, I will!' I lifted a pan from the shelf and trotted out the eggs from the refrigerator.

'Oh no you don't!' She fairly hurled herself at me, grabbed the pan and filled it with water. 'I'm the cook here, not you.'

'But you just said . . .'

'Never mind what I just said. I'm on to all your little tricks! You'd just love me to walk out, wouldn't you? Well, let me tell you, Mrs Clever-Clogs, I could get a job anywhere in this one-eyed town.'

'Could you?'

She had the grace to blush. 'Sure I could,' she retorted, but she didn't sound any too certain.

I finished washing the lettuce while Daisy banged and clattered, and swore defiantly under her breath.

Gabriel was serving beer to the locals in Dirty Dick's Parlour, and glancing nervously over his shoulder to make sure that nobody was waiting to be served in the cocktail lounge. No wonder the poor chap bit his fingernails to the quick. What he needed was someone behind the bar with him to ease the strain. A pensioner could do the job nicely, I thought – one of those old fellows playing dominoes for instance.

Upstairs in the dining room, I saw from the window a coach draw up in the rear car park. From it streamed a crowd of men wearing knitted caps and rosettes who surged towards the side door of the hotel, laughing and shouting at the tops of their voices. I counted at least thirty-six bobbing heads, like corks on a fishing-line, jostling to get in. Two or three of the heads started singing a bawdy rugby ditty to pass the time as they clustered, waiting their turn to get inside the hotel.

'Ye gods,' I muttered, 'poor Gabriel,' and dashed on to the landing. But it wasn't Gabriel who needed sympathy. I flattened myself against the wall as the knitted caps came gallumping up the staircase and swept past me into the dining room where they began fighting for seats.

I stood in the doorway feeling that all the starch had gone out of my pinny, bemused by the noise and the sheer weight of hungry young bodies wanting sustenance.

'Hi, there. You the waitress?'

I nodded.

'Well, we're famished, see? What's for eats?' Their spokesman, a fair-haired youth with acne, picked up a menu. 'Mock turtle soup with sherry? We'll have a basin full of that for a kick-off!'

'No, you can't have that! It – it's a set menu for coach parties!' I said desperately the first thing that came into my head.

'Fair enough. What's the set menu?'

'Egg mayonnaise, tomato soup, chicken and chips, and trifle.'

'Sounds OK. How much?'

'Two fifty a head.'

'Right. Let's be having it!' He grinned, revealing two broken front teeth. 'And what about beer?'

'Beer?' I hadn't a clue about beer. That was Gabriel's department.

'Don' tell me you never heard of *bee*-er.' He sounded shocked. 'It's brown, see, with froth on top.'

He was making game of me and I knew it, but not unkindly. He was simply showing off. It occurred to me that he had had far too much brown stuff with froth on top already. 'Yes, of course,' I said. 'How many pints do you want?'

'Pints!' He roared with laughter. 'You mean gallons, don' you? Look, lady, this ain' no pussycats' picnic. Get some crates up *hee*-er, an' get 'em up fast. Got it?'

I'd got it all right. I had a first-class emergency on my hands, and the sooner I warned Gabriel and the rest of the staff the better.

I flew downstairs to Dirty Dick's Parlour. 'We've got to get some crates of beer upstairs,' I told him breathlessly. 'There'll be a riot if we don't.'

Gabriel's face turned a whiter shade of pale. 'We can't,' he said, having a quick nibble at his fingernails. 'It's impossible. I can't leave the bar, and even if I could, how the hell do you expect me to lump beer-crates upstairs on my own?'

'Look, Gabriel. If you don't get some crates of beer upstairs, those Welsh rugby types in the dining room will come down and assault and batter us.'

'My God,' he muttered hoarsely, 'what on earth am I going to do?'

'I felt like Horatio at the bridge as I called out to the denizens of Dirty Dick's Parlour, 'Excuse me, but is there an ex-barman in the house?'

'I kept the Old Barn at Hardington for thirty-odd years,' said one old chap, getting to his feet. 'What do you want me to do?'

'Are you any good at humping beer-crates?'

'Naw.' His face fell. 'I can pull a pint as well as the next man, but my back ain't what it used to be since I slipped my disc.'

'There's now't wrong with my back!' The next man to stand up was well over six feet and burly to boot. 'I'm an ex-copper,' he said proudly, 'and as fit as a lop.'

'Tell you what, Gabriel,, I said, 'why not let the Old Barn at Hardington stand in for you behind the bar, while you and the ex-copper get the crates upstairs?'

'Well, I don't know . . .'

I didn't stop to argue. My legs were trembling as I hurried to the kitchen to warn Daisy that the Red Lion had suffered a Welsh invasion. But there was no need. As I skidded through the swing door, 'Land of my Fathers' to a descant of 'Why are we waiting?' was floating down the dumb-waiter.

Polly barged into the kitchen by the back entrance. 'What the hell's the matter?' she demanded, rolling her fag end across her bottom lip. 'It sounds as if *Star Wars* is going awn in the dining room.'

'There'll be more than *Star Wars* if we don't get a move on,' I said. 'There's a Welsh rugger crowd up there – thirty-six of them – as hungry as hunters, and not in the best of tempers.'

'Bloody hell!' Daisy Burns sat on *Doctor Tim* in the stress of the moment. 'You shouldn't have let 'em in. Why didn't you stop 'em?'

'Stop 'em! I might as well have tried stopping a steam-roller with my bare hands. In any case, this is a hotel. We are here to provide food if people want it, aren't we?'

Daisy's bottom lip quivered and she burst into tears. 'It's all very well for you,' she wept. 'All you have to do is stand up in that bleedin' still room and shout orders at me. I'm the one that has to do the rotten work. Well, I can't cook thirty-six meals an' that's flat. Not with *my* feet!'

I stared at her in disbelief. What had her feet to do with it?

She blurted out, 'They're hot, an' they *hurts!*'

Polly leaned against the door, her turbanned head to one side, her mouth gaping open, and her cigarette hanging from her bottom lip by some miraculous centrifugal force – or possibly just saliva.

'I'm sorry that you feet hurt, Mrs Burns,' I said, glancing uneasily at the dumb-waiter down which the strains of Cymn Rhondda could now clearly be heard, 'but why don't you take your boots off? No wonder your feet are hot in fur boots.'

Daisy began wailing like a banshee. 'I suppose you think I wear these boots for fun?' she bawled.

I glanced at her feet encased in scuffed suede edged with moulting fur. By no stretch of the imagination could Daisy's foot-gear be described as 'fun' boots.

She mopped her eyes on the edge of her nylon overall. 'It's all right for you an' Polly,' she sniffed, 'but you ain't got no bunions, fallen arches, and two 'Faroukas' into the bargain. These boots are all I can wear, so now you know!'

Polly clicked her tongue sympathetically. '*Two* 'Faroukas' You pore thing. Where are they?'

'Under me fallen arches,' Daisy sobbed.

I felt like bursting into tears myself as I slipped a comforting arm round Daisy's shoulders. 'Never mind,' I said, 'if you can't manage, you can't.' After all, I thought, two bunions were bad enough, but to have 'verrucas' under your fallen arches as well must be the very devil. 'I'll just have to go up and break it to those Welshmen that they're not going to get anything to eat after all. Seems a pity, though. The only cooking involved would be chicken and chips. I've already told them it's a set menu.'

'Eeyah,' Polly called after me as I headed for the door, 'what did you tell 'em was awn the menu?'

When I'd told her, she bustled forward, jettisoned her fag end into the sink-basket, and took control of the situation. 'Now just you stand up at the stove, Daisy love,' she said, 'an' see to the chicken an' chips, while I slap these eggs into the salad cream. The soup's made, ain't it, and so is the trifles.

You get up to the still room, Mrs Sam, an' I'll give you a shout up the dumb-waiter when the soup's awn, only don't jerk at it this time.'

'No, I won't.'

'Eeyah. Tek these bread buns with you,' she yelled after me, thrusting a tray into my trembling hands.

I raced upstairs to the dining room where Gabriel and the ex-copper were unbottling beer as fast as they could go.

The brown stuff with froth on top was having a two-fold effect on the imbibers. Some had reached saturation point and were sitting there quietly befuddled, while the rest of them grew more rowdy by the minute.

I saw, with horror, that the more voracious element had stripped the cheeseboard of everything except the doilies, and that one of them was running round the room with it, weaving unsteadily between the tables, and shouting, 'A penny for the guy.'

'Where the hell's the grub?' Gabriel muttered as I tripped over a crate.

'It's on its way.'

The next thing I knew, the chicken from the sideboard whizzed past my left ear as a burly lad with bright auburn hair plucked it from its china stand and booted it towards the fireplace.

'Goal!' Someone applauded wildly.

'Did you say goal? If that was a goal, boyo, my name is David Lloyd George, look you.' Acne grinned.

'It was so a goal.'

'And I say it wasn't. You cuddn't kick a goal, Dai Jones, if the goalposts came out an' met you!'

'Who cuddn't?' Dai scrambled for the chicken, tucked it under his arm, and looked round bemusedly. 'I could if I 'ad some proper goalposts.'

'You 'aven't though, 'ave you? So why don't you sit down, man, an' take the weight off your legs?'

Dai's eyes lit up wickedly when he caught sight of me hiding behind the ex-copper.

At that moment Polly appeared, all of a fluster, to tell me that she had been shouting up the dumb-waiter for the past five minutes, and why the hell hadn't I answered.

With a cry of triumph, Dai lunged forward, grabbed the

bewildered Polly with one hand, and me with the other. 'Goalposts, is it?' he bellowed, standing us six feet apart. 'Here's my goalposts. Now I'll show you. Stand still, the pair of you.'

He paced the length of the dining room, propped the chicken on its parson's nose, took aim and fired.

There was a full-throated roar from the spectators as the chicken whistled squarely between Polly and me and landed with a thud on the mantelpiece.

'My Gawd,' cried Polly, bursting with righteous indignation, 'I've done some things in my time, but I ain't never been used as a goalpost before.' She wagged her turbanned head alarmingly. 'It's not awn! Now, you lot, just cop an earful of this. Sit down an' behave yourselves or you'll get nawthin' to eat at awl. The very idea!'

As the din subsided, Polly turned her wrath on Gabriel and the ex-policeman. 'As for you, you should think shame on yourselves. Call yourself a cawper? You should be drummed out of the fawce!'

With that she turned and marched out of the dining room, whilst I followed at a safe distance.

'Now just yet into that still room,' she threw at me over her shoulder as she strode downstairs, 'an get hawling on that rope in two seconds flat, or I'll be awf to the Job Centre before you know what's hit you!'

'Yes, Polly.' I stared at her in admiration. At least when the chips were down, one of Mrs Amor's 'incompetent fools' had turned up trumps.

Chapter Seventeen

I was stuffing pound notes into the till when Mrs Amor came back.

'One hundred and thirty, thirty-one, thirty-two . . .'

'Been playing Monopoly?' she asked in that brittle way of hers, but I could tell that she was intrigued.

'Hmmm. It was rather more exciting than Monopoly.'

'What the hell's been going on here?'

'Oh, by the way, you'll need to deduct Basil and Ernie's wages,' I said, 'otherwise you're quids in!'

'If you don't tell me what's been going on, so help me I'll . . .'

'Why don't we go through to the kitchen and have a nice cup of tea?' I suggested.

'Cup of tea be damned,' she snapped, 'what I need is a stiff gin and tonic.'

'Honestly, I think we should go through to the kitchen.'

'All right, all right, I can see you need humouring, though personally, I think you've flipped your lid.'

She stopped dead in her tracks when she heard the sound of laughter. 'Hell's teeth,' she said, 'you've all flipped your lids. Nobody ever laughs in this hotel.'

I pushed open the door. 'An' I said to him,' Polly chortled, holding her aching sides, 'I've done some things in my time, but I ain't never been used as a goalpost before. That was after the chicken landed on the mantelpiece an' awl the stuffing spilled out of it.'

I put my fingers to my lips. Nobody had noticed we were there.

'An' I'll never forget when Daisy told Mrs Sam about her bad feet.' Polly kinked with laughter again. 'Why don't you take your boots awf Mrs Sam asked her, an' Daisy said she couldn't becawse of her faroukas an' fallen arches. Lawf. I thought I'd have died lawfing.'

'You wouldn't laugh if they was your faroukas,' Daisy spluttered.

'I've never slipped eggs out of their shells so fast in awl my life,' Polly continued, 'but when I shoved them an' the soup on to that blooming dumb-waiter, could I make her hear? Not likely! But of cawse the pore soul is a bit deaf, so we must excuse her.'

'Mrs Sam may be a bit deaf,' Gabriel butted in, 'not that I've ever noticed it, but she certainly ain't daft, or we'd never have got Basil and Ernie here to help us.'

'It was what you might cawl a team effort,' said Polly. 'An' the funny thing is, I enjoyed it. Yes, I did!'

'So did I,' Daisy admitted. 'She was ever so nice about my feet once I'd told her what was the matter with them. She put her arm round my shoulders. Kind of broke me up, that did, seein' I'd been calling her everything from a pig to a dog beforehand.'

Mrs Amor and I slipped out of the kitchen at that point.

'That,' she said, 'is the weirdest conversation I've ever heard in my life. Now, come on, spill the beans.'

When the beans had been well and truly spilt, she said, 'Now I'll tell you my news.'

'You mean about putting the hotel on the market?'

She laughed. 'You can wipe that worried look off your face, Mrs Sam. I didn't go to see the estate-agent after all.'

'You – didn't?'

'No.' She frowned and ran her fingers through her hair, 'I was actually on my way upstairs to his office when I remembered what you said about the Red Lion not being a tuppeny-ha'penny hotel stuck away in a side street . . .'

'And?'

'Well, it simply occurred to me that if you could see a future for it, why shouldn't I? So I walked out of the estate-agent's and went to see my bank-manager instead. Had lunch with him, as a matter of fact, and he couldn't have been kinder or more understanding.'

'You mean . . .?'

'Yes, Mrs Sam, he's going to lend me enough money to put this place on its feet.'

'Thank the Lord for that.' I felt like a child with its first kite, laughing as the wind tugged at the strings, and the whole multi-coloured wonder of it sailed up into a blue sky.

'Hi-up! What do you think you're doing?'

'Who? Me?'

'Yes, you!'

I stared up at the sky, half expecting to see a prophet of the Lord glaring down at me and stroking his white beard – or whatever prophets did when they were put out about something.

'Nay, I'm not on the chimbley.' The voice of the prophet sounded more than a little put out. 'I'm *here*.'

'Where's – here?' I asked.

'Behind the fence. Near that bush you just rove up out of the ground. Hang on a minute while I fetch another box from the shed. I'm a bit on the short side, you see, but I can see fine what you're up to through this 'ere knot-hole.'

Oh no, I thought. Not the Gaffer. But it was.

Talk about 'a scraping aside of pickle-tub boards'. When he finally hoisted himself up high enough to see over the fence, I came face to face with a human garden gnome, white whiskers, pointed cap and all.

'Now then,' he said, 'what for are you shifting them bushes?'

'Because I want them over there,' I said meekly, 'if you've no objection.'

'They'll dee, the lot of 'em,' he spat out. 'I've been gardenin' all my life, and I *knows*!'

'I'm sorry, but I can't bear to see them so overgrown. I just thought that if I dug deep enough holes and filled them with water, then dug up the bushes and rushed them across to the holes, they'd never know they'd been moved at all.'

His wizened face crumpled. 'I knew I shouldn't have come to live here,' he sighed. 'I should've gone last September when me carbuncle bust. It was touch and go at the time, now I wish I'd gone.'

'But people don't die of bust carbuncles, do they?' I asked uncertainly, wishing I'd been a bit more charitable.

'They does if sceptre-sepia sets in,' the Gaffer said gloomily.

'And did – er – septicaemia set in with you?' I asked.

130

'Naw, but I wish now that it had. I'd have been out of everyone's way then. Just a little mound in the graveyard. They'd all have been sorry then, wouldn't they? All of 'em weepin' and wailin' and gnashin' their gums.'

He smiled suddenly, revealing his own gums, bare save for one indomitable bicuspid which had defied the ravages of time. 'But I didn't go after all. I'm still here, though her in yonder,' he jerked his thumb in the direction of the kitchen window, 'would've been the first to plant a few crocus bulbs atop of me if I had.'

He gave a wheezy chuckle. 'She hates me, Darr does, cos I waint conform. Keeps her on the hop, I does. Interferes with her arrangements accidentally on purpose. It makes life more interestin'.' His face puckered up again. 'The truth is, I feel like a fish out of water since I came ti live 'ere. I 'ad a nice little bit of a house over Hardington way. Enjoyed potterin' round it fine, I did. It were a bit mucky, but it were mine.'

He sighed. 'Used to hev some grand times down at the Old Barn pub near the river. Ah'd cook mesen a bite to eat then nip off as nice as ninepence. Burnt a few saucepans, o' course, an' couldn't get the burnt bits off. That upset Darr, an' it weren't no use tellin' her that I liked the taste. She said it weren't healthy eatin' all them germs. Weren't no way I could convince her that they'd all be dead anyway by the time they'd been boiled up again.'

His gnarled fingers clung like grappling irons to the top of the fence. 'Seems to me they dain't exactly want me to dee, but they dain't exactly want me ti live neither. They wants me to be what they calls "comfortable in me old age". By the way, hev you seen my cat?'

'No, I don't think so. What does she look like?'

'Now't on earth,' he said. 'Longish legs an' a biggish belly. All over black except for her chest. That's white, an' so is her whiskers, but she's got the bonniest green eyes. Found the pore little devil in a dustbin. Suppose whoever wanted rid of her thowt a dustbin were the best place for her, but she's the best pal I ever had. Come on, Dodgy, show the'sen.'

'Dodgy?'

'Aye, her name's Dodgy Knees. She's a bit lame, you see.'

My heart warmed towards the Gaffer.

'Darr don't like her cos she sharpens her claws on the

furniture, but I waint part with her as sure as my name's Oliver Rumbold. When she goes, I goes.'

He scrambled down from his pile of boxes. 'Got to go an' get me dinner now.' He pulled a face. 'Stew wi' no burnt bits. An' you mark my word about them bushes. They'll sag if you shifts 'em, sure as eggs is eggs.'

He turned back to grin at me, 'But you'll shift 'em anyway, waint you? Well, I dain't blame you. Once you starts obeyin' the rules, you're done for.'

I was up at the crack of dawn the next day, peering through my bedroom curtains, expecting to see all the bushes I'd transplanted lying flat on the ground. But they weren't! They hadn't even wilted. Every white pompom blossom, every yellow bud was lifting its head to the pearly morning air, and a thrush was singing its heart out on the upstanding japonica.

'Come in, my dear. You have no idea how much I've looked forward to seeing you again. You'll have a cup of coffee before you start, won't you?'

The sitting room of Nurse Pintuck's cottage had a deep, flower-filled window-shelf, chintz curtains, an old-fashioned kitchen range where a fire glowed despite the heat of the day, a walnut dresser crowded with blue and white Spode china, and a high mantelpiece arrayed with photographs of smiling young women, plum-pudding babies, serious-faced lads, and wedding invitations.

She had obviously gone to a lot of trouble to prepare for my visit. Blue and white cups were spread on a pristine white tablecloth, and the kettle was singing on the hob.

'I hope you don't find it too warm in here,' she said. 'I'm obliged to keep a fire going to heat the range, though I do have a gas-ring in the kitchen. I'll just go through to the pantry, if you'll excuse me for a minute. I set the milk there for the cream to rise, knowing you were coming today.'

'Amelia used to set the cream to rise in the pantry when I was a little girl,' I said. 'One of the delights of my life was watching her spoon off the cream with a separator.'

Nurse Pintuck smiled. 'Yes, she told me all about you. Amelia once said that if she'd had a daughter she'd have wanted her to be exactly like you.'

My eyes misted over as I looked out of the window at the

garden, catching, through the open lattice, the scent of thyme, mint, roses and pinks.

'If you're admiring my garden, I have Ambrose Lanfeard to thank for keeping it shipshape,' Nurse Pintuck said when she came back with the cream. 'He comes in two or three times a week to chop wood and see to the privy.'

'Greater love hath no man . . .' I turned, caught Nurse Pintuck's eye, and we began to laugh.

'Ambrose is no oil painting,' she chuckled, 'but I think he'll get a good pew in heaven.' Her face saddened, 'I'll miss him, you know. He's always been sweet on me, but I never could get sweet on him. Strange, isn't it?'

I couldn't take my eyes off her. As she poured the coffee I noticed again her lovely bone structure. Although her skin had aged, it hadn't sagged and was so delicate that her wrinkles seemed like the finest lace threads spread on pink linen.

Here was a woman who had obviously cared all her life for her small treasures, that much was evident by the shine on the furniture, the gleam of the silver. In winter, summer, spring and autumn throughout the years she must have closed the door against the world with a feeling of thankfulness for a warm fire and four stout walls. Lizzie Nugent had told me how Rebecca used to cycle round the villages in all weathers and at all hours on that old sit-up-and-beg bike of hers, and I could just imagine her, an indomitable figure in a navy-blue uniform, battling against wind and rain with her nurse's bag in the carrier basket strapped to the handlebars.

With remarkable intuition, she knew exactly what I was thinking. 'You mustn't feel sorry for me, my dear,' she said quietly. 'If I were twenty years younger I'd have fought to stay here, but I'm past fighting now and, after all, I've had a fairly good innings.'

'Then it's high time someone else did the fighting for you!'

She smiled. 'But it isn't as if I owned this cottage. It belongs to Lady Nettlefold, and if she says I must go – well then.'

'That's all very well on the face of it,' I said, 'but I think that her ladyship would have helped other people too by letting you stay on here.'

'Other people?'

'Well yes, Miss Handyside for one. She fainted in church,

and it was all because of worry. She said she was afraid because what could happen to one elderly person could easily happen to another. Apparently she lives in fear of being turned out of her home.'

'I hadn't thought of it in that light,' Rebecca said.

'I'm sorry, I shouldn't have mentioned it, it's just that I . . .'

'I know, my dear,' Nurse Pintuck smiled, 'you have a warm heart and a compassionate nature. I realised that the minute I met you.'

She paused, frowning slightly, 'But I really am sorry about poor Beth Handyside. I had no idea she was so worried. Even so, I really am very weary.'

She got up stiffly from her armchair. 'Now, my dear, where shall I sit to have my hair singed?'

Chapter Eighteen

Why was it, I wondered, that the word 'gardening' brought out the Mastermind instinct in the male population? Bert Rumbold was usually to be seen hanging over the fence when I was doing my Trader Horn stuff in the jungle near Amelia's shed. Then the Gaffer had started putting in his two cent's worth of wisdom. Now the Archangel Gabriel was drawing diagrams on scraps of paper to illustrate the exact method of pruning roses.

'You needn't bother doing that,' I said. 'I haven't got any pruning scissors.'

'You mean you haven't got any secateurs?'

'No, I haven't got any of those either. And I haven't got any roses worth mentioning, unless you'd call all those briars cluttering up Miss Cox's fence, roses.'

'That's the whole point,' Gabriel said, loftily, 'if they'd been properly pruned, they wouldn't be briars. All the goodness is going into the shoots.'

'There's nothing good about those shoots, I can tell you. They'd give you a course of acupuncture as soon as look at you! Besides, what would I do with them if I did prune them? There's a limit to the amount of rubbish one garden can contain, and mine has reached saturation point. I can't move for all the nettles and weeds I've scythed, not to mention the clematis I've pulled down from the telephone wires. And my garden shed's full of rubbish, too.'

'Then why don't you burn it?'

'What? The garden shed?'

'No, the rubbish.'

'You mean – set fire to it?'

'How else could you burn it?'

135

Gabriel, I thought, was getting too big for his breeches since he'd stopped chewing his fingernails so much.

'But you needn't burn your grass-cuttings,' he continued, 'you could use those for mulch.'

'Mulch?'

'Compost, then.'

'You mean that stuff you spread on the ground to make things grow faster than they're growing already?'

'You'd need to mix them with compound manure, of course,' he said, with the panache of a Percy Thrower.

'Mix *what* with compound manure?'

'Your grass-cuttings.'

'But I haven't got any grass-cuttings.'

'Don't be daft,' he said, 'everyone has grass-cuttings.'

'Well, no, I haven't, because I haven't got any grass, unless you count that Tarzan stuff near the garden shed as grass. What I have got is lots of broken concrete, but I couldn't mulch that, could I?'

'I'd better go down and see what they're short of in the kitchen,' Gabriel muttered.

I caught the bus to Bagdad Corner fired with enthusiasm. Why hadn't I thought of burning all the roots and shoots and bits of dried wood, wizened apple boughs, and the rest of the rubbish before? Not to mention raking together the dried up nettles, wilting clematis fronds, and jungle grass; mixing them with compound manure – whatever that was – and making them into mulch.

Then, when I'd got them all well mulched and spread about, I might have an even better crop of nettles next year.

Now was the time for some level-headed thinking. An experienced gardener would have got rid of the rubbish as she went along. I'd been sadly remiss in coping with my rubbish, but I was prepared to mend my ways.

'Now what the devil are you up to?'

I looked up to see the Gaffer and Dodgy Knees peering over the fence at me. The Gaffer was standing on a couple of boxes, with his little pot-bellied cat perched on his shoulder.

'I'm making a compost heap.'

'You should've done that last back-end,' he said.

136

'I might have done, but I wasn't here last back-end,' I explained.

'And what's that other heap of rubbidge over yonder?'

'Oh, that's my bonfire. At least it will be when I've found some coal and newspapers to get it started.'

The Gaffer tottered backwards with laughter. 'Dost tha' hear that, Dodgy? She's gonna use coal an' newspapers to start a bonfire!'

'What's wrong with that?' I was getting what my mother would have called 'hikey'.

Bert appeared at the back door. 'Tea's ready,' he shouted, 'so you'd best come in Dad an' have it whilst it's hot. Darr wain't make two lots! An' you can leave that danged cat of yours out of doors. It's been sharpening its claws on the hoss-hair sofa again!'

As soon as the Gaffer had gone, I got down to business; hurriedly rolled newspapers into spills, found sticks and a few lumps of coal from the garden shed, made a pyramid, and struck a match which promptly blew out.

Six matches later, I still hadn't got the fire started. Well, was it my fault that the wind had changed direction?

The Gaffer's cat mewed piteously from the garden fence.

'I know what you're trying to tell me, Dodgy,' I said in what I hoped was pussy-cat language. 'I should move the darned thing to a more sheltered position, shouldn't I?'

I spent the next ten minutes shifting the bonfire to a less exposed site near the garden shed, struck another match, and watched, with a feeling of having conquered Everest, as the newspaper took hold and the sticks began to crackle.

My bonfire was going great guns now; fairly devouring the dried up nettles and clematis fronds. The smoke from it kept blowing sideways and getting up my nostrils; swirled in gusty, billowing circles as the wind rose and tongues of flame shot out at unexpected angles.

I was wiping my streaming eyes on a strip of kitchen-roll when the Gaffer came back.

'So you've got it goin', have yer?' He sounded put out.

'Looks like it,' I replied as airily as possible, seeing that I was on the point of choking to death.

'You're goin' blue in the face,' he remarked. 'Why don't you go indoors an' hev a cup of tea? I'll keep an eye on it for you.'

'Thanks very much, but I think that's enough for one day. I'll let the fire go out now.'

'Let it go out? Whativer for? Tha's only just got it goin'! You wants rid of all that there rubbidge, don't you?'

'Yes, but not all at once. There's far too much for that, and besides, it is getting rather late.'

'Late? It's only just gone seven.'

'I know, but I haven't had my supper yet.'

'*Supper?* Don't tell me you're off ti bed already. Only babbies go ti bed at seven.'

'No, of course not, but I have a cooked meal in the evening.' I wondered if I should fill in a questionnaire and have done with it.

'Some fowk have funny habits.' He shook his head. 'Why don't you have tea like sensible people?' He clambered down from his boxes. 'Ah well, if you won't let me keep on eye on the fire, that's that. Seems to me I'm neither use nor ornament now – just tekkin' up good oxygen. Ah should've gone when me ulcer went peptic . . .'

'Just a minute,' I called after him. 'I didn't mean to upset you. Of course you can look after the fire. Go round to the gate and I'll let you in.'

My heart melted at the sight of him – four feet ten, in Chaplinesque trousers and a wrinkled pullover, with his pom-pommed hat stuck jauntily atop his white curls.

'Give us hold of that rake,' he said gleefully, 'an' you needn't hurry back neither.'

'You will be careful, won't you?' I said, remembering all those burnt saucepans he'd told me about.

'Women,' he chuntered, 'can't leave a feller alone five minutes without givin' orders!'

He'd made his point. I went indoors.

An hour later, what met my eyes was a cross between the *Towering Inferno* and the burning of Atlanta in *Gone With the Wind*. Flames were shooting high into the darkening sky, and the Gaffer looked like a demented pin-man as the roof of Amelia's shed took hold.

I stood open-mouthed for a second, then Bert came rushing through my back gate carrying a bucket of water. At the same instant, Frances Cox cantered down her garden path and stood gawping over her fence looking for all the world like a racehorse at a starting gate.

As I flew down the path to the scene of the holocaust, she screeched, 'I knew it. I *knew* it! I saw it coming. But I shall send for the police, make no mistake about that.'

That did it! I'd had enough of Frances Cox and her silly, wagging tongue. 'For God's sake, woman, stop blathering and fetch some water,' I yelled. 'Do something useful for once in your life!'

'How dare you speak to me that way? You'll live to regret it!'

'It may come as a surprise to you, Miss Cox, but I already regret the day I met you,' I snapped. 'Now, are you going to fetch some water, or stand there and watch your fence go up in smoke?'

She disappeared without more ado.

Meanwhile Bert had hared back to his own garden to fetch a hose-pipe. 'Here,' he shouted, 'fix this on your kitchen tap, an' turn it on when I tell yer. As for you, you danged ould fool, chuck that bucket of water on the fire.'

The Gaffer complied. The trouble was, he forgot to let go of the handle.

I raced back to the house, dragging the hose-pipe with me, and jammed the end on the cold tap.

'Now, turn on!' Bert yelled.

The hose promptly parted company with the tap.

'What in tarnation are you doing? Nowt's coming through!' He appeared at the kitchen door and stared at the soaking wet figure confronting him.

'By heck,' he said with feeling. 'How the hell did you get as wet as that?'

How indeed! 'The pipe shot off the tap,' I explained, mopping my face with a tea-towel.

'Then hold it *on*,' he snapped. 'Of all the dateless lasses!'

I bunged the pipe back on the tap, and stood there like Peter at the Dyke as the hose writhed like a python and drenched Bert at the other end of it.

'By hell,' he puffed when the fire was out, 'that shed of yours were nearly a goner. I thowt you'd hev had more sense than to keep chuckin' rubbish on that bonfire when you could see with your own two eyes what was 'appening!'

The Gaffer's wrinkled prune of a face appeared round the kitchen door. 'Daint go on at the lass, Bert,' he began, 'it were all my . . .'

'Bert's quite right,' I interrupted, 'I should have known better. Now why don't you sit down, and I'll put the kettle on.'

The old man heaved a sigh of relief, smiled and said, 'I could do with a nice cup of tea.'

'By heck,' said Bert when we were dripping together on kitchen stools, 'you gave that long-nosed ould biddy next door a fair goin' over.' He chuckled. 'About time, an' all. She ain't 'ad a roastin' like that since Amelia were alive.'

'But, I thought . . . That is, Miss Cox told me that she and Miss Beatty had always lived in harmony.'

'So they did,' Bert nodded, 'because Amelia wouldn't put up with her nonsense for a minute. If her an' ould Fanny Cox lived in harmony, it was because Miss Cox was scared stiff of Amelia.'

'Really?'

'Aye, Amelia didn't give a tinker's cuss for nobody when she wus in the right. I mind that time Lady Nettlefold wanted the duck-pond down yonder filled in, an' the trees in front of her house cut down.'

'What happened?'

Bert grinned. 'What happened? Why, Miss Beatty called a meetin' in the village hall; took some ould deeds along with her, proved that the land belonged to the people of Tootington, an' marched down there at the head of a procession. By gum, I nivver enjoyed owt so much in me life as the look on her ladyship's face when she knew she'd been bested.'

Suddenly my heart lifted as I thought of the indomitable Amelia, not only walking at the head of a procession, but 'besting' the fearsome Lady Nettlefold.

As Gran would have said: 'What man has done, man can do.'

I didn't understand what she'd meant at the time, but I understood now.

Chapter Nineteen

I wondered how a woman who had just given birth to a baby could possibly fit into a pair of skin-tight jeans and look so attractive.

'I'm feeding Fern myself,' Julienne Douglas said, 'that's why I haven't time to go into Carnelian Bay to get my hair done. Hope you don't think I'm making a convenience of you.'

'I'd better warn you,' I said lightly, 'I haven't set anyone's hair for ages.'

'Oh I don't mind that. You're bound to be better at it than I am.' Julienne smiled engagingly.

I had thought that the wife of a television producer might be too high-flown for the likes of me, but she wasn't. She reminded me of the young Judy Garland at the start of her Hollywood career – before she became too famous.

Julienne Douglas's nose wrinkled in that same delightful way, and her smile was as warm as newly-made toast spread with heather honey.

'Would you like to look at my baby?' she asked.

'She's beautiful,' I said wistfully, as the baby's fingers curled round mine.

'Actually she's just a tube,' Julienne sighed, 'as fast as I feed her at one end, it all runs out at the other. Well I expect you know what it's like. I guess you've had children of your own.'

'No, I haven't.' I turned my head away as I spoke.

'Oh, I thought . . . But perhaps you didn't want children.'

I smiled brightly as I turned to face her. 'Yes, I did as a matter of fact, but my husband didn't. At least not until I was too old to have any, then he changed his mind.' I paused briefly. 'Julienne's an unusual name, isn't it?'

She matched her smile to mine. 'It's more than unusual, it's absurd! Would you believe it, my mother was reading a cook-book when the pains started? Still, I suppose I'm lucky that she wasn't looking for the Salamangundi recipe!'

'And you'd like a gamin-type fringe?' I said briskly. 'Just as well perhaps. I don't think I could cut a straight fringe if my life depended on it.'

The moment was weighted with unspoken words like, 'I'm sorry,' and 'it doesn't matter.' We were being very brittle and businesslike. Then, suddenly, we let things ride on a tide of laughter which seemed to me a far more sensible thing to do than to rake over the dead ashes of my past life.

I had never met anyone like the Douglases before. They appeared to float on the choppy sea of life on a kind of unsinkable hovercraft, spanking along at a rate of knots, whilst never actually touching the surface.

'You've made a great impression on Dominic,' Julienne said when I was twiddling her hair on fat rollers. He's all set to go ahead with the film, and he's got Go-Go Shingles interested in the deal. What he intends to do is superimpose Go-Go against a background of village life. Get him to sing with the Tootington Church Choir; take tea with Lady Nettlefold and the Vicar; find out how a character like Go-Go views the English village scene. What do you think?'

'It will never work,' I said, sensing disaster. 'Lady Nettle-fold would as soon take tea with the devil.'

'Oh.' She frowned. 'I thought it was your idea to get Go-Go in on the act.'

'Well yes, it was,' I admitted, 'but I never really thought that . . .'

'Look, Sally,' she said, 'I might as well come clean with you. Dominic and I are flat broke. We really need this film. Things were different when we lived in London. Dominic had lots of contacts there. Now I'm feeling guilty because I persuaded him to move to the country. You do understand what I mean, don't you?'

'Meet a fellow member of the flat-broke club,' I said.

So sparks were about to fly after all. But as I listened to Julienne's praise for the way I'd done her hair, I had no idea what a blaze those sparks would cause. If I'd known that, I might have caught the next train out of Carnelian Bay.

* * *

The sparks were fanned by a headline in the *Carnelian Bay Advertiser*. I'd bought a paper from a disabled news-vendor in the town square – a smiling individual called Buddy, whose hands had been crippled since birth. Not that he minded.

'I see we're in the news at last,' he grinned, as I put 10p into his bag, 'and not before time, if you ask me. I just hope that Go-Go Shingles has a word or two with me, that's all. If he does, I'll tell him that this is the finest place on earth to live, and we don't want outsiders messing about with it. What do you say?'

'I couldn't agree with you more.' But what would Buddy think if he knew that I had been instrumental in bringing Go-Go Shingles to the quiet Carnelian backwater?

On the bus, I opened the paper, and read: 'Local Man to Make Film. Mr Dominic Douglas, a local film producer, today confirmed that he expects to start work on exterior shots within the next few days.'

It was all there, spilled over the front page in that halting, non-committal way that reporters adopt when dropping bombshells. There was even a picture of Go-Go Shingles leaving the court on his last drug-addiction charge.

I wanted to curl up and die.

Life was getting complicated. Apart from all the hassle about Dominic's film, Mrs Amor had told me that Mrs Billy Watson was coming back to the Red Lion.

'I'd love to keep you on, Mrs Sam,' she'd said with the air of a tragedy queen. 'As a matter of fact I've been trying to pluck up my courage to tell you about Mrs Billy . . .'

'That makes us even,' I said, 'because I've been trying to pluck up enough courage to tell you about the man in Room Five.'

'I don't get it.'

'No, he was the one who got it – teapot, hot water, milk, sugar-lumps – the lot! But that's not the half of it! I owe you money!'

So now, to add to my troubles, I was about to become unemployed again, but I understood that Mrs Amor couldn't afford to take on more staff until the alterations were completed. In any case, the job at the Red Lion had been only a temporary one. I'd always known that.

As I got off the bus at Bagdad Corner, I scarcely knew

which to worry about first – Dominic's film, *Go-Go Shingles* or being made redundant.

A man followed me off the bus – a man with greying hair, carrying a small leather case. We stood together on the kerb, waiting for a couple of cars to pass. He smiled at me uncertainly. 'Excuse me,' he said, 'but does the pub take in visitors?'

'You mean the Spotted Dog? Well yes, I think so.' I wondered why he seemed so nervous, and noticed as we crossed the road together that he walked with a slight limp.

'There isn't another pub or hotel further down the village, is there? One not so close to the main road.'

'No, there isn't. But you might find accommodation at one of those cottages on the far side of the common. I believe Mrs Pickles does bed and breakfast.'

'Thank you. I'll try the pub first.'

He was an unremarkable man, quietly dressed in grey slacks and a navy blue blazer, so why did I have the feeling that I should start worrying about him too?

That evening I rang my sister.

'Now what's the matter?' she asked.

'There are times,' I said, 'when I wish you'd make nice cooing sounds on the telephone. Did I say that anything was the matter?'

'You didn't have to. I could tell by the way the bell rang!'

I wouldn't have been a bit surprised if she could. Holly and I might have made a nice living as a mind-reading act, I thought.

'What's wrong? Go on, get it off your chest and on to mine.'

'Nothing much, apart from the fact that I'm unemployed again. Oh, and did I tell you that my garden shed caught fire, and I nearly came to blows with Miss Cox, and . . .'

'Phew,' she said when I'd finished. 'Well, that's what comes of being incident-prone. You know you never could stay out of trouble for five minutes on end, but I thought you might have managed to keep your nose clean in a country cottage.'

'So did I,' I said dolefully.

'Why don't you come home for a few days?' she suggested. 'It would do you a world of good. Jim and I are dying to see you, and your canine nephew is trying to get to you down the telephone at this minute.'

'Really? Maxie!' I gave a couple of woofs over the wire, and imagined Holly's black and tan dachshund pricking up his ears as I did so. 'Give him a kiss on the lips from me.'

'You're kidding, of course! But seriously, why don't you come over for a while?'

'I'd love to. There's nothing I'd like more right this minute, but I can't. Not yet, anyway.'

'Why not?'

I wasn't joking as I said, 'I don't really know. It's just a feeling I have that something is going to happen. Something odd, and that I'll be needed here.'

'Well, you know best, love. But just remember, there's a bed here any time you want to come.'

'I know that. Bless you.'

Half-an-hour later, I answered a knock at the door.

'May I talk to you?' Avril fairly fell into my arms. She'd been crying, that much was easily discernible.

'Of course. Come in. What's happened? What's wrong?'

'Oh, Sally, I can't stand much more of this! I've told Arthur that we'll simply have to move away from here! I'll go off my head if we don't!'

How odd, I thought, as I led Avril to the settee, that a little while ago I was unburdening myself to my sister, now here was the Vicar's wife unburdening herself to me.

'Arthur and Lady Nettlefold have had the most awful row,' she sobbed. 'It was terrible, really terrible. She came to see us in a flaming temper. She'd read the evening paper, you see, and as good as blamed Arthur because that Go-Go whatever his name is, is coming to Tootington.'

'Oh, Lord,' I murmured.

'All because he has given Dominic Douglas permission to take some exterior shots of the church, and said that he wasn't averse to the cameras going inside it either.'

'Oh dear.'

'She actually *shouted* at him, Sally! Shouted at my husband! Said how dare he give his permission to allow filming in *her* church! That's when I got so wound up that I shouted back at her, "*Your* church? Just who do you think you are, Lady Nettlefold, God Almighty?"'

'You *didn't*.'

'I most certainly *did*!'

'Good for you!'

Avril blew her nose hard. 'But that's not the worst of it! She told Arthur that she would demand his resignation as Vicar of Tootington, and then she said, on her way out, that she wasn't prepared to stand for any more nonsense, and that's why she'd given Nurse Pintuck seven days' notice to quit her cottage.'

'You mean, she's actually going to turn Rebecca out of doors?' Anger took hold of me. 'But she *can't*! It's – inhuman!'

'That's just the trouble, I'm afraid she will, if something doesn't happen to stop her.'

I thought, when Avril had gone, that I'd been a fool to turn down my sister's offer of a few days' holiday. I felt like ringing her up again to tell her I'd changed my mind; that I'd just work my last day at the Red Lion, pack a suitcase, and be on my way, but I couldn't.

Sitting on my sprawly settee, looking up at Amelia's print of Leigh Holman's *Light of the World* over the mantelpiece, I knew that I was committed to Tootington and the people who lived there, as I had never been committed to anything before.

It seemed to me that this quiet backwater village reflected all the drama of the outside world, and that to turn my back on it now would be a shameful thing to do. Amelia would never forgive me.

But the day's trauma wasn't over yet. I was getting ready for bed when Lizzie, pale faced and watery eyed, knocked at the door.

'I just had to come,' she said hoarsely, 'May I talk to you?'

It occurred to me that I might open a little consulting room as I led her to the settee and waited for her to dry her eyes.

'Promise you won't tell Mother,' she said when she was more composed. 'Whatever happens, she mustn't know . . .'

'Of course I won't tell her, but perhaps you'd better say what it is that she mustn't know, or I might let it slip without knowing.'

'You couldn't do that,' Lizzie said, 'because you don't know what it is yet. I didn't know myself until this afternoon, and I've never had such a shock in my life. I mean – I've often dreamed of it happening and planned what I'd do if ever it did, but now that it has happened, I don't know what to do at all.'

'Are you trying to tell me that you've won the Pools?' I

lowered my voice just in case anyone was listening at the window.

Lizzie's face was a study. 'W-won the Pools?' She sounded as mystified as I felt, 'But I don't fill in the coupons. No, it isn't that. It – it's Leo, my young man. He's not dead, after all. Well, I mean he couldn't be, could he, because he walked into the shop this afternoon . . .'

'Gosh!'

'The awful thing is,' Lizzie went on, 'I didn't even recognise him at first, then when he broke his name to me I turned giddy and knocked a stack of baked beans flying.'

'Was he carrying a suitcase?' I asked, light beginning to dawn.

'No, I don't think so. I mean, he wasn't selling anything.' Lizzie started to tremble.

'He must have left it at the Spotted Dog, then,' I nodded. 'Tell me, did he walk with a limp when you knew him before, or did he get that in the Army?'

'I don't understand,' she said bemusedly. 'I came here to tell you a secret, and now you seem to know more about it than I do. You haven't got a crystal ball by any chance, have you?'

'Hmmm, yes. I carry it round in a kind of sporran under my skirt.'

Lizzie heaved a deep sigh. 'I don't know why it is,' she said, 'but every time I start a serious conversation with you, I end up wanting to laugh.'

'I'm very sorry, I didn't mean to sound insensitive,' I said, 'it's just that I felt I should worry about him when he got off the bus. Now I know why. Go on, Lizzie. What happened after you'd knocked over the baked beans?'

'Oh, he helped me pick them up, and then he told me how he was wounded at Dunkirk . . .'

'I think he might have written to you,' I said, 'or got someone else to do it for him.'

'Yes, so did I,' Lizzie flushed, 'but apparently he met a nurse at the hospital they sent him to, and to cut a long story short, they got married. Now he's a widower, and . . .'

'Don't tell me. Let me consult my crystal ball . . . I suppose he's here to plight his troth, or to press his suit or whatever.' I felt rather annoyed with Leo. 'Did he hand you all that guff about never having forgotten you, and wanting to start again where you left off?'

'Well yes,' Lizzie admitted. 'But in all fairness, he must have remembered me, or he wouldn't be here, would he?'

'I suppose not.' I gave her hand a squeeze. 'And how do you feel about that?'

'That's just it, I don't know.' Lizzie wrinkled her forehead. 'But it doesn't matter much how I feel, does it? The whole thing's impossible. What about Mother? She'd raise the roof if she so much as suspected he'd turned up again. But the truth is, I should like to go out with him – just to see if . . .' She sighed. 'Oh Lord, what a mess!'

'But surely you could do that, couldn't you? What's to stop you meeting him somewhere one evening? You could always nip down to the cinema in Carnelian Bay, and sit on the back row.'

'I've already thought of that. But I haven't been to the cinema for at least twenty years, and don't you think Mother would smell something fishy if I told her I wanted to go to the Roxy to see a double horror bill? Besides, I can't leave her in alone at night. Living with an old person is like having a permanent baby on your hands.'

'I know. I really do sympathise with you. But what if I came to sit in with her?'

'Thanks, but that wouldn't be any use either. She'd want to know where I was going and why and who with, and she's so cute she'd know in a minute that something was going on.'

'Wait a minute. I think I've got an idea.' I ran my fingers through my hair to clear my mind. 'Listen. How would it be if you arranged to meet Leo on your half day? No, don't interrupt. Your mother wants me to do your hair, doesn't she? Well, why not come down here on Wednesday afternoon and have it shampooed and set? You could say quite truthfully that it would suit me better to do it here than to fag up the road carrying my equipment. Et voilà! Then Leo could nip in the back way as I nipped out, and the pair of you could have the cottage to yourselves for a couple of hours!'

A look of relief spread across Lizzie's face. 'That's a wonderful idea,' she said.

'Good, that's settled then.'

'But – but what if Miss Cox saw Leo coming in the back gate?'

'There are times,' I said sternly, 'when you've got to grasp the nettle danger, even if you end up getting stung. Besides, she wouldn't know him, would she? Or perhaps we could winkle him in with a blanket over his head the way they get prisoners in and out of court rooms.'

Lizzie was now strung between hope and indecision. 'It's funny you should say that Frances Cox wouldn't know Leo, but she might.'

'Why?'

'Because, when he was stationed here during the war, he took her to the pictures a couple of times before he got to know me, and, well, it was Frances Cox who felt it her duty to tell Mother about us. She was crazy with jealousy, when he dropped her. In fact,' Lizzie's face puckered again, 'I often think that's why she's so bitter and twisted now.'

'Surely not?'

'It could be,' Lizzie said. 'You see, she was mad about him, and film-struck into the bargain. You know how everyone practically lived at the cinema during the war years? Well, Frances lived in a make-believe world in those days, and she wasn't bad looking either. Leo told me at the time what a job he'd had to convince her he wasn't Humphrey Bogart, and that she wasn't Ingrid Bergman or Greer Garson.'

'But even you didn't recognise him when he walked into your shop . . . Oh no, Lizzie. Stop worrying and start thinking positively for a change. After all, when you've been alone with him for a couple of hours, you might decide you don't like him as much as you thought you did, then the problem would be solved anyway!'

'But what if I like him more than I thought I did?' Lizzie insisted.

What indeed? 'Look, Lizzie,' I said firmly, 'let's cross that hurdle when we come to it.'

When she had gone, I sank down exhausted. Apparently I was right when I told my sister about my premonition that something odd was going to happen. I didn't know the half of of then!

Chapter Twenty

If only something good would happen to me for a change, I thought the next morning, as I struggled into my black tights, skirt and jumper and caught the bus to Carnelian Bay. Depression hung over me like a cloud. Trust me to lose my job just when I'd made friends with Daisy and Polly, I thought. But I was sick of thinking. I'd been thinking all night; dozing, having nightmares, getting up and wandering down to the kitchen to make cups of tea, going back to bed, dozing, then having nightmares all over again.

'You're a bit down in the mouth this morning, Mrs Sam,' Polly gave me a sharp look as I leaned against the draining-board. 'Cawse, I can see why you might be, what with Mrs Billy Watson comin' back to tek over from you. But we'll miss you, won't we Daisy?'

I didn't catch Daisy's reply. I was too tired and preoccupied for that. 'Pardon?' I said.

Polly clicked her tongue. 'You really ought to go up to the hawspital with you ears. They cleaned our Eadie's out a treat.' She folded her skinny arms across her bosom and warmed to the subject. 'You wus in the war, wasn't you?'

'Yes. What's that got to do with it?' I was miles away.

'I blames the war for everything,' Polly said. 'That's when my husband's spleen started. An' his brother went into the parachute regiment, took one jump an' punctured his ear-drums. Cawse, he never got no compensation. They said his ear-drums was punctured when he went in, so they was bound to be punctured when he came out. But it don't seem right, do it? I mean, someone should 'ave said his ear-drums was punctured when he had his medical. An' they wouldn't take his liver an' kidneys into account at all.'

150

Polly's brother-in-law, I thought, had all the makings of a mixed-grill by the sound of things.

'Now there's you an' your ears,' she went on.

'But I wasn't in the parachute regiment,' I said dully, my mind on other things, 'I was in the Wrens.'

'Must have been all the gun-fire, then,' Polly said decisively. Perhaps she thought I'd been in the Battle of Trafalgar, I reflected.

The kitchen door swung open at that moment, and Mrs Billy Watson limped in, fifteen stone with skinny legs, a full set of gleaming false teeth, and a chip on her shoulder.

'Oooh, you wouldn't believe what a night I've had with my legs,' she said. 'Played me up something terrible they did.'

'You pore thing,' said Polly, lighting a fresh cigarette. 'Well, here you are, back on the jawb, an' this is Mrs Sam who stood in for you whilst you was poorly.'

'Pleased ter meet you I'm sure,' said Mrs Billy Watson coldly. 'Oooh, my legs gave me gyp last night in bed. Ached something shocking they did. I said to my husband, "If my legs hurts me like this termorrer morning, I'll have all on ter get up ter that still room."'

'Daisy's got faroukas under her fallen arches,' Polly announced, 'an I expect they hurts her something shocking, too.'

'I expect they does,' Mrs Billy said sharply, 'but faroukas an' broken legs are two different things entirely.'

'Well, if you'll excuse me a minute.' I backed out of the kitchen and rushed up to the still room feeling like Mary Queen of Scots on her way to the scaffold; stood there for a moment or two; said a silent farewell to the dumb-waiter, the tomato-soup and custard stalactites, and the washing-up liquid that brought the skin off my hands, then wandered through to the dining room and bade a fond farewell to the cheese board and the latest chicken.

I t had been fun after all, at the Red Lion, I thought mistily. But I was one of those fools who always felt that a part of me was trapped for all eternity in any room I entered, and that the words I'd spoken there were destined to be uttered again in the spiralling galaxies of time. In short, I hated saying goodbye to anything that had become a part of me, and the Red Lion had certainly done that.

* * *

'And so, Mrs Sam,' Polly said, 'we have much pleasure in presenting you with a little token of our esteem. We all hopes – that is, Gabriel, Daisy, Basil, Ernie an' me – that these raffia tablemats will always remind you of us, your friends and colleagues at the Red Lion.'

'Oh, how marvellous!' I clutched my farewell present ecstatically to my bosom. 'How on earth did you know that I wanted a set of raffia tablemats more than anything else in the world?'

'Well,' said Polly, 'you did go awn a bit about not winning any at that village fête you went to, didn't you?'

'Did I? I hadn't realised that.'

'Where's the Missis?' Gabriel asked. 'She should have been here when you made the presentation.'

'She's over yawnder in her apawtment,' Polly said tartly. 'She an' Mrs Billy went across to settle up about the cawmpensation form. S'pect they'll be down in time for the sherry.'

She produced a bottle of British best and six glasses. 'Well, go awn, Gabriel,' she adjured him, 'give 'em a cawl before those dozy shift-relievers come awn duty.'

Gabriel assumed his wind-resistance stance, and ducked obediently through the back door to give Mrs Amor and Mrs Billy a shout.

Suddenly a piercing yell rent the air.

'My gawd, what wus that?' Polly slopped the sherry as the shriek was followed by a loud wailing noise, two 'Oh, hell's', and a couple of other naughty words usually written up in bus shelters.

We all rushed to the door and rounded the corner to find Mrs Billy Watson spreadeagled on the cobblestones.

'Ooooh,' she yelled. 'Ooooh, me arm! I've busted me arm!' She glared up at us. 'Well, don't just stand there. Send for the ambulance!'

'She slipped on the steps and grabbed at the hand-rail,' Mrs Amor explained desperately, running her fingers through her hair.

'More cawpensation,' Polly muttered darkly.

When the unfortunate Mrs Billy Watson had been carted off to the hospital, I felt obliged to return the raffia tablemats to their donors.

'You'd better keep them for me until the next time I leave the Red Lion,' I said.

'Aye, an' we'd better keep the sherry an' all.' Polly said, pouring it carefully back into the bottle.

Somehow I had the feeling that that sherry would be vintage wine before I got around to sampling it.

Well, I thought on the bus, at least one problem has been solved. I'm not unemployed any more.

I passed Miss Cox on my way down the lane to April Cottage.

'Good afternoon,' I said, but she threw up her head and stalked past me as if I were less than the dust beneath her feet.

Then a truck and a Landrover appeared, loaded with what I took to be camera equipment, and Dominic Douglas's film crew. Five or six men in all, and a long-haired blonde girl who waved to me in passing.

Now for all the Scarlet Pimpernel business, I thought. Hair wash'n sett'n; heads under blankets, and me nipping through the back gate as Leo nipped in. I just hoped that Lizzie hadn't got cold feet at the last minute and that Miss Cox wouldn't be looking out of her back room window when he arrived.

'You won't cut too much off my hair, will you?' Lizzie asked nervously as I stood there with my scissors poised.

'Can't promise a thing,' I said airily. 'Didn't you know? They used to call me the Demon Barber of Neat Street. Now I'm called the Cliptomaniac of Carnelian Bay.'

'Oh, *Sally*.'

'I know, Lizzie, but if you're nervous, well, so am I.'

'What if he doesn't come?'

'Of course he'll come. Don't be so daft!'

'I feel the way I did when I was eighteen,' Lizzie admitted. 'I know it's silly of me, but Leo is the only man I've ever cared for. And now, even though he's so much older, I still think of him as that young man I once held hands with under the stars.'

'I bet he still thinks of you in the same way too,' I said, putting her under the dryer.

When she looked at herself in the mirror afterwards, she touched her hair and cheeks in a kind of wonderment. 'Why, I look twenty years younger with my hair short,' she said.

'So you do, at that.' I handed her a pot of tinted foundation cream, my lipstick and pressed powder compact. 'Now, go to town, make yourself beautiful, Miss Nugent, and don't worry about a thing. Just enjoy yourself for a change.'

'I don't know what to say.'

'Best say nothing then. I'll be off now. Have a nice time with your young man.'

'Won't you wait to meet him?'

'No. It might make him feel, well, you know what I mean? See you around six o'clock?'

I had no way of knowing, as I marched down the garden path in my old grey slacks and a sweater, that I wouldn't be seeing Lizzie, or April Cottage again for the next three days.

Chapter Twenty-One

How odd, I thought, that June had slipped into July without my being aware of it. It was three months since I came to April Cottage, and now the trees were in full leaf, and the grass on the common was looking a little parched for want of rain.

As I walked towards the church, I kept my fingers crossed for Lizzie and Leo. If anyone deserved a bit of luck it was Lizzie. I felt light-hearted because I'd been snatched from the jaws of redundancy, not that I had wanted Mrs Billy Watson to break her arm on my behalf, but seemingly the poor woman was just as accident as I was incident prone.

Security was a tenuous thing anyway, I decided as I strolled along; a butterfly commodity that was there one minute and gone the next. Sometimes I thought of myself as a walking disaster-zone, then – poof – troubles flew out of the window and all was serene again. If only one could have seen what lay ahead round the next corner . . .

I came down to earth with a jolt when I did see what lay around the next corner – in the turning just before the church, outside Nurse Pintuck's cottage.

A furniture van was drawn up with its wheels on the grass verge, and three aproned furniture removal men were carrying Rebecca's belongings down the garden path.

I dodged a couple of men carrying a chintz-covered settee, and walked through Rebecca's front door to find her trying to pack a tea-chest; wrapping her precious blue and white Spode china in bits of newspaper.

'Rebecca,' I cried, 'what's happening?' It was a fatuous remark, because I could see very well what was happening. The trouble was, I'd never really believed that it *could* happen. 'Where are they taking your things?'

For the first time, I saw Rebecca Pintuck as a tired old woman. And yet she squared her shoulders bravely as she turned to face me, but her hands were trembling, and I knew that she had been crying.

'They're going to the saleroom,' she said, 'at least all save my most personal belongings, my clothes and my photographs.' She glanced up at the mantelpiece. 'I couldn't bear to part with my photographs.'

The last time I'd been in this room it was a home, now it was a shambles. I saw, with a sense of shock, the clean patches on the wallpaper where her pictures had hung, and the ashes in the grate of her once bright and welcoming hearth.

A deep, overwhelming feeling of anger surged through me. I had never felt so angry in my life before.

'Sally, my dear,' Rebecca said, catching my expression, 'what are you going to do?'

'I'm not sure right at this minute. But I'm going to do *something*!'

'There's nothing you *can* do,' she said, laying a restraining hand on my arm.

'Isn't there? We'll see about that!' I took her hand in mine. 'Do you trust me, Rebecca?'

She smiled faintly. 'Of course, child, but it's too late.'

'No it isn't. Not yet. Not quite yet. It might be in an hour from now, but not yet.'

'I wish you'd tell me what's in your mind.' She shrank back a little as the removal men stumped in and manhandled a couple of armchairs towards the door.

'I don't know myself at the moment,' I confessed, racking my brains. Then my eyes fell on the key to Rebecca's front door. A big black key in a hefty-looking lock.

'Where does the back door lead to?' I asked urgently.

'Only to the back garden and the privy,' she said. 'Why?'

'I want to lock your back door,' I said, 'and I'm going to lock the front door and take the key with me. That way nobody will be able to get in, will they?'

'No. But I don't quite see . . .' She frowned. 'Really, Sally, I think I have the right to know what you're up to.'

'I'm going to see Lady Nettlefold,' I said. 'I intend to appeal to her better nature. Meanwhile, it might be as well, don't you think, if those removal men couldn't get into your cottage?'

She laughed suddenly in that enchanting way of hers. 'Oh Sally, Sally,' she murmured, 'you remind me so much of Amelia.'

I stuck Rebecca's key in the pocket of my slacks as I marched down the garden path.

'Here,' said one of the removal men as I whistled past him, 'what's your little game? Why've you shut an' locked that door? How the 'ell do you expect us to load up the old girl's furniture if we can't get into the cottage?'

'Ah well, that's the whole point,' I said, 'you won't be able to.'

He was an elderly man wearing overalls, an old hand experienced at his job. 'You can't do that,' he said. 'We've got to get that lot shifted to the saleroom, an' be back at the depot by five.'

'Yes, I see your problem, but this is terribly important.' Whilst I was appealing to better natures, I thought I might just as well appeal to his. 'Do you realise that the old lady whose furniture is being taken away is about to be put into an old folk's home?'

'Is that a fact?' His mates had now wandered up to listen to the conversation. 'Well, that's a shame. She seems a nice lady, but that doesn't alter the fact that we have our job to do.'

'Couldn't you have your tea-break or something?' I pleaded.

'We've already had that.'

'Haven't you got a few bloater paste sandwiches left over?'

'Go on,' butted in one of his mates, a shock-headed younger man who obviously liked the idea of another tea-break, 'I could nip over to that shop opposite the village green and buy a couple of pork pies.'

'That's all very well, but where are you going, an' how long are you going to be gone? The foreman admonished, 'we can't hang about here indefinite. I shall hev to find a telephone box an' ring the depot. This delay'll play hell with our time sheets.'

'I'll be as quick as I can,' I promised. 'I'm only going as far as that big house opposite the duck-pond.

My feet sank in the gravel as I walked up to the front door of the Hall. I was just about to reach for the knocker when a blonde girl wearing jodhpurs and a white blouse called out to me.

'Who on earth are *you*?'

This time I actually remembered my own name. 'I'm Sally Shelton,' I replied, 'who are you?'

'My name is Natalie Nettlefold if it's any of your business. The servants' entrance is round the back by the way. You should have gone down the path over there.'

'I might have done if I happened to be looking for a job,' I said coolly. 'As it happens, I've come to see Lady Nettlefold.'

'You'll be lucky. Granny never sees anyone without an appointment.' She gave her boots a taste of her riding whip as she spoke.

'Then I'll just have to sit on the steps until she decides to let me in.'

'You work at the Red Lion, don't you? she asked. 'You're the one who had to dash off to the kitchen because you hadn't any smoked salmon.'

'Oh yes,' I said, 'and you and your friends hadn't the manners to wait until I came back.'

'Touché!' She smiled unexpectedly. 'I rather like you, Sally Shelton. Come with me.'

I followed her into a hall that looked rather like an oak penitentiary with oil-paintings.

'She's in the drawing room with Uncle Alfred,' Natalie said. 'I say you're not armed, are you?'

'My name is Shelton, not Al Capone,' I said pleasantly.

Natalie flung open a door. 'There's someone here to see you, Granny,' she announced. 'Her name is Sally Shelton, and she hasn't got a revolver.' She slipped away to a window-seat giving me a solemn wink en route.

Lady Nettlefold was ensconced in a high-backed chair with a sandwich half-way to her lips. She looked even more ferocious without her hat, and her hair was obviously a wig, with every strand severely in place. If only she hadn't put it on just a little askew, so that it favoured her left ear a little more than her right.

'Please forgive this intrusion,' I said, 'but I just had to speak to you about Nurse Pintuck.'

Alfred sprang up, clicking his tongue in irritation at my

158

unexpected appearance. 'Really, Natalie,' he snapped, 'you should have known . . .'

'Oh, do sit down, Alfred,' her ladyship rumbled. 'You irritate me past bearing at times.' She fixed me with her steely eye. 'Haven't I seen you before?'

'Yes, Lady Nettlefold, I'm a member of the church-choir.'

'Humph! Now I remember you. You're the wretched woman who caused all that commotion! Well, speak up. What do you want, eh?'

'It's about Nurse Pintuck,' I said.

'What about her?'

'I've come to appeal to you . . .'

She rose from her chair and stood over me like a monolith.

'I have no intention whatever of discussing Nurse Pintuck's future with you or anyone else,' she bellowed, thumping her walking stick on the Axminster. 'The very idea! The impudence! Alfred, remove this person at once.'

'There's no need for that, your ladyship.' I fended off Alfred and started backing towards the door as a matter of expediency. For all I knew she might have the Hound of the Baskervilles chained up somewhere. 'And – I think it high time you did discuss Nurse Pintuck's future.'

'*Alfred*!'

'Yes, Aunt.' But he looked uneasy as he edged towards me again.

Suddenly I remembered that Amelia had once got the better of these people, and took courage from the thought.

'Very well,' I said, 'you can have me thrown out if you want to, but not before I've said what I came here to say. Put yourself in Nurse Pintuck's place at this minute. Just think how you'd feel if a furniture van drew up in the drive out there, and a gang of removal men started dismantling your home. And suppose someone came along and told you that you were about to end your days with nothing but a few photograph albums, and all that was left to you was in a locker beside your bed – and that even the bed and the locker didn't belong to you either. What would you do then?'

'Sentimental twaddle,' snapped Lady Nettlefold. 'Rebecca Pintuck should feel grateful that she is going to be looked after from now on. She'll be given three meals a day. What more does she want?'

'A great deal more, I'd have thought. Is that all you want from life, your ladyship, three meals a day?'

Natalie butted in. 'Mrs Shelton's right,' she said. 'You'd want six, wouldn't you, Granny?'

Lady Nettlefold chose to ignore her grand-daughter's ill-timed remark. She lumbered past me towards the door, prodding her stick into the carpet. 'I shall not stay to listen to all this rubbish,' she said. 'Alfred, if this person is not out of my house in five minutes, you will send for the police . . .'

'Don't worry, I'm going.' I felt like bursting into tears, but I didn't. 'I simply thought that I might appeal to your better nature. Now I see that you haven't got one. All you've got is money and position. I feel sorry for you, Lady Nettlefold, because you haven't got a friend in the world. If you died tomorrow, the only people to attend you funeral would be solicitors.'

At last I'd got through to her. She turned at the door, quivering with indignation. 'How dare you speak to me that way? How dare you?'

'I'm sorry if I've offended you, but I just happen to think that someone in your position holds all the aces. Take the Hollies, for example. That house in the village with a For Sale notice in the garden. That belongs to you, doesn't it? Just think how many grateful people would come to your funeral if you let your heart rule your head for once, and made it into the kind of old people's home that is really needed here. Have you any idea, Lady Nettlefold, just how many old folk there are in need of the kind of security and independence that you could provide for them, if you wanted to?'

Suddenly all the fight went out of me. I'd overstepped the mark and I knew it. I felt my legs shaking as I walked across the hall with its frowning portraits, broad oak staircase and black and white tessellated floor.

As I fiddled with the catches, Natalie appeared at my elbow.

'I thought you said you weren't armed,' she murmured as she showed me out.

Now what, I thought as I marched back across the bridge to Rebecca's cottage. Perhaps it had been a foolish idea to beard Lady Nettlefold in her den, and it hadn't done a ha'porth of

160

good – quite the opposite, in fact. Now Rebecca's time was nearly up. As soon as the cottage was cleared, she'd put on her hat and coat and wait for the welfare worker to come for her. An hour from now and it really would be too late to do anything. Once Rebecca's furniture was in that van and off to the saleroom there'd be nothing left of her home.

Then I began to think more clearly. What was it my father had said when Holly and I had argued about who should get the first bite from a chocolate bar? 'Possession is nine-tenths of the law', that's what he said.

I knew nothing about tenancy laws, but it seemed reasonable to suppose that if Rebecca stayed put, even Lady Nettlefold could scarcely hustle her bodily through the front door.

As I turned into the lane and saw the furniture van again, I knew that Rebecca must remain in the cottage at all costs; that we must play for time. After all, there may be some legal angle to all this which had never even been explored. All we had to go on was her ladyship's declaration that the cottage was her property, and that Rebecca must leave it. But suppose that wasn't true?

'Oh there you are,' said the removal foreman. 'About time too. Hurry up an' get that door open so we can finish loading. It's past four o'clock.'

'Ah well, there's a snag,' I said, backing in through the gate.

'A snag? What, another one? Nay, damn, we ain't got time for no more snags.'

'I'm afraid you'll just have to make time. You see, you can't load the rest of the furniture. Nurse Pintuck isn't leaving, after all.'

'You what? Then what the hell are we to do with the furniture we've already loaded?'

'There's only one thing you can do with it if you want to get to the depot by five o'clock. Carry it back indoors!'

'Hi-up,' he said. 'I'll have to phone the depot about this.'

'Aw, give up, Jack,' said the shock-headed one. 'I'd just as soon shove that furniture back indoors and get going. I'm not struck on this job anyway. I don' like turning old folks out of doors.'

'Me neither,' said the third man, picking a bit of pork pie from his teeth.

Apparently I'd appealed to someone's better nature after all.

161

Chapter Twenty-Two

Rebecca's Siege, as I thought of it afterwards, turned out to be the biggest thing to hit Tootington since the Vikings landed, and it all started with the removers unloading the van and struggling back into the cottage with the stuff they'd just nicely taken out of it.

That turn of events bewildered Rebecca. She hadn't known until the men turned up at her door that they were coming, and a letter by the morning post had informed her that a welfare officer would arrive at five o'clock to see her settled into the Anchorage Rest Home for the Elderly in Carnelian Bay. Lady Nettlefold, it seemed had lost no time in setting the wheels in motion, but she hadn't had the decency to warn Rebecca beforehand.

Rebecca's lips trembled when she saw her cretonne-covered settee and armchairs again. 'I don't understand,' she said. 'I thought they were on their way to the saleroom.'

'Well they're not. They're back where they belong, so why don't you put the kettle on, and make a cup of tea.'

'But there won't be time, my dear,' she said helplessly, 'the welfare officer is coming any minute. She's taking me to the home . . .'

Rebecca's mind, as crystal clear as a glass bell, under normal circumstances, hadn't quite grasped what was happening. Lady Nettlefold had a lot to answer for, I thought grimly.

'Dear Rebecca,' I said, putting my arms round her, 'the welfare officer isn't taking you anywhere. You are staying right here where you belong. Don't worry your head about anything for the moment. Do you think you can manage to make the tea? We'll give the welfare officer a cup as well when she arrives.'

I kept harping on about tea because I wanted Rebecca to

162

keep busy doing something familiar and ordinary like getting out the cups and spoons. Besides, a cuppa would do her the world of good.

The tea was brewing when there was a sharp rat-tat at the door. A dark-haired woman with a brisk, Come-along,-let's-have-no-more-nonsense air about her, stood there. I noticed that she had parked her Mini near the gate and had left the engine running.

'I'm Miss Binns,' she said, glancing at her watch.

'I'm Sally Shelton. Won't you come in? You're just in time for a cup of tea.'

'Tea? Oh, I haven't time to stop for tea. Is Nursey ready?'

Maybe 'Nursey' was meant to soften the blow, but it put my back up. I wondered if Miss Binns had ever been a governess – one of those efficient ladies who could jolly along a classroom full of obstreperous children with cries of, 'Now, you know very well we don't allow that kind of thing,' and 'if you don't stop that at once, no bikkies for tea'.

'No, "Nursey" isn't ready,' I said. 'As a matter of fact, she's had an extremely harassing day and she's sitting with her feet up.'

'Sitting with her feet up? But she shouldn't be doing that now. Tea's at a quarter to six at the Anchorage, and Matron won't be best pleased if Nursey's late. What I mean is, Matron is very particular about time. She has to be in her position. What do you suppose would happen if everyone had tea when they felt like it?'

Miss Binns was getting hot under the collar of her blue linen dress, and her spectacles were beginning to mist over.

'I don't think Matron need worry about Nurse Pintuck being late for tea, because she isn't going to the Anchorage after all,' I said.

'Not . . . ?' Miss Binn's mouth sagged on its hinges. 'But this is most irregular. Arrangements have been made!'

'I'm afraid they'll have to be cancelled, then,' I said with the sweetest of smiles. 'So if you haven't time to stay for a cup of tea, there's really nothing more to be said, is there?'

She bridled. 'There's a great deal more to be said. I shall contact my department immediately and get a ruling on this matter. You'll be hearing from us again. Have you any idea of the waiting list there is for accommodation at the Anchorage?'

I kept my smile firmly fixed in position, although Miss Binns had lost my sympathy when she referred to Rebecca as "Nursey".

'In that case,' I said, 'I can't see where the problem lies. All you'll have to do is cross Nurse Pintuck's name off the list, and move the next one up a peg. Good day, Miss Binns.'

As she marched down the path and backed her car, missing the church wall by a couple of inches, I noticed that Mrs Pickles and Mrs Tucker were standing with their heads together at the end of the lane. They jumped as the car shot past them, and watched with interest as it roared up the road towards Bagdad Corner.

The tea had done Rebecca a power of good, but I could see that she was worn out. Bed would be the best place for her, I reckoned, although I had all on to convince her of the fact. What she needed most was a good night's sleep, and to wake up in her own bed in her own home.

'I expect you're right,' she said at last. 'But what if that – Miss Binns comes back? I don't think I could cope with her.'

'You won't have to,' I reassured her, 'because I'm not leaving you alone. I'm staying right here tonight. I'll just tidy up a bit, and light the fire.' Then I trotted out one of Gran's sayings. 'You'll see, everything will look better in the morning.'

When I'd lugged the furniture round a bit and got the fire going, I popped upstairs with a cup of cocoa and a few biscuits, but Rebecca was fast asleep.

As I drew the curtains, I saw that Mrs Pickles and Mrs Tucker were back, and that they had been joined by a few more women, some of them with pushchairs.

The Tootington bush telegraph system had been at work with a vengeance, I thought, but I wondered what they expected to see. Everything was quiet and yet there was a strange air of expectancy, as if they were waiting for something to happen.

They didn't have long to wait. Half-an-hour later, a car nosed into the lane and Alfred Nettlefold got out of it.

So the bush telegraph system had really been at work. But what if Alfred crossed the threshold? If I let him in, there was no telling what might happen. Alfred, I decided, might be the thin edge of a very large wedge, and I didn't want him hammering at the door either – that would wake Rebecca and upset her even more, so I called to him through the letter-box.

It was a novel experience, holding a conversation through a letter-box, and I couldn't help wondering, as Alfred and I hissed at each other throught the aperture, what kind of a picture he presented from the rear. The audience in the lane must be enjoying enormously the sight of little Alfred doing a contortionist act on the garden path. I had the ridiculous notion of a confessional with Alfred as the supplicant, and I wondered what he'd do if I gave him three Hail Mary's and a how's your father?

What he said was that his aunt was seriously displeased by the turn of events, and would be even more displeased when she learned that he had been obliged to hold a consultation through a letter-box.

'There's such a thing as the law of trespass,' he muttered. 'If you think that her ladyship will let matters rest here, you are very much mistaken.'

His legs must have gone into cramp at that moment. He turned groaning, and I watched from the sitting room window as he did a kind of Toulouse Lautrec back to his car, watched by an ever growing crowd of village women, one of whom gave him a derisory cheer as he scrambled into the driving seat.

'G'arn, Mister,' someone shouted. 'Go home an' tell yer Auntie!'

That was all very fine, but I didn't like the law of trespass threat one little bit. Suppose I'd landed Rebecca in a worse mess than ever?

I felt a sudden urge to spend a penny, and remembered that the loo was at the end of the garden. I thought of the ignominy of being arrested on my way to answer a call of nature, and realised how vulnerable Rebecca and I were in that respect. Lady Nettlefold would have worked out that one, I felt sure, as I unlocked the back door and peeped out. If a heavy hand fell on my shoulder and a voice said, 'Now then, what have we here?' I'd faint dead straight away.

Apparently someone else had thought of the loo angle too. As I sprinted up the path, a head appeared over the back gate. But it wasn't the constabulary, it was Stan Tucker, one of the Tootington band trombonists.

'How do?' he said conversationally. 'Nice evening.'

'What on earth are you doing here?' I asked in amazement.

'Standing guard.' He grinned. 'Heard tell the pore old lady was in a bit of a fix, so we decided to lend a hand.'

'We?'

'Aye,' he said laconically. 'Ambrose Lanfeard is out front. It was his idea, tha knows. Thinks the world of Nurse Pintuck, does Ambrose. When he heard she was in trouble there was no holding him.'

That's how Rebecca's Siege started, slowly at first then gradually gaining momentum.

Back indoors, I looked out of the sitting room window to see the indomitable Ambrose mounting guard over Rebecca's gate, armed with a pitchfork.

Now the fat really was in the fire, I thought. But the fat hadn't even begun to bubble at that stage.

As dusk was falling, Dominic and his film crew arrived and started setting up their lighting equipment, run from a generator in the Landrover.

'Ye gods,' I muttered under my breath as I pelted upstairs to take another look at Rebecca, 'she'll never sleep through all this.' But I was wrong. She looked as peaceful as the Sleeping Princess in the fairy tale, with her white hair spread on the pillow, and a cup of cold cocoa on the table beside her.

It was eleven o'clock when Dominic and his gang packed up their equipment, and called it a day, and even then there were a few sightseers left in the lane. I recognised Miss Fanshaw from the church-choir, with no fewer than six dogs on various leashes, those stalwarts from the afternoon, Mrs Pickles and Mrs Tucker, and Oliver Rumbold – the Gaffer.

But pride of place went to Ambrose Lanfeard – that 'fair hummer on the euphonium' – whose pitchfork remained resolutely at the ready to repel boarders.

At midnight I flopped on to Rebecca's settee, totally exhausted. The last thought that crossed my mind before I fell asleep was, I hope Lizzie and Leo aren't still waiting for me to come home.

I woke to the scent of bacon and eggs.

'Ah, you're awake, child,' Rebecca said, setting down a tray beside me. 'And you were quite right about things looking better in the morning. I feel like a new woman today. Now, eat your breakfast before it gets cold.'

I struggled into a sitting position, still wearing my slacks and jumper, with my hair hanging over my face. 'What time is it?' I asked.

'Seven o'clock,' she said. 'But would you believe it? When I went out to the loo just a few minutes ago, there was a young man leaning on the back gate.' She smiled. 'A very *nice* young man. But what was he doing there?'

'Listen Rebecca,' I said.

The Rebecca Siege entered its second day.

At nine-fifteen, a car drew up in the lane. A car with a Press notice pasted to the windshield, then another Press car, and yet another.

At ten o'clock Dominic Douglas's crew re-appeared. By half-past ten, the sightseers had started to re-group. At a quarter to eleven, old Ambrose was prised from his pitchfork and led away by young Andy Appleby, protesting, as he was packed into a van and driven home for a rest, that he was good for the next twenty-four hours, and that he'd sort out anyone who said he wasn't.

Before he went, there was a changing the guard ceremony, when the Gaffer took charge of the pitchfork. All these events were being recorded for posterity by Dominic's cameraman, a gangling youth with flapping fair hair who carried the camera on his shoulder, rather like Rebecca at the Well.

'My goodness, isn't it exciting?' my Rebecca said.

Around noon, Miss Binns reappeared accompanied by a fussy young man in a pale blue shirt and trousers. I listened to their exchange with the Gaffer through the open window.

'Stand and deliver,' he commanded, waving his pitchfork.

'Stand and deliver what?' snapped Miss Binns. 'This isn't the milkman, you know. This is Mr Peake, Carnelian Bay's Head of Social Services, come to speak to Nurse Pintuck.'

'Well, Mr Peake can just push off,' the Gaffer retorted. 'Mr Peake can't speak to no one, an' neither can you, so bugger off, the pair of you!'

'Did you hear that, Mr Peake? Not only threatening behaviour, but foul language into the bargain! The police must be informed at once!'

We'll all end up in jail, I thought, as sure as my name's Sally Shelton. What's more, we were running short of food. I scribbled a note and hared to the back gate with it.

At half-past two, a Panda car parked outside the church, and a young constable got out of it.

'Afternoon, sir,' said the Gaffer, leaning on his pitchfork. 'Nice day, ain't it?' Hs smiled encouragingly. 'If you've come about the rumpus . . .'

'Which rumpus?'

'You mean you ain't heard?' The Gaffer gave a sigh of relief. 'Why this rumpus. The one you're lookin' at this minute.'

The constable scratched his head. 'You mean the filming? I wouldn't exactly call that a rumpus. Why? Has anything happened that I should know about?'

'Eh?' said the Gaffer, cupping his hand round his ear.

'I said . . . Oh, never mind! I'd better ring my Sarge and find out.' The young constable hurried back to his car.

I thought gloomily of all the people sitting at desks; in newspaper and welfare offices; police stations and old people's homes; making rulings, subbing, and generally trying to sort out the affairs of one old lady. The ramifications seemed endless, and no doubt a few lawyers and barristers would soon get in on the act.

At three o'clock, Commander Bruce strode down the lane carrying a box full of groceries which he handed to the Gaffer, who sagged at the knees and staggered up the path with it, and handed it to me through the window. In it was a note which read: 'Well done. Keep the flag flying. Hope there's enough here to keep you going. If not, let me know, and remember – whatever you may need, I'm ready, willing and able! Regards, Howard B. P.S. I'm on the pitchfork rota. P.P.S. Lizzie Nugent has asked me to say that the 'balloon has gone up'. What on earth can she mean?'

'Dear Howard,' Rebecca said softly, 'he's such a comfort. He's been very kind to me, you know.' She paused. 'It's such a pity about Kay.'

168

'Kay?'

'Yes dear, his wife.'

I asked the question diffidently, 'Why? What's wrong with her?' I didn't want to pry, but I just had to know.

Rebecca glanced across at me, understanding that my question was necessary to me. She would not have answered it had she believed otherwise. Her voice was very tender as she confided, 'Their only son was killed about five years ago. He was such a fine young man; every bit as handsome and kind as his father. It was a terrible tragedy.'

'Wh-what happened?' My throat felt so constricted that I almost swallowed the words.

'He had just joined the Army,' Rebecca said slowly. 'He was an officer cadet, and his father and mother were so proud of him. He was one of my babies, you know. Dear Charles. He came to see me just before he set off on those maneouvres . . .' She shivered suddenly. 'He looked so fine in his uniform.'

Her old eyes stared back into the past. 'He walked into this very room, kissed me, and said, "Well, Rebecca, how do I look?" "Very handsome," I said, "and well you know it, you young monkey!"'

'I never dreamt that I would never see him again. He stood by that door and saluted me before he went out. We heard later that he had died leading his fellow cadets across some kind of a chasm – on ropes – you know the kind of thing I mean? He was half way across when the ropes gave way.'

Rebecca's eyes filled with tears as she went on. 'He lay there, joking and laughing, until an ambulance arrived. The poor boy must have been in agony because, you see, his back was broken. He was dead by the time that ambulance arrived at the base hospital.

'Poor Kay Bruce. She couldn't accept the fact that her son was dead.' Rebecca reached out her hand for me to hold. I clasped it firmly as she continued, 'After the funeral, she started drinking heavily, the poor soul, and who could blame her?'

'Oh, how terrible! Poor Mrs Bruce. Poor Commander Bruce!' Tears came into my eyes too.

'Now she's a total recluse,' Rebecca said sadly. 'She never goes anywhere; never sees anyone. It's such a shame. She was so beautiful, you see. But now . . .'

'I'm sorry. So very sorry.'

'So am I.' Rebecca sighed deeply. 'Sorry for both of them, but especially for Howard. That accident robbed him of the two people he cared most for – his son, and his wife as she used to be. That's why I admire him so much. Any other man might have reacted quite differently to seeing a once beautiful woman become fat and apathetic, but he has remained absolutely loyal to Kay.'

She smiled and her eyes kindled. 'I always think of Howard Bruce as a kind of knight in shining armour, throwing down the gauntlet in the face of his enemies. People can be very unkind, you know.'

'Unkind? But that's monstrous!'

'Even so, my dear, he has had to face some snide remarks from time to time. You know the kind of thing I mean? "Your wife not with you tonight, Commander? Not feeling well? Never seem to see anything of her these days!".'

'How could they! How unfair! How cruel!'

'But people can be cruel, Sally dear. Perhaps they don't mean to be, but they are so often.' She smiled sadly, 'In one sense, Howard became withdrawn too. That is why he is so well thought of by what some people call "the common folk" of the village; decent folk, compassionate folk. People like Ambrose Lanfeard.'

'Yes, I see,' I said eagerly. 'I sensed that the first time I met him; the way he smiled at Ambrose, the way he helped Miss Handyside when she fainted.' I paused.

Rebecca was wise enough to change the subject at that point. Perching her spectacles on the end of her nose, she said, 'And Lizzie Nugent's "balloon has gone up" has it? I expect she's had another upset with her mother.'

'Yes,' I said uncomfortably, 'I expect she has.'

'Poor Dolly Nugent,' Rebecca sighed, 'she can be a trial when she feels like it, and she does so often feel like it. I think she enjoys keeping Lizzie on the hop, just to add a little spice to her own life. It's very naughty of her. I must speak to her about it when I go to see her again – when all this is over.'

Then Rebecca asked the jackpot question. 'When do you think that all this will be over? I know that I was rather confused yesterday, and that worried me a good deal; made me think, as a matter of fact, that perhaps it is time I went into

170

a home. But now, although I feel perfectly well physically, I'm still not quite sure what is going on. What *is* going on, child?'

'I'm not quite sure about that myself any more,' I confessed. 'I was yesterday when I went to see Lady Nettlefold, but that seems like a hundred years ago now.'

By half-past four, Rebecca and I were inundated with groceries; packets of teabags, cartons of cornflakes, bars of chocolate, jars of coffee, tins of baked beans, home-made cakes and bread-buns. One kindly soul had even sent us a bottle of washing-up liquid and a jar of hand-cream.

Then the flowers began to arrive. Posies from children labelled, 'With love and kisses'; masses of pot-plants; a half-wilted bouquet from Beth Handyside, and a fearsome looking cactus from Cynthia Fanshaw.

'My goodness,' said Rebecca, 'I'm beginning to feel like the Cenotaph.'

At six o'clock, Ambrose Lanfeard took over his pitchfork again, and stuffed a newspaper throught the letter-box. 'Cop a load of the headlines,' he hissed.

'ARMED VILLAGERS PICKET LOCAL COTTAGE', I read.

'Good gracious!' Rebecca remarked. 'We sound like a national strike!'

'It gets worse as it goes on. Listen to this.'

'Villagers armed with pitchforks yesterday took the law into their own hands in a bid to prevent the eviction of retired district nurse, Rebecca Pintuck (82) from her home in Tootington-by-Carnelian-Bay.'

'Eighty-two?' Rebecca interrupted. 'But I'm only eighty-one!'

'The quiet village of Tootington was invaded by crowds of people angry because of an eviction notice served on Miss Pintuck by Lady Eunice Nettlefold (84) of the Hall, Tootington, who refused to comment on the situation.'

'Eunice Nettlefold will throw a fit when she reads that,' Rebecca butted in. 'She's only eighty-two!'

171

'Well you know what newspaper reporters are like,' I consoled her. 'They have to exaggerate a bit or they'd be out of a job.'

'What else does it say?'

I drew a deep breath.

'While Lady Nettlefold was unavailable for comment, Mr Ambrose Lanfeard (81) a native of Tootington said: "It's a crying shame that Nurse Pintuck should be turned out of her home. She has always kept the premises clean and tidy even though she has no indoor sanitation or hot running water".'

'Just you wait until I see Ambrose Lanfeard. He makes me sound like a second-rate plumber!'

'Mr Dominic Douglas, a television film producer and a resident of Tootington, at present engaged in making a film about village life, told our reporters: "Here is not only a prime example of the feudal system at work in 20th century England, but a miscarriage of justice to boot. We cannot allow individuals to be threatened in this way, particularly the elderly and infirm. I applaud what is being done here on behalf of old people the length and breadth of this land." Mr Douglas then went on to say that he hopes to interview Miss Pintuck tomorrow.

"Her reminiscences of the village and its inhabitants," said Mr Douglas "will make a valid contribution to my film which is due for general release around Christmas".'

'Well,' said Rebecca, 'there's a turn up for the book. So I'm going to be a television star at last, am I?' She chuckled. 'And Mr Douglas is quite right about my reminiscences of the village and its inhabitants. I could tell a tale or two if I wanted to. I wonder what Eunice Nettlefold will think when she reads *that!*'

'But surely,' I laughed, catching Rebecca's tongue-in-cheek humour, 'Lady Nettlefold hasn't any skeletons in the family closet, has she?'

'Oh hasn't she? She won't sleep a wink tonight for worrying about whether I'm going to spill the beans about her father. A real old roué he was. Oh, I daresay that Eunice was born between the sheets of the family residence, but her sister, Meg, certainly wasn't.'

'I can't believe it!' I said.

'Oh, it's perfectly true, my dear, and I know you won't let it go any further, but Meg Nettlefold was Sir Horace's daughter by a barmaid over at Hardington. That's why she and Eunice never saw eye to eye over anything. Meg was just as nice as could be.' She sighed, 'But I don't suppose she'd have been given house-room except that the real mother died when she was born, and rather than have a scandal on her hands, Eunice's mother adopted the baby . . .'

'Hang on a minute,' I said. 'I don't quite get it. If Lady Nettlefold married, and I assume that she must have done since she has a granddaughter, how come that her name is still Nettlefold?'

'Ah well,' Rebecca nodded mysteriously, 'she married her first cousin, Will Nettlefold, but he was as nutty as a Dundee cake. Then poor Meg got herself pregnant by the Reverend Mr Parker, and Eunice, to save another scandal, adopted *that* baby. Of course, Will Nettlefold was in a mental home by that time – only they didn't call them mental homes in those days, they called them asylums.'

'Ye gods,' I said with feeling. 'So, let me get this straight, Natalie Nettlefold is the progeny of Meg. But haven't we skipped a generation? What happened to Natalie's mother who, I presume, was Lady Nettlefold's adoptive daughter?'

'No, child, you've got the wrong end of the stick,' Rebecca said. 'Meg's baby was a boy, not a girl, so he naturally took the name Nettlefold, which he would have done anyway seeing that his mother was called Nettlefold. Now have you got it?'

'No, I mean yes.' Family trees were like arithmetic and psalters so far as I was concerned – totally unfathomable.

'Of course,' Rebecca went on, 'poor Natalie's parents were killed some years ago. I don't know if you've ever met her, but if you did you might wonder why she doesn't favour Eunice's side of the family at all.'

'I have met her,' I said weakly, 'and I did wonder . . .'

'Why don't you sit down, child?' Rebecca said. 'You look rather odd. Is anything the matter?'

173

Chapter Twenty-Three

I spent my second night on Rebecca's settee dressed in a voluminous cotton nightgown, but I didn't sleep a wink. What did Lizzie mean by 'the balloon has gone up'? Just what would be the outcome of Rebecca's Siege, and what was I doing dressed in a Victorian nightgown?

I wished that all I had to worry about now was being made redundant. I hadn't read out the last paragraph of the newspaper report to Rebecca, the bit that said Mrs Sally Shelton, a friend and neighbour of Nurse Pintuck's, was in the cottage with her, and that it was she who had apparently sparked off the villagers' insurrection in refusing admittance to Miss Letitia Binns, a social welfare worker and her colleague Mr Desmond Peake, Carnelian Bay's Director of Social Services.

Ah well, I'd always had the feeling that I'd end up picking oakum – but insurrection! Could I possibly end up in the Tower of London? Insurrection smacked of sabotage and treason – and all I'd ever wanted was justice for one old lady.

Now, teasing the back of my mind was The Hollies, that house facing the village green with the For Sale notice in the garden. Lady Nettlefold's house with the smiling bay windows and conservatory, and all the old people I knew who might be happy to spend the rest of their days there if only I'd been able to persuade her ladyship of that fact.

I could just imagine the dining room set with little tables, and people like the Gaffer and Ambrose Lanfeard, Dolly Nugent and even Rebecca herself being looked after not in a kind of old folks' concentration camp, but in a warm, loving, homely atmosphere.

The kind of home I envisaged would cater for pets, too, and

feather beds. Every room would be a little home in itself, so that no one need get rid of all their treasured possessions to live there. After all, possessions meant a great deal to old people – I knew that from Gran and that old earthenware jug of hers, and her samplers and photograph albums; that little beaded footstool she was so fond of, and the teaset – or what was left of it – that her mother had given her for a wedding present. Possessions meant memories to old people, and memories were all that were left to most of them.

But what was the use of thinking? I'd botched that interview with Lady Nettlefold and said unforgivable things to her when I should have been charming and diplomatic.

Once I was on the trick-cycle of thought, I couldn't dismount. I started to worry about how Mrs Amor was coping without me, and about my nettles, my vendetta with Frances Cox, and about the Commander's wife. Most of all about Go-Go Shingles.

I was still awake when daylight appeared through the curtains. I got up and inhaled the freshness of the morning. 'Lord,' I said, 'I'm in a bit of a jam, and so are a lot of other people. Anything You can do to help, I'll be much obliged.' It wasn't much of a prayer, but it came from my heart.

So commenced the third day of Rebecca's Siege.

The Press cars were the first to arrive.

'Oh my,' said Rebecca, 'there's more than ever this morning. If that nice Dominic Douglas doesn't hurry up, he won't find a parking space.' She had slept well and was as bright as a button, whilst I felt as if I had just completed an Olympic marathon.

'I'm going to put these trews in the dustbin when I get back to April Cottage,' I declared, 'and this sweater.'

'Why?' Rebecca asked, pouring me a cup of tea.

'Because I feel as if they've been soldered on me.'

She glanced at me shrewdly. 'I've been thinking, my dear. We really can't go on like this for much longer. Perhaps I'd better send word to Miss Binns . . .' Her fingers trembled on the handle of the teapot. 'It occurs to me that I'm being very selfish causing all this upset.'

'You'll upset that teapot if you're not careful,' I said. 'Oh look, there's the postman.'

'Hmmm. He's getting too old to ride that bicycle,' Rebecca commented, crossing to the window to collect her mail. 'Now then, Able, how's your leg this morning?'

Able, as an official of Her Majesty's Postal Service, hadn't been threatened with a pitchfork, and he appeared to have forgotten about his leg in his excitement.

'Hi-up,' he said, 'have you seen what's goin' on round the corner on the common? There's caravans parked there, an' a feller with an ice-cream cart has just come up from Carnelian Bay. By gum, the coppers'll have summat to say about that. It's like Bank Holiday Monday out yonder.'

By ten o'clock the lane was awash with sightseers. One enterprising couple edged their car to the end of the cul-de-sac and started cooking their breakfast on a Primus stove, and when Dominic and his gang put in an appearance, they were obliged to park in the road fronting the church.

The driver of a television van that appeared around eleven was more foolhardy. He tooted his horn until he had managed to clear a pathway – and who, I thought, was going to argue with a television van?

'Here! Mind my bodywork,' yelled one of the Pressmen. 'If you come any closer you'll put a dent in my wing!'

The television van driver wound down his window, and a heated exchange occurred between the pair of them, then Primus-stove wandered up munching a bacon butty and started doing the old 'down with your left, now straighten up a bit' lark, as if he was bringing in an aircraft on the deck of a carrier. All he needed was a couple of yellow ping-pong bats.

The pitchfork had now been handed over to Ould Gabby, who had retreated to a safe distance halfway up Rebecca's garden path. Then I saw Half-Pint's and Herbie Parrott's heads bobbing along by the hedge. They'd come, I guessed, to keep Ould Gabby from falling backwards into the rose bushes. Half-Pint gave me a beaming smile and the thumbs-up sign when he saw me at the window.

'I've never seen anything like this in my life before,' Rebecca said. 'If that man in the yellow car comes any nearer he'll knock my fence down.'

'It's a matter of self-preservation,' I replied. 'He's trying to get out of the way of the television van.'

'I don't know why he doesn't drive straight up the path and

have done with it. And what will happen when he's finished his reporting? How will he get out of the lane?'

'He won't,' I observed, 'unless Dominic moves his Land-rover.'

It wasn't until Dominic and his helpers had run the gauntlet of Gabby and his pitchfork, and Rebecca had given permission for them to be allowed into the cottage, that I discovered he couldn't move his vehicle either. The road beyond the church, Dominic said, was choc-a-bloc with cars, and a couple were stuck on the bridge.

'There's a Panda car somewhere back,' Dominic told us cheerfully, 'and it's stuck too as far as I can make out. Isn't it marvellous? I never dreamt when I started shooting my film that things would turn out this way. It's a film producer's dream come true. The way things have developed, it doesn't even matter about Go-Go Shingles.'

'You mean – he's not coming after all?' I asked breathlessly.

'Afraid not. He's blotted his copy-book again.' Dominic grinned. 'His case comes up next week!'

A feeling of relief swept over me. I felt light-headed with relief, or perhaps I was simply over-reacting after a sleepless night. 'I'll make some coffee,' I said weakly as Dominic set the wheels in motion for his interview with Rebecca.

I'd need seven cups, I figured. One for Dominic, one for the nice girl with blonde hair who kept scribbling notes, two for the lads doing the lighting, one for the cameraman, one for Rebecca and one for me.

Conversation floated through to me from the sitting room as I waited for the milk to heat.

'I'm doing a marching sequence with the Tootington Village Band on Sunday,' Dominic said. 'The uniforms should be here any day now . . .'

Uniforms, I thought happily. Thank you, Lord. I know I didn't mention uniforms for the band when I spoke to You earlier this morning, but Thank You anyway.

'And to think I asked Dominic when we came here,' the blonde girl said, 'whatever happened in a place like Tootington.'

I glanced out of the window on my way through with the coffee. The television crew, I noticed, were interviewing

Primus-stove and his wife, and the Press men were interviewing Ould Gabby. I wondered vaguely as I set down the tray how the Panda car was doing, and if the ice-cream vendor on the common was having a busy time.

'Right,' said Dominic, who had obviously made a hit with Rebecca, 'we'll just have our coffee, then we'll get cracking, and don't feel nervous, Nurse Pintuck, just be your natural, charming self, and you'll come across beautifully.' He gave her hand a little squeeze. 'Let's make this an interview to remember, shall we?'

I turned away from the window. 'Famous last words,' I said.

'Why? What do you mean?' Dominic asked.

'Perhaps you'd better take a look.'

'Christ Almighty,' he said, twitching back the curtain, 'if it isn't Lady Nettlefold and company – and it looks as if she's brought the undertaker.'

'What?' Rebecca hurried to the window. 'Oh that's Mr Wellbehave, her lawyer,' she said.

'She's brought the Vicar and friend Alfred as well,' Dominic remarked. 'Looks as if we're in for the Last Rites. Oh Lord, that old chap isn't going to spit her on his pitchfork, is he?'

'Dear me,' Rebecca gasped, knocking on the window, 'he mustn't wave that pitchfork in Lady Nettlefold's face like that, especially with her solicitor watching. Let them pass, Gabby,' she called to the doddering old chap on the path.

'Eh?' he shouted. 'What say?' But Half-Pint and Herbie Parrott got the message, and hauled Ould Gabby into the rose bushes before he could do any permanent damage to her ladyship's violet tongue.

'I knew it would come to lawyers sooner or later,' I murmured. 'I'll bet she's come about that law of trespass Alfred was chattering on about. I've felt quite poorly ever since he mentioned it.'

'Well, my dear, it can't be helped,' Rebecca said firmly. 'This matter has always been between me and Eunice Nettlefold, and I expect she has realised that, too. So no more fuss and bother. The time has come to take our medicine, so we'd better get it over with.' She smiled at me. 'Would you mind opening the door for her, Sally?'

So here is the thick end of the wedge at last, I thought as her ladyship stumped into the cottage and stared at the lights and cables, then at the cameraman.

'Have you talked into that contraption yet, Rebecca?' she demanded, waving her walking stick at the microphone.

'Not yet. I was just about to do so,' Nurse Pintuck replied, 'and I think it would be as well if you sat down before you fall down. Young man, please help her ladyship to step over that cable, and find her a chair – preferably a high-backed one with stout legs.'

Lady Nettlefold shook off the young electrician's helping hand. 'I intend to sit in that chair,' she bellowed, choosing the one Rebecca was to sit in for the interview.

'I'm afraid you can't sit there, Madam,' said Dominic briskly, 'that is the interview chair.'

'Then I shall certainly sit in that one, for I intend to be interviewed. I have something very important to say.'

I caught Arthur Abercromby's eye and did a double-take. Something had happened to the Vicar but I couldn't put my finger on what was different about him. He gave me a solemn wink – and then I knew. He'd got rid of his nervous tic. That hunted look had completely gone, his forehead was smooth and he looked ten years younger.

Lady Nettlefold hadn't been inside the cottage five minutes and already she had taken charge. She prodded her way to the interview chair and thumped hard on the seat to make sure it would stand her weight before she sat down on it. I had to hand it to her, Eunice Nettlefold was a force to be reckoned with.

When she had settled herself and demanded a footstool, she glared round at us. 'Well, why are you standing there like a lot of tailor's dummies?' she demanded. 'Get on with the interview, Mr Douglas.'

'But we haven't discussed the format,' he said. 'I usually go through the questions I'll be asking first . . .'

'Questions?' She bridled. 'I don't intend to answer questions at this stage, young man. I have an important announcement to make.'

Mr Wellbehave cleared his throat and began to hem. He was well named, I thought, and looked rather like a cadaver in clothing. His long doleful face was crowned with three strands of grey hair which had been arranged carefully on his forehead to give the appearance of more abundant locks.

'I really think that you should pay some attention to Mr – er – Douglas's requirements, dear lady. After all, he is the expert in such matters,' he said.

'Oh stuff and nonsense, Alistair! I shall say what I have come to say without wasting any more time. Now, Mr Douglas, shall we get on with it?'

But what had Lady Nettlefold come to say? That's what worried me. Then I noticed that Rebecca was looking anxious too, and I slipped my hand comfortingly into hers.

'Right,' said Dominic briskly, bowing to the inevitable. 'Lights. Camera. Go ahead, your ladyship.'

I stayed with Rebecca to read the evening paper and watch the regional news on television. Stayed with her until all the excitement was over; until the couple with the Primus stove had packed up their gear and called it a day, and the caravans had gone from the common; until the ice-cream merchant had taken himself and his soft-whipped and chocolate flakes back to Carnelian Bay, and the backlog of motor cars had gone from the bridge.

Rebecca was still as excited as a child, but she wouldn't need me tonight. Lady Nettlefold had gone down – neither bloody nor bowed – but in fine fettle. Indeed, in allowing Nurse Pintuck to stay on in her cottage she had not merely bent to the pressure of public opinion, but had somehow managed to emerge as the heroine of the hour, and I guessed that the cadaverous lawyer, Alistair Wellbehave, had managed to convince his recalcitrant client that a straightforward statement regarding her future intentions would not only be advisable, but that some extraordinary gesture of goodwill was necessary to prove her claim to the title of benefactress, for her ladyship had hammered that word into the ground during her confrontation with Dominic Douglas's camera.

'My family and I, throughout the years we have lived here,' she'd said, 'have always considered ourselves to be the guardians of a sacred trust. My father, and his father before him, have seen ourselves as leaders – benefactors . . .'

Hmmm, I'd thought, no wonder she wanted to get her two cent's worth in before Rebecca's. What Eunice Nettlefold hadn't realised was that Rebecca would not have referred, however obliquely, to all those skeletons rattling in the Nettlefold closets, but Lady Nettlefold didn't know that because she didn't know Rebecca as I knew her.

The newspaper headlines referred in bold type to 'LAND-LADY'S CHANGE OF HEART', and heartily commended Lady Eunice Nettlefold's generosity, while the television newscaster had commenced his spiel with the words: 'Pitch-forks have been laid aside in the quiet village of Tootington. Thanks to a kindly action by local benefactress, Lady Eunice Nettlefold, retired district nurse, Rebecca Pintuck, can sleep easily in her own bed once more.'

'They do talk a lot of twaddle, don't they?' Rebecca commented. 'I didn't lose a wink of sleep. You were the one who lost sleep, Sally dear.'

I yawned. 'Yes, but I intend making up for it tonight.'

Rebecca put her arms round me. 'Sleep well, child,' she said. 'Amelia would have been so proud of you.'

Rebecca's Siege was over.

It was dusk when I walked back to April Cottage. The air smelt sweet and fresh in my nostrils, and I was almost too tired to put one leg in front of the other, but it was a pleasant tiredness engendered by happiness and laced with a 'this is too good to be true' feeling.

I stopped and leaned my back against a tree; looked across the common at pinpricks of light from cottages where people would be busy doing little ordinary things – watching television perhaps, or putting children to bed.

Then I looked up at the sky, and somehow the stars seemed like lights of home too, not millions of light years away, but warm and friendly, as thickly sprinkled as the sleeping daisies near my feet. I had the feeling that I could hold up my hands and gather a handful of stars tonight.

What a day it had been. None of us had known what Lady Nettlefold was going to say when she started speaking into Dominic's microphone, except Mr Wellbehave, Alfred, and the Vicar, and that was her ladyship's trump card which she played like a professional gambler.

She'd taken her time coming to the point. First she'd said that she was prepared to let Rebecca stay in her cottage, and

181

then added 'for the time being', which swung us to a feeling of relief one minute, despair the next. Surely, I thought, we won't have to go through this siege business all over again. That's when I caught Arthur Abercromby's eye, and wondered what he was looking so pleased about. He'd actually winked at me again.

Then Lady Nettlefold had cleared her throat and unleashed her ace of diamonds. She had been thinking for some time, she said, staring at me over her pince-nez spectacles, of the need for permanent accommodation for old people in Tootington. That is why she had decided to withdraw from the market a valuable property called The Hollies which she intended, in her role of benefactress, to turn into a residential home for the elderly.

I'd stood there with trembling lips, and then above all the chatter and applause, I'd heard a thrush singing its heart out in the branches of the lilac tree.

Chapter Twenty-Four

All I wanted when I got indoors was a cup of tea and a good night's sleep, but I had forgotten that the milk would be sour. I ordered milk when I needed it as an economy measure, leaving a note for the milkman along with the money. I hadn't been there to leave any money so Joe hadn't left any milk. It was as simple as that.

Never mind the tea, I thought, just let me get to bed. Then I noticed a couple of gingham-topped jars on the table, which hadn't been there when I left home a thousand years ago. Bleary eyed with tiredness, I picked up a scrap of paper beside them, and read: 'At a meeting of the Tootington Women's Institute yesterday afternoon, it was decided that some acknowledgement was due to you in connection with Nurse Pintuck. Yrs. truly, F. Cox, (Chairperson).'

A gesture from Frances Cox! Well at least it wasn't a rude gesture. But why piccalilli of all things? Why hadn't my tetchy next door neighbour left me a couple of jars of damson jam or a nice tin of dried milk? Then it occurred to me that there weren't all that many places left in the world where one could leave the front door unlocked for three days without being burgled or vandalised and where one might even end up richer by two jars of chopped vegetables in hot mustard sauce.

'You ungrateful wretch, Sally Shelton,' I told myself severely. 'Don't you realise what this means?' Frances Cox had actually crossed my threshold of her own free will at last, and I'd eat every scrap of that piccalilli if it gave me heartburn for a year. My eyes began to water at the thought.

Well, if Frances Cox could make a gesture, so could I. The bottle of milk in my refrigerator might be on the turn, but I'd show her that the milk of human kindness hadn't gone sour.

There wasn't a light in the fair Frances's front window, so she must be round at the back. This was the moment to make a reciprocal gesture of my own. I'd march up her garden path and give her something to remember me by. But what? I thought wickedly of my old grey bags, and giggled. I always felt an urge to giggle whenever I was really tired. My mother had packed me off to bed when I showed signs of hysteria with the firm directive, 'Go to bed, Sally, you're getting silly'.

No this was no laughing matter, I had to give Miss Cox something she'd appreciate. Then it struck me! I'd give her Amelia's Victorian tiles. I guessed that she'd had her eye on them all along, and she'd said herself that they were valuable.

Just as well I am wearing my old grey slacks, I thought, as I climbed over her back gate and picked my way up her garden path. She had a loggia too, of sorts. Not as fine as Amelia's, more of a conservatory, and her plumbing seemed a little odd as well, so far as I could make out. She had a drain with a round cover over it, only *her* piping disappeared through the wall of *my* cottage.

Her conservatory and kitchen doors were open, and I could see a thread of light showing round the edges of the back room.

I knocked, but there was no reply. Little wonder. Her television set was on full blast, and I didn't need my Sherlock Holmes hat and magnifying glass to realise that she was watching *Casablanca*.

'Miss Cox. Are you there?'

I peeped round the edge of the door. The fearsome Frances was sitting in an armchair, crying her eyes out.

I stepped back, meaning to leave without her seeing me, and sent a stool clattering to the ground.

'Who's there?' she called hoarsely, getting up.

'It's only me, Sally Shelton. I didn't mean to frighten you.'

'How dare you come prying?' she cried. 'You had no business to come in without knocking.'

'I did knock. You couldn't hear me for the television.' I stared past her at the screen. It was the famous 'Play it again Sam; as time goes by' sequence, and Miss Cox's voice faded as I remembered my sister and I sitting in the one-and-nines at our local Odeon, blowing our noses on a couple of Dad's handkerchiefs. We'd always rifled his top drawer whenever we were going to see a weepy.

'Well, really . . .'

'Oh, would you mind terribly if I just watched this bit?' My lips began to quiver, and I felt up the sleeve of my sweater for a hanky.

'What's the matter?' she snapped.

'I can't find my handkerchief.'

'Here,' she said, handing me one of hers.

'Thanks.' I blew my nose hard. 'I'll boil it before I give it back to you.'

I could see that she was embarrassed because I had found her in tears, but *Casablanca* always touched me too. It was that 'Here's looking at you, kid', bit that got me, and Humphrey lighting two cigarettes. But far more than the film itself were the memories it invoked when the wartime world was full of pseudo Humphrey Bogarts trying that lighting two cigarettes lark and bringing the skin off their lips, as a result.

Perhaps my next-door neighbour was reliving old memories too, perhaps some young Air Force chap had brought the skin off his top lip for her once – or perhaps she was thinking of Leo.

I glanced round the prim little room in which we were standing. Frances hadn't asked me to sit down – and even that was evocative of those "standing room only" days at the Odeon when we would crowd behind the blue velvet curtains until seats became vacant. The room was like its owner – no soft touches anywhere. The armchairs were made of slippery rexine, the fireplace looked like – potted brawn, the lamp beside her chair was brass with a conical shade. The only flamboyant note was struck by the high, wide and handsome colour television set.

It crossed my mind that my critical gossipy next-door neighbour had not outgrown her passion for make-believe. She'd outgrown her youthful prettiness and charm, possibly even hope of ever meeting a man she could marry and be happy with, but she hadn't outgrown her passion for old black-and-white movies, and she was angry with me because I had discovered her Achilles heel.

In the middle of a tender scene between Ingrid Bergman and Paul Henried, my right leg went to sleep, and I started hopping on my left to wake it up again.

'Now what's wrong?' she muttered.

'My leg's gone funny.'

'You had better sit down then. But please keep quiet. If you intend watching this film, remember that I wish to do so as well. As a matter of fact I prefer to watch television on my own.'

'So do I – so that I can have a good cry if I want to. I'm sorry if I've spoilt your enjoyment. Perhaps I'd better go now.'

'No it doesn't matter. Only for goodness sake sit still.'

When the aeroplane was about to take off, and Humphrey Bogart was saying his farewell to Ingrid Bergman, I noticed that Miss Cox was in tears again, only this time she didn't seem to mind the fact that I knew she was weeping – we both were.

She got up and switched off the set. I'd never seen her without her hat before except briefly in the garden, but standing there in the lamplight without it, she seemed much more vulnerable.

Perhaps she thought that I seemed more vulnerable too, for she said, 'I must say that you have surprised me, Mrs Shelton'.

'Have I? Why?'

'Well, it isn't easy to put into words, but I had formed the opinion that you were a flighty kind of person, both thoughtless and flippant. But what you did for Rebecca Pintuck was kind – very kind.' She flushed and the tip of her nose quivered. 'As a matter of fact, I owe you an apology. I've said some unpleasant things about you, and I'm sorry.'

She turned her head away and dabbed her eyes with a handkerchief. 'You're not the only one, of course, that I've said unkind things about. I'm afraid I've done something to Lizzie Nugent of which I am deeply ashamed. Something despicable. I realise that now.'

'Lizzie?'

Miss Cox nodded. 'We had – words – about it. Lizzie accused me of being a vile, gossipy old bitch, and she was justified in her assessment of me.'

She hesitated, and I guessed what it had cost Frances Cox to make that confession. 'If you must know, that is why I was crying when you came in. It took *Casablanca* to make me realise how much I have changed over the years. I was remembering those days when life seemed much sweeter than it does now.'

'Don't say any more, Miss Cox.' I murmured, 'I'm sure Lizzie will forgive you . . .'

'I don't think she will. You see, I discovered that an old

186

admirer of hers had turned up. Someone I once cared for too, and I actually wrote to Lizzie's mother about it. Yes, I did. Now I daresay that I'll lose everyone's respect when word gets around. Gossip is one thing, but poison pen letters are abhorrent, and I actually set pen to paper; I could cut my hand off.' She began crying in earnest again.

'For what it's worth,' I said quietly, 'you haven't lost my respect. Far from it. It takes a lot of courage to admit to making a mistake. In any case, what makes you think that word will get around? Lizzie Nugent isn't the kind of person to heap coals on a bonfire.'

'I know, but I have ruined her chance of happiness. You see Mrs Nugent was so upset by my letter that Lizzie sent her "young man" away and promised never to see him again.'

So that's what Lizzie meant when she said the balloon had gone up. What a ghastly situation, I thought.

'Yes, I can see that has shocked you,' Miss Cox said, blowing her nose and stuffing the hanky up the sleeve of her jumper. 'I imagine you're sorry you came now and won't trouble to come again.' Then she frowned. 'Why did you come in the first place?'

'Huh?' I'd almost forgotten in the midst of so much drama. 'Well, I really came to offer you Amelia's Victorian tiles, and to thank you for the piccalilli.'

'The – what?'

'You know, the piccalilli you left on my kitchen table.'

'But I didn't leave any piccalilli on your kitchen table,' she said.

'You didn't? But the note was in your name.'

'I know that, but the choice of a gift and it's delivery was left to someone else.'

'Oh.' I felt deflated. 'Who?'

'As a matter of fact it was Mrs Pickles,' she said weepily.

'Mrs Pickles?' My lips began to twitch, and I knew that I was in for a touch of the 'you're getting silly, Sally's'. But then I was very tired.

'If you want those tiles, Miss Cox,' I said, trying hard not to smile, 'I'll stack them near your shed tomorrow. Oh, and could you possibly spare me a cup of milk? Mine's gone sour.'

'Yes, of course.' She bit her lip. 'But I don't quite understand. You mean that you still want me to have those tiles
after what I've just told you?'

'What you have just told me is between ourselves, Miss
Cox, and has nothing whatever to do with Amelia's tiles.
Thanks for the milk and – for *Casablanca*.' I laid my hand on
her arm. 'I'll see you tomorrow. Good night Frances.'

Chapter Twenty-Five

I thought the phone would never stop ringing.

At nine o'clock the next morning, Edward Connery, the editor of the local paper, rang up to ask if I would talk to one of his reporters.

I was sitting on the bottom step of the stairs yawning my head off. 'What for?' I asked, wondering if anyone had ever swallowed a telephone before.

He chuckled. 'Because you're news, that's why. Or didn't you know?'

'But Rebecca's Siege is over,' I mumbled.

'Rebecca's Siege. I like that,' he said.

'That's because you weren't there, Mr Connery. It was a bit of a shambles really.'

'Was it? I'm sure my readers would be interested in your point of view. We'd like a photograph of you as well, by the way.' He paused. 'Shall we make it eleven o'clock this morning?'

'I'm not having my photograph taken with my hair like this,' I protested.

'Couldn't you wash it?' he asked persuasively.

'Yes, I suppose so, but . . .'

'Thank you so much, Mrs Shelton. Eleven o'clock, then?'

'Oh, all right.' I was too tired to argue.

I was making myself a cup of tea when the phone rang again. It was my sister this time.

'Sally. What on earth's been happening? We switched on the television last night and there you were in the news! Jim had to give me a glass of sherry to bring me round! We tried ringing the cottage but there was no reply. Where were you?'

'I was next door,' I said, 'watching *Casablanca*.'

'You mean at Bert Rumbold's?'

'No, at Miss Cox's.'

'But I thought you and she weren't on speaking terms.'

'We weren't, but we're now on crying terms which is far more important.'

'I wish you'd *say*,' Holly muttered.

'I will, honestly. I'll ring you tonight and tell you all about it, but I'll have to go now because the kettle is boiling its head off, and I have to wash my hair and have a bath because the reporter's coming at eleven, and I haven't even switched on the immersion-heater yet.'

I was draped in a towel with my head in a turban when Avril rang.

'Oh Sally, isn't it marvellous news?' she said. 'I still can't quite believe it. How do you feel about it?'

'Very wet at the moment.' I took up my telephone station on the bottom step and began drying my feet. 'As a matter of fact, I can't believe it either, about The Hollies, I mean. I suppose Lady Nettlefold did mean what she said about turning it into an old people's home?'

'There isn't the slightest doubt about it. Arthur's with her now, discussing what's to be done.' I'd never heard Avril so happy before.

'By the way,' I asked, giving my hair a good rub, 'what has happened to Arthur? I couldn't believe he was the same person when I saw him yesterday.'

Avril laughed. 'It was that row with her ladyship that turned the tide. You remember the day she came round here and shouted at him? When she said she would demand his resignation as Vicar of Tootington?'

'Yes, of course I do. That was the day you asked her if she thought she was God Almighty, wasn't it?'

'Yes, well I wanted Arthur to resign, but that husband of mine is as stubborn as a mule when he feels like it. "If I resign now" he said, "I might as well say goodbye to all I've worked for," and he was quite right. The next thing I knew, he had torn Lady Nettlefold's choice of hymns to pieces. "From now on," he said, "I'm choosing the hymns myself." Then he marched round to the Hall and told her ladyship that he had no intention of resigning. Oh Sally, I was so proud of him.'

'Glory Hallelujah!' I sighed.

'And while you and Rebecca were incarcerated in that cottage down the lane,' Avril continued, 'Arthur was busy instructing Lady N in her Christian duty towards her fellow men, whilst I was busy inflaming righteous indignation in the bosoms of the Women's Institute. I even got Miss Cox to write and sign a note on their behalf, and inveigled them into sending a gift to you. Did you get it, by the way?'

'Yes, I did. As a matter of fact I'm thinking of throwing a cheese and piccalilli party in the near future.'

I was twiddling my hair on heated rollers when the phone rang again.

'Mrs Sam? Where the hell have you been?' Mrs Amor asked. 'No, don't bother to tell me, I know.'

'I'm terribly sorry I couldn't let you know about not coming into work,' I said, squatting on the bottom step again and stuffing a lump of cotton wool under a roller that seemed likely to leave the mark of Cain on my left ear, 'I couldn't get to a telephone'.

'Do you realise what you've done?'

'Apart from causing several traffic jams and nearly ending up in jail, you mean?'

'The Rotarians are coming back!'

'That's wonderful.'

'The president rang me yesterday and wanted to know if my general assistant was *the* Sally Shelton. I said you were, and that you'd be delighted to speak to them about your experiences when we've finished altering the dining room.'

'*What?*' My eyebrows nearly disappeared into the heated rollers. 'But I can't. I mean I couldn't possibly. I've never "speaked" in my life.'

'No, well, you'll be all right when you've polished up your grammar. When are you coming back to work, by the way? Polly's got out that wretched sherry of hers again. If you play your cards right, you might even get another crack at those tablemats.'

'I'm not coming back at all if I have to speak to those Rotarians,' I retorted.

'You sound a bit het up, Mrs Sam. Are you feeling all right?'

'I was feeling fine until you rang up.'

'You know your trouble? You lack self-confidence,' she said.

191

'I know that. I take after my mother. She daren't even go to the bank to draw out her money in case the manager asked her what she wanted it for.'

Dominic rang when I was applying a little Vaseline to my sore ear. 'Sally, me darlin',' he chortled. 'Just thought I'd say thanks a million for all you've done. The film should be a wow! By the way, I'm doing the band marching sequence on Sunday. You will be there? Oh, just a sec, Julienne's making eating signs. She says why don't you come in time for coffee on Sunday, and have lunch with us, and could you possibly do her hair as well?'

I'd just nicely got out of my towel and into my beige suit when the reporter and photographer arrived.

'My name's Stan Trent,' the reporter said, 'and this is Jinks.'

'Hi, Jinks,' I said, 'won't you come in? Only don't start taking photographs just yet, I haven't combed my hair.'

The phone rang again. 'You don't know me,' said a quavering voice, 'but I'd like to book a nice big room on the first floor. My name is Mrs Wittering, and could you tell me how much it will cost? Not that I'm short of money, it's just that I have run short of relatives. I'm not a faddy eater, you know but there are certain things that I really mustn't eat. The doctor has warned me off fats, so I wouldn't want bacon or butter, just plenty of nice lean meat with all the fat removed, and I mustn't eat chicken skin either . . .'

'I'm terribly sorry, Mrs Wittering,' I said, 'but are you sure you've got the right number? This is Sally Shelton, April Cottage, Tootington.'

'Yes, I know, dear, but you are the lady to do with the old people's home, aren't you? I saw your name in the paper.'

'I'm very sorry, Mrs Wittering, but the home isn't open yet. Perhaps you'd better write a letter to Lady Nettlefold – or better still, ring her.'

'I see. Thank you, my dear.'

'And – Mrs Wittering – I do hope you'll get your nice big room on the first floor.'

'So do I, dear, and you will see that I'm not given any fat bacon or chicken skins, won't you?'

When Mrs Wittering had rung off, I turned to Stan the reporter with a bright, determined smile. 'Now then, what do you want to know?' I asked, hoping he wouldn't realise how nervous I felt.

'I don't actually . . .' he flushed crimson, '. . . that is to say . . .'

I laughed and relaxed. 'Don't tell me this is Trent's first case?'

'Well yes, it is as a matter of fact. I've never interviewed anyone before, and I don't quite know where to start.'

'Why not try opening your notebook and licking your pencil? That's what reporters usually do, isn't it?'

A slow smile spread over his face. 'Yes, I suppose it is.'

The phone rang again. It was Commander Bruce. 'I've been trying to ring you since nine o'clock this morning,' he said. 'Apparently you're a very busy lady these days.'

'I think I'm being pressurised,' I laughed.

'Don't get too pressurised,' he said, 'because we're going to need you.'

'Who's we?' I knew that he was being deliberately mysterious by the chuckle in his voice.

'The Hollies house committee.'

'I didn't know there was one.'

'There is now. I just thought you'd like to know that we're not letting the grass grow under our feet, I've just come from a meeting at the Hall – a rather hurried meeting because Mr Wellbehave had to get back to London – but a very successful one. To cut a long story short, I've been elected chairman of The Hollies committee. Her ladyship's the president, of course . . .'

'Of course,' I chimed in.

'Alfred's the treasurer, and George Brassington the secretary as things stand at the moment.'

'That's marvellous news,' I said. 'But what did you mean about needing me?'

'Because we want you on that committee, my dear – and Dominic Douglas . . .'

'But I've never been on a committee in my life! I haven't a clue about committees,' I protested, 'except that they're always having rows and resigning, and I'm sure Lady Nettlefold wouldn't like it one little bit if I went on to her committee.'

The Commander laughed. 'That's the whole point, Sally, it

193

won't be her committee, but I'll talk to you about it another time and explain everything to you then.'

When Stan and Jinks had departed, I made myself some coffee. Throughout all the phone calls and the interview my mind had been niggling over Lizzie. Life, it seemed to me, was just one damned thing after another what with Rotarians and committees and traffic jams and Victorian tiles. How the hell did I get mixed up in all this, I wondered. All I'd ever wanted was to get rid of a few nettles.

Lizzie was just hanging the 'Closed for Lunch' sign on the door as I hurried up the road.

'Come in,' she said without a glimmer of her old twinkle. 'It seems years since you did my hair, doesn't it? Well it was a waste of time. Everything was a waste of time.' She gave a dry, bitter little laugh. 'I had such high hopes of that afternoon, and I knew that things hadn't changed between Leo and I. We spent three hours together talking over old times, and we even got round to discussing the future as well. Oh we both knew that we couldn't do anything more than keep in touch for the time being, but we came to an understanding that we wanted to get married one day, and it was so wonderful knowing that he would be there waiting.'

'But surely, Lizzie nothing can change that?'

'You don't understand,' she said dully. 'I've told him not to wait. I'm never going to see him again. You see, Frances Cox saw him and recognised him when he came that day, then she wrote a letter to Mother . . .'

'I know,' I said softly, 'she told me about it, and she's deeply ashamed . . .'

Lizzie turned on me. 'Frances Cox told *you* that? You mean to say the pair of you have been gossiping about me?'

'Don't jump to conclusions, Lizzie. It wasn't like that at all.'

'I don't want to hear any more.' She flushed scarlet, 'I thought you at least were my friend. Well, my mind's made up. I'm going to sell this shop and I don't care what Mother says.' Her voice was rough with tears, 'I'll sell up and buy one of those new flats in Carnelian Bay – and stay there until we both rot.'

'Lizzie Nugent, I've never heard such twaddle in my life!' I felt more than a little irritated with her. 'Honestly, I wish I'd never set eyes on that wretched piccalilli.'

'Piccalilli?' Lizzie stared at me in amazement. 'What on earth has piccalilli got to do with it?'

'I found some on my kitchen table when I got back from Rebecca's last night,' I said with some asperity. 'I thought Miss Cox had put it there so I went round to thank her for it. She wasn't very pleased to see me either. As a matter of fact she nearly snapped my head off at first. Now I'm getting my head snapped off again, and it's really too bad!'

'I'm sorry,' Lizzie was still a bit snappish, 'but how was I to know about the piccalilli?'

'I'd have told you if you'd given me half a chance. Then Miss Cox told me about writing that letter. That was after Ingrid Bergman and Paul Henried had gone off on the plane together.'

'Oh dear,' Lizzie sighed, 'what a mess!'

'It's a funny thing,' I said, sitting down on the bentwood chair near the counter, 'the way people have of thinking they'll get out of one mess by creating an even bigger mess. You're not thinking very clearly, are you?'

'Do you wonder?' Lizzie wiped her glasses. 'I don't know whether I'm coming or going. Mother's treating me like a naughty child, I had a flaming row with Frances, now Leo's gone for good, and I've upset you . . .'

'Ah, but I'm like one of those plastic dolls with a rubber bottom,' I said. 'You know the kind I mean? The harder you hit them the quicker they bounce up again. I had one when I was a kid, and it got on my nerves. In any case, Leo hasn't "gone for good" as you put it. I'll bet you a hundred pounds to a hayseed that he, poor soul, doesn't know whether he's coming or going either. Miss Cox said you'd sent him away, but you don't imagine he'll stay away, do you?'

Lizzie's face was a study, a blend of hope and despair. She stopped wiping her glasses. 'I hadn't thought of that. But no, it's impossible. I left him in no doubt about my feelings . . .'

'Come off it, Lizzie,' I said. 'Your feelings didn't come into it. You sent him away because you hadn't the gumption to have a show-down with your mother, and yet you've got the gumption to tell her that you intend selling the shop. You just said so yourself, remember? You said that you'd made up your mind to sell the shop, and you didn't care what your mother said, so if you're going to have a good old bust-up anyway, why not fight for something worth fighting for? As for packing up the shop and getting a flat in Carnelian Bay, you'd hate it and so would your mother.'

'Lizzie! Lizzie, what are you doing? I want my dinner!' Mrs Nugent's voice was accompanied by the rapping of her walking-stick on the ceiling over our heads, and I noticed that Lizzie winced at the sound of her mother's voice and that insistent thumping.

'I know you mean well, Sally,' Lizzie said, 'but you see what I'm up against? I might have had a show-down with Mother, but always, at the back of mind, is the fear that she might have a heart-attack. Then I'd never be able to forgive myself.'

'Yes, I know. I'm sorry. I shouldn't have said what I did, but for what it's worth, I know that Frances Cox is really upset, because she sent that letter, and I'm still your friend.'

'I know that. Please, *please* forgive me.' She hesitated with her hand on the door. 'What would you do in my situation?'

'I'd write to Leo and tell him I loved him for a start,' I said. 'I'd make certain that he knew that. You need him, and he needs you. Then I'd clear the air with Frances Cox, and forget about selling up the shop. That way you'd have only one problem left.'

She actually smiled. 'Thanks, Sal,' she said.

'Don't mention it – Liz.'

I was back in my gardening gear. I had a stack of Victorian tiles to shift, and I really must do something about all that concrete.

The Gaffer popped his head over the fence. 'We showed 'em, didn't we?' he chuckled.

'Yes, we did.' I felt short and snappish.

'Your phone's ringing,' he said.

'Let it ring!' I was tired of answering the telephone. 'I don't suppose you've got a wheelbarrow and a pick-axe, have you?'

'Eh? Whativer for?'

'I'm going to get rid of this concrete and plant grass seed,' I told him, 'and I'm going to shift those concrete pudding basins and that rockery while I'm about it.'

196

He grinned. 'Goin' to work off a bit of steam, are you?'

'Yes. That's exactly what I'm going to do.'

He nodded. 'I'll ask Bert. Daren't touch nothing in his shed without askin' him first. I'd cop it good an' proper if I did.' He climbed down from his boxes and went indoors.

Frances Cox appeared at that moment. 'Good afternoon, Sally,' she said, peering over the fence. 'Do you want a hand with the tiles?'

'Thank you, Frances.' I felt it my duty to lift my face into some semblance of a smile. 'I'm trying to borrow a wheelbarrow and a pick-axe.'

'I've got a pick-axe,' Frances said, 'if you'd care to borrow that I'll be happy to lend it to you.'

'I'd better warn you first. I intend getting rid of Amelia's concrete.'

'Yes, well, it is rather unsightly, isn't it?'

'Nah then, Ruby,' Bert sprang up like a jack-in-the-box on my left-hand side. 'Wantin' a wheelbarrer are yer? Just oppen the back gate an' I'll trundle it through.'

His mouth sagged a little as he caught sight of the smiling Miss Cox.

'Good afternoon, Mr Rumbold,' she said pleasantly.

'Afternoon, ma'am,' said Bert, then sotto-voce, 'Bloody hell, what's come over her?'

It all had to do, I decided, as I whipped the tiles into the wheelbarrow, with Rebecca's Siege and getting my name into the newspapers. That – and *Casablanca*.

Chapter Twenty-Six

After Sunday lunch at Dominic's, Jill, the fair-haired girl who told me that she was in charge of P.R. – which in her book was short for Possible Ructions – Neddy their cameraman, Robin and Tobias who were responsible for the lighting, Armand the sound engineer, who looked a bit like a youthful Omar Sharif, Phil the driver, Dominic and I got into the truck and the Landrover and set off for the cliffs above Tootington Cove.

'So you all know what you've got to do?' Dominic was standing on a knoll with the fringe of his tunic flapping in the breeze. 'Hold your heads well up, and start marching.'

'I ain't got no choice but to hold me head up in this collar,' said Ambrose, 'me head feels as if it's in a vice.'

'Yes, well, never mind that,' said Dominic. 'You look very smart.'

'I feel smart an' all. These trousers are cutting me in half.'

'Right then. Neddy. Camera!'

The camera started whirring, the band started marching.

'Cut! Hold it!' Dominic leapt down from his knoll.

'What's up?' Bert demanded. 'Weren't we marchin' right?'

'You were marching fine. But you weren't playing.'

'Ah, well,' said Bert, 'you told us to march, you niver said nowt about playin'.'

'That's the whole point of having the band in the picture,' Dominic explained, 'otherwise we could have got a juggler and a couple of trick cyclists.'

Bert said there was no need to take that attitude as they were naturally nervous this being their first experience of marching and playing at the same time, and some of them were having difficulty in reading the music, a) because it was about a foot from their nose-ends and some of them hadn't got their long-distance glasses on, and b) because some of it had blown away, and c) because old Lukey Tidmarsh had never been able to read music anyway.

Dominic said, 'Fine, fine,' and asked Bert if they'd all mind moving back a bit and starting all over again, only this time he'd be obliged if they would march and play at the same time.

The band moved back to their starting position and set off again.

Dominic yelled, 'Cut! Hold it!'

'Now what's up?' Bert wanted to know.

Dominic said that they had marched quite nicely that time, but did they think they could all start playing at roughly the same time.

Bert said there was a little problem about that because they hadn't got a proper conductor. It was different when they were all sitting down because then he gave them the nod, but he didn't fancy marching backwards to give them the nod, and if he gave them the nod with the back of his head he'd hit his forehead on his instrument.

Dominic said he didn't quite understand what Bert meant, but they'd better devise a method of all starting at the same time, so it was decided to get the drummer to march in front and the rest would keep their eyes on his drumsticks.

Somebody said that if the drummer was going to march in front, hadn't he better take off his woolly cap and wear the correct headgear? The drummer said that he'd tried on the correct headgear but his head wasn't big enough to fill it and it kept slipping round with the peak at the back which wasn't very comfortable, and made him look like a legionnaire.

Jill said she'd brought a reel of Elastoplast just in case, and couldn't they stick the drummer's hat on with that? She felt that no one would notice because the Elastoplast was roughly the same colour as the drummer, whereupon the drummer said indignantly that he wasn't having his hat stuck on with Elastoplast because it would cause him considerable pain when it was removed, and he knew all about the adhesive propensities of Elastoplast because he had once had a carbuncle on the back of his neck.

Dominic said the matter could easily be got over it someone

199

would exchange caps with the drummer. Ould Gabby said it weren't no use him swapping caps because his hat was already resting on his lugs and he had a big head to start with.

Jill said that she happened to have a roll of toilet tissue in her hold-all, and why not stuff the drummer's hat with that, and gave the drummer such a charming smile that he agreed.

'Now then,' said Dominic when all that had been seen to, 'let's make a film here.'

Having the drummer in front worked quite well up to a point – the point being that his beat was erratic, he couldn't see where he was going and caught his foot in a rabbit hole. When he'd been set back on his feet and the toilet tissue had been stuffed back into his cap, he said he thought he'd had enough. Dominic said that he knew just how he felt, then Jill and I led the little fellow away for a drink of tea from the flask in her hold-all and laced it with a drop of rum.

Ambrose Lanfeard said he wouldn't mind getting his foot caught in a rabbit hole if he could have a drop of summat as compensation, and Dominic said that they'd all be compensated in due course when the marching sequence was in the can, because he'd brought a crate of beer along in the back of the Landrover.

Ould Gabby said they'd likely march better if they had the beer at once, and it was unanimously agreed that this was so. Bert said that he for one would step livelier with a bottle of beer under his belt, and the reason things weren't going right was because they'd missed their lunchtime session at the Spotted Dog.

Dominic told Jill and me that he felt he'd made a grave mistake in mentioning the beer. Robin said he felt that Dominic had made an even graver mistake in mentioning a marching sequence, while Neddy wanted to know what was against his idea of having a sitting round in a circle sequence instead.

'Apart from the fact that we haven't got any chairs,' Dominic said, 'what I'm after is fluidity.'

'You got that the minute you mentioned beer,' Neddy reminded him.

'What I want is movement,' Dominic went on.

'You'll get that too in a little while,' said Neddy, 'when they all start rushing for the bushes.'

'Perhaps you should do a boy-scout sequence instead,' Jill said, as Herbie and Half-Pint arrived with their bogie.

At that point, Ambrose Lanfeard asked Bert if he knew the buttons had come off his jacket.

Then Durking Pickles spoke up and said that there was only one thing for it so far as he could see. He'd better take charge of the drum as he was the right size and shape and he had no trouble keeping his hat on.

Everyone cheered. Then Ould Gabby said to hang on a minute because the tacking threads had come out of his trouser bottoms and he'd break his neck if he attempted to walk in them.

Jill said she just happened to have a needle and thread in her hold-all, and she'd whip them up again in a jiffy.

Dominic said this was ridiculous, and he might just take up pig-farming in earnest, whilst Wilkins Pickles was heard to say that he didn't know why the tacking threads didn't fall out of his trouser bottoms and trust Ould Gabby to have all the luck.

When Ould Gabby's trousers had been sewn up, and Bert's buttons stitched back on, the band lined up again with Durking in front carrying the drum. Two abreast behind him came Ted and Tucker, Wilkins Pickles and Ambrose, Bert and the one called Lukey Tidmarsh who couldn't read music, Ould Gabby and a chap called Tom Oldway, followed by Half-Pint and Herbie Parrott pulling the bogie.

'Listen son,' said Dominic patiently, 'I don't want that bogie in the film. What do you need it for anyway?'

Half-Pint explained that his great-grandad's legs might pack up which they did sometimes. Dominic said all right, but to keep the camera off the bogie if at all possible.

'Let's get it right this time, shall we?' He sprang up on his knoll. 'Look, all I want you to do is march in a fairly straight line to that clump of trees over there, playing your instruments as you go. Have you got it?'

Lukey Tidmarsh said it wasn't all that easy marching on the cliffs as there were tussocks of grass all over the place, and various other things he couldn't very well mention with ladies present, only did Dominic realise that Farmer Appleby's cows sometimes had a wander along there?

'An' there's another thing you haven't tekken into consideration,' said Lukey, 'that's the way the ground slopes down sudden like in places. When that happens I kind of tilt over sideways and I get a touch of the *verdigris*.'

The Gaffer said he wished he'd gone when he had his tonsils removed because life wasn't worth living now he wasn't going to be on television.

Jill said that it did seem a shame, and couldn't he just walk along behind the rest pretending to play a mouth organ or something now that they had got the problem of his hat settled, to which Dominic replied that he must want his brains testing, but all right if it would make everybody happy, but if the Gaffer went in, the bogie would have to come out, and if Ould Gabby's legs packed up he'd send out a rescue team.

'Now, for somebody's sake, get cracking and let's get it right this time.'

They trooped forward like the remnants of an undefeated army. Perhaps they gained confidence from young Durking out front, or, as Dominic remarked later, perhaps they were all smashed out of their minds with the beer. Whatever the reason, Armand kissed his fingertips to the wind and murmured, 'C'est magnifique'.

The Gaffer was heard to say in the bar of the Spotted Dog that evening that things had started to go right when he stepped in as the band mascot but he'd always been a lucky little devil – known for it he was over Hardington way. One had only to look at his brushes with death to spot that.

I'd never been into the pub before, but that night I was borne there on a tide of spiritual uplift and goodwill. Everyone was in a state of euphoria after the marching and attacks of vertigo, falling into rabbit holes and cowpats.

Bert said it was the beer that got them going, and there was nowt like a drop of ale to set a fellow on his feet, even though Ould Gabby had ended up on his back.

Even Julienne came along to share in the jollification, having found a babysitter for a couple of hours, and sat on a high stool looking as if she had just stepped off the cover of *Vogue*. Jill said that Julienne's hair really did look smashing, and she'd love me to do hers if I could fit it in.

'Do you do a lot of hairdressing?' she asked, and I explained that things were building up quite well in that direction, not that I'd intended doing hair at all, but if was funny how word got around – in fact word got around faster than I did, and it would be nice if I could afford a car, just a little car, nothing very expensive.

Durking said I should go round and have a word with Nick Fadden at the garage just along the main road, and he'd mention that I was coming if I liked.

'Well, I'm not sure,' I said, 'in any case I'd only be able to afford a banger.'

'Nick Fadden only sells bangers,' said Durking, smiling at Jill.

Everything seemed possible at that moment. Standing there in the packed bar parlour with its cases of stuffed pike, I had not felt so happy for years. Gin and tonic was quite a nice drink, I thought. My eyes seemed to be seeing more than usual, and people seemed nicer too, it really was kind of them to keep on sending me glasses of gin and little bottles of tonic, I had six of them lined up on the mantelpiece.

'I feel fine,' I hiccuped to Julienne.

'Mmmm, so I've noticed,' she replied.

Suddenly I spotted a familiar face near the door, but I couldn't for the life of me remember where I'd seen him before until he pushed his way through the crowd to the bar and I noticed that he walked with a limp.

'Leo,' I said.

He turned and smiled at me. Yes, I thought, he has a nice face – an indeterminate sort of face, a little careworn, but kindly and pleasant.

'I'm Sally Shelton,' I said, 'Lizzie's friend.'

I thought for a moment he was going to kiss me; instead he grabbed my hand and shook it warmly, relief flowing through his fingertips.

'I really am pleased to meet you,' he said, 'let me get you a drink.'

'Thank you, but I have plenty to be going on with. Did you get Lizzie's letter?'

'Letter?' The poor fellow looked bewildered.

'No, you couldn't have done, and she may not have taken my advice after all . . .'

'Advice? What advice?'

'About writing to you. But now there's no need. You're here. Oh, I'm so glad, and Lizzie will be pleased too. You see she thought you'd gone for good, but I told her you'd be back . . .'

'Do you think so?'

'I'm sure of it.'

'But she said . . .'

'I know what she said, but I'm sure she didn't mean it.'

'I had to come back,' he said, 'I couldn't leave things as they were. I wouldn't have gone away at all except that she seemed so upset I thought I'd make matters worse if I stayed.' He rubbed his forehead. 'Now I don't know what to do.'

'Why don't you go and see her?'

'What, now? But I couldn't possibly do that. What about the old lady?'

'I expect she'll be in bed by this time.' I felt very resolute, a bit devil-may-care. Really gin and tonic did have a marvellous effect on one. 'I'll go with you if you like.'

'I say, would you really?'

Lizzie's face was a study when she opened the door.

'Why don't you and Leo take a stroll down the cliff path?' I suggested.

'But I can't leave Mother,' Lizzie protested in a fierce whisper. 'She insisted on staying up a bit longer tonight, and I don't think she's gone to sleep yet.'

'I'll stay with her,' I said.

'But what if she wants me?'

'Don't worry, I'll think of something. Just put your coat on and go.'

Lizzie gave up the struggle. 'Well, just for half-an-hour,' she sighed.

When she and Leo had gone, I sat in Mrs Nugent's chair near the fireplace and watched the hands of the clock, remembering what I'd said to Lizzie about grasping the nettle danger even if you ended up getting stung, knowing that she needed her half-hour with Leo to get things straight between them, and that if she had any sense at all she'd tell him how she really felt about him.

Suddenly there came a rap on the ceiling, then another, followed by a querulous demand for a drink of water, and a tattoo of raps.

'Lizzie. Come up at once,' Mrs Nugent shouted.

There was nothing else for it. I went slowly upstairs.

Mrs Nugent was propped up in bed, clawing her walking-stick with one hand, the sheets with the other, and I guessed that she had hidden her false-teeth in the bedclothes because they certainly weren't in her mouth.

'Good evening, Mrs Nugent,' I said, feeling as if my stomach had gone walk-about.

Her mouth gaped open. 'Where's Lizzie?' she demanded.

'In the cellar,' I said.

'In the *cellar* at this time of night?'

Ye gods, I thought, now what? I sat down on the edge of her bed, looked her straight in the eye and said, 'No, she isn't in the cellar. She's gone out for a walk with her young man, if you must know, and if you intend having a heart-attack you'd better have it now and get it over with.'

'Eh?' I thought for a minute she was going to clout me over the head with her walking-stick.

'Well, you did say you liked people who got down to the essentials. What I have never understood is why you like everyone else to get down to the essentials except Lizzie.'

'That's different,' she croaked, 'Lizzie's my daughter.'

'All the more reason, I'd have thought. Or perhaps you want her to end up a lonely old maid.'

'Eh?'

'You should be happy that Lizzie has found such a nice man to care for her,' I said, 'and Leo is a nice man.'

'*Leo*!' she spat out. 'He sounds like a lion-tamer to me.'

'Mmmm. Just as well, perhaps.'

'What do you mean by that remark, Miss?' She glared at me with those sharp old eyes of hers. 'Well, I'm not having any lion-tamers coming here telling me what to do at my time of life.'

'Leo may sound like a lion-tamer,' I said, 'but he isn't. He's just a nice, ordinary man who could make Lizzie happy if you'd give him a chance.'

'Hoity-toity,' she cried, 'well why doesn't this nice ordinary man have the gumption to show himself to me? I don't like people who go by way of London to get to Newcastle.'

'I'm sure Leo has plenty of gumption,' I said. 'He also has feelings. In any case, what would you have said if he'd barged in without being invited? You'd have bitten his head off. You know you would.'

She burst out laughing. 'Well, that's what lions do, isn't it? Bite lion-tamer's heads off.'

'If you invited him to tea tomorrow afternoon,' I said, quaking inwardly, 'you could bite his head off in person couldn't you?'

'Yes, I'd like that,' she cackled. 'I'll tell him exactly what I think of him making sheep's eyes at my daughter; filling her head with a lot of nonsense at her age. She's been like a dying duck in a thunderstorm ever since he turned up.'

'Then – you mean he can come to tea?'

She glared at me. 'I've just said so, haven't I? Just you wait. I'll give him a taste of tongue-pie.'

'You won't if you've got the sense you were born with,' I said, getting up as I heard the quiet closing of the side door. 'There's Lizzie now.'

'Is that lion-tamer feller with her?' Mrs Nugent demanded.

'I shouldn't think so.' I noticed that her false teeth had slipped off the bed, picked them up and handed them to her. 'Hadn't you better put these back where they belong?' I said. 'You'll be losing them once too often if your not careful. I mean to say, you couldn't very well bite anyone's head off without any teeth, could you?'

'Hoity-toity,' she said, jamming the teeth in her mouth. 'Who says I'm going to bite anyone's head off? Don't you tell me what to do, Miss. And tell Lizzie not to make any of those slimy cucumber sandwiches, when she brings that lion-tamer to tea, she knows very well I can't chew them!'

Chapter Twenty-Seven

I stood in Amelia's garden on a pearly end of October day and looked at it with a sense of achievement. All the nettles had gone, so had the concrete pudding basins and what had always been more of a brickery than a rockery.

I'd spent the past weeks pick-axing Amelia's broken concrete, assisted by two small labourers – Half-Pint and Herbie Parrott – who appeared at the back gate after school and started filling the barrow, then trundling it to the tip near the garden shed. By the time they had fairly broken into a gallop where the ground sloped down a little, they and the barrow had gained so much momentum that they didn't need to unload it, they simply let go of the handles and the barrow unloaded itself.

When the concrete and the pudding basins, the 'brickery', Amelia's 'runny' paths, and the rusted clothes-posts had gone, and the Carnelian Bay borough council had sent a pick-up truck for the rubbish, I had laid a pathway of pink and grey stepping stones to the end of the garden, and started pipe-dreaming about myself in a gardening hat tied becomingly under my chin, wandering down my fairy stepping stones gathering flowers for the house. Not that I had any flowers to speak of, but I would have when I'd planted some – and I hadn't a gardening hat either.

Now I was about to plant grass seed, despite the Gaffer's gloomy prediction that it would never grow in a thousand years, not at this time of year.

'And what the heck hev you stuck in that border over yonder?' he asked darkly. When I told him that Frances Cox had given me a few roots of Myosotis, marigold and Aaron's rod, he seemed likely to fall backwards off his boxes. 'Humph,' he said to Dodgy Knees, who was sitting on his shoulder, 'd'you hear that? She's planted a border full of danged weeds.'

'But I like forget-me-nots and marigolds,' I said.

'Tha should've planted tatties,' he said crossly. 'You can boil up tatties a treat, but you can't boil up a pan full of bloomin' marigolds. Not that ah'd put it past you to try if you felt like it.'

'We plough the fields and sc-hat-ter', I sang as I broadcast the grass seed, watched by a row of beady-eyed sparrows on Bert's fence, remembering the look on Lady Nettlefold's face when, during the harvest festival service in church, Ambrose Lanfeard had set the rafters ringing with his 'joyful sound to the Lord'. I'd thought for a moment that she was going to thump the floor with her walking-stick, but perhaps her ladyship had come to the conclusion that she couldn't fight City Hall.

Things had certainly changed since I came to April Cottage on that sunshine and showery day seven months ago, I thought. Lizzie looked ten years younger these days in her new glasses, and happiness fairly sparkled from her since she and Leo became officially engaged and it had been arranged that her mother would go into The Hollies when it became functional next spring.

'In fact,' croaked the indomitable Dolly Nugent, 'I'll be glad to get out of this place when Lizzie gets married. I'd much rather be with Rebecca anyway because Rebecca and I understand each other.'

'Honestly, Mother,' Lizzie had retorted, 'you'd think that I had never understood you at all.'

'No more you do,' the old woman chuntered, 'you poke-stick about too much for my liking. I like people to be more decisive – like Leo. He gets on with things does Leo. Has he sold that bungalow of his yet?'

Lizzie had already had an offer for the shop from a couple called Ramona and St John Benedict.

'Strewth,' I said when Lizzie told me that item of news, 'they sound as if they should be buying a mission, let alone a corner shop.'

'They plan to whip out all the counters,' Lizzie said, 'and put in deep-freeze units. I expect they'll have shopping trolleys too, and a check-point Charlie.'

'Hmmm,' I sighed, 'and I bet they'll stick up the windows with those 2p-off cornflakes notices.'

Yes, change was in the air, I reflected, shooing away the sparrows. Mrs Amor was back under the cottonwood trees of Tara, ogling her Rotarians beneath blue-shadowed eyelids, and she appeared to be doing quite nicely with her new chef, Larry – who knew all about Dickensian game pies and haunches of venison – and a few other things as well, according to her.

I'd even managed to get up on my hind legs to speak to the Rotarians, fortified by a stiff gin and tonic and clutching my notes like a lifeline. Then, after the first ghastly five minutes, I'd started spouting like John Martin Harvey in *The Bells*.

'Good God,' Mrs Amor said afterwards, 'I thought we'd need a hook to get you off! Was your mother frightened by a Shakespearean actor by any chance?'

Since then I'd been besieged with phone calls from ladies who wanted to know if I'd speak at their luncheon club meetings. I'd said 'Yes' because they paid five pounds and gave me a free meal into the bargain, and free meals weren't to be sniffed at.

Money, or the lack of it, was my main problem in life as usual, despite my growing hairdressing clientele and the articles I'd had published in the *Advertiser* by that nice editor Edward Connery.

I was even starting to get the hang of those interminable committee meetings presided over by Lady Nettlefold, and we were getting things hammered into shape at last. It had never occurred to me how much there would be to discuss: fire regulations, running costs, how much rent to charge the tenants, how many people we'd need to run things, but at least I'd carried the vote when I stood up and said that I felt that we didn't want too many rules and regulations; that The Hollies should be a real home in the true sense of the word.

And yet I felt that something was missing from my life, and I didn't know what it was. Perhaps I was just tired. I couldn't even explain what ailed me when I went to visit Holly and Jim for a long weekend in August.

'It strikes me,' said that clairvoyant sister of mine, 'that you're either sickening for a dose of the flu, or you're in love.

It's got to be one or the other: fevered brow, restlessness, irritability . . .'

'I'm not in the least irritable,' I'd snapped. 'I feel perfectly well, and I'm most certainly not in love. Well, I mean to say, who could I possibly be in love with?'

'I just thought – Commander Bruce,' she said placidly, 'seeing you've mentioned him in every other sentence since you came here.'

'Don't talk such utter tripe!' I'd nearly bitten her head off. 'The Commander is a married man. Moreover he has a sick wife whom he adores, so how could I possibly be in love with him?'

'Quite easily, I'd have thought, knowing you. After all, you've always been inclined to let your heart rule your head, haven't you?'

'Not any more,' I said. 'Have you an aspirin, by the way? I've got an awful headache!'

When I came back from that weekend, there was the harvest festival service to look forward to, with corn-dollies, loaves of bread, flowers on every available windowsill, glowing berries and dusty sheaves stacked near the altar against a glorious background of chrysanthemums, gladioli and dahlias.

Moreover there were all those men who normally wore jeans and open-necked shirts and drove tractors, suddenly serious and nearly unrecognisable in dark blue suits with knife-edged collars and Adam's apples restraining ties, filing into church with their wives and children.

I'd gone home afterwards and felt the loneliness of April Cottage for the first time; even wondered how Hugo and his new wife were getting along together; remembered Ambrose Lanfeard belting out the Harvest Anthem, and the way the Vicar had walked forward so confidently to address his congregation.

Perhaps I'd been a little unfair, glancing across at George Brassington, in thinking that it was just as well he wasn't in the Crusades because they'd never have found a tasset to fit him. He really was '*Misericordiam et judicum*' to the life, with his proud look and high stomach.

Ah well, it was all part of life's rich pattern, the loneliness, the sudden longing, the memories, the wishing and the waiting, I decided. But waiting for what?

* * *

October faded into November, November slipped quietly into December, and my grass seed had started to sprout.

'Ah suppose you'll be mowing it afore Christmas,' said the Gaffer with a gusty sigh. 'Well, all ah can say is, the Lord must be on your side. Ah've niver heeard tell of grass seed sproutin' in November afore.'

'It looks a bit uneven though, doesn't it?' I said, trying to soften the blow.

He perked up a bit at that. 'Aye, it does now you come to mention it.' Then he sighed again. 'Ah wus wonderin'. When The Hollies gets goin', do you think I could get a room there? Truth to tell, ah'm fed up with Darr. It's nowt but mutter, mutter, chunter, chunter from morn till night. I wish our Bert had married a wumman who didn't carry on so, an' that's a fact.'

I just had to ask him, 'What is Darr short for, anyway? I've racked my brains but I can't think of a thing.'

The Gaffer pulled a face. 'Bert'd skin me alive if I told you.'

'In that case you'd better not tell me.'

'Ah don't aim to.' He scowled. 'That wumman's got Bert on a piece of string. Costs him a fortune in hairpins, she do; wain't hev her hair cut neither, just cos that soft gobbin of a Bert tould her, when they was courtin', that he liked long hair. Pity, as things turned out, that he didn't tell her he liked an Eton crop. He'd be well off now if he had.'

'Now, Oliver,' I admonished, 'don't get all bitter and twisted.'

'Bitter an' twisted!' He pulled an even longer face. 'It meks me feel porely the way he runs after her. Why, if she told him her foot had gone to sleep he'd put it ti bed for her! Calls him 'Bertie', she does. 'Bertie' – I ask you!' He clambered down from his pile of boxes. 'Well, I'd best be gettin' indoors afore ah catches me death of cold.'

Suddenly he gave a wicked little chuckle, winked his eyes, and went off up the path singing, 'You're the Darr-ling of my heart, sweet Adeline' at the top of his voice.

Chapter Twenty-Eight

Julienne managed to look elegant even when she was wheeling a barrow full of pig swill. I'd just finished setting her hair, and she had tucked it inside the hood of a fur-edged parka. Dominic was in London putting the finishing touches to his film – 'Whatever Happens in a Place Like This' – that is why Julienne was left to cope with Miss Piggy and the hens.

The film title, she told me, came from Jill, Dominic's 'Possible Ructions' girl, who kept saying the day before the shooting started, 'I simply can't imagine whatever happens in a place like this.'

'I bet she got the shock of her life when she did find out,' I laughed.

'Hmmm,' Julienne remarked as I grabbed the other handle of the swill bin and we struggled with it into the pig pen. 'Jill's coming over for Christmas, by the way. I think she's got something going with Durking Pickles. Can't say I blame her, he's quite dishy in a bucolic sort of fashion, isn't he?'

When we'd tipped the contents of the bin into Miss Piggy's trough and she was standing blissfully with her front trotters in it, Julienne asked me if I was going away for Christmas.

'No, I'm staying put,' I said. 'For one thing I'm working on Christmas Eve morning. The Rotarians are having a special do at the Red Lion, so it would be a bit of a rush to get to my sister's afterwards. I'm going there for New Year instead.' I leaned my elbows on the railings and gazed at Miss Piggy. 'As a matter of fact, I wish Christmas was over and done with. The awful thing is, I used to love Christmas once upon a time. I don't know what's come over me nowadays.'

As we trundled the barrow back to the shed and went indoors for a cup of coffee, Julienne asked if I was feeling quite well. 'You've seemed a bit out of sorts recently,' she said. 'Is anything the matter? You've gone broody all of a sudden.'

The truth was, my sister had shaken me to the core when she'd suggested that I might have fallen in love with the Commander, but I couldn't very well tell Julienne that.

'Listen,' she said when the coffee was perking, 'why don't you come here on Christmas Day? I'm asking Nurse Pintuck as well, and any other spares that happen to be lying around . . .'

'Spares,' I said bleakly.

'Oh Sally, I didn't mean it! Why the hell did I say that?'

I gave a lop-sided smile. 'It doesn't matter. Anyway, I suppose it's true, isn't it?'

'No, it isn't bloody well true, and you know it.' She ruffled her newly-set hair in agitation. 'I could bite my tongue off . . .'

'I think I can hear Fern crying,' I said, changing the subject. I knew that Julienne hadn't meant what she said, but I couldn't help thinking about it afterwards. To be called a 'spare' had hurt just a little.

Writing Christmas cards that afternoon, my mind kept wandering back to my Hugo days. They hadn't been a ball of fun at times, but at least I'd belonged to someone; had someone to care for. Doing things for one's self all the time seemed a little empty, I thought.

Human beings, I reckoned, needed to touch now and then, not just mentally but physically too. The warmth of a human hand was worth a thousand kind thoughts.

I lit a cigarette and sat on my sprawly settee, gazing into the fire, then I gave myself a good talking to. 'Oh fine,' I muttered, 'this is going to get you a long way, isn't it?'

Julienne had hit the nail on the head when she'd said I was broody, and who on earth wanted broody people around them? Perhaps I'd feel better when I'd had a cup of tea.

Waiting for the kettle to boil, I went through a few of the old adages; 'Laugh and the world laughs with you, cry and you cry alone'; 'Count your blessings'.

It had slipped my mind for a moment what a lucky person I was. Whatever would Amelia think if she could see me now? I looked in the mirror and pulled a Cheshire Cat face. 'Keep going, you fool,' I said.

Sipping the tea, I thought about Hugo, and about Howard Bruce. Perhaps if Hugo had been more like the Commander, we'd have made a go of our marriage. My sister was right when she said I'd mentioned his name in every other sentence, but that was simply because he possessed all the qualities I had hoped to find in a man, kindliness, loyalty linked to a sense of humour, compassion laced with forthrightness. I sighed.

Well, no use dwelling on that. Even if I fell in love with him ten times over, what good would it do me? He wasn't the least bit in love with me.

I stared out of the window. The common was rimed with sparkling white frost under a star-sprinkled sky, and there, on the far side of the wide triangle of starched grass, was a lighted Christmas tree in Mrs Pickles's front window, alert with winking blue and green lights.

I smiled suddenly. Well, at least this year I could have a real Christmas tree, I thought, not one of those silver-paper things like a folding umbrella, with no-one to complain because the needles would ruin the pile of a new carpet. Come to think of it, I'd never felt at home in that bungalow with the pseudo carriage lamps and all that concrete. I'd buy lots of holly, too, and stick it behind the pictures, the way my mother used to when I was a kid. Hugo hadn't liked holly, either. In fact he'd scoffed at the whole idea of Christmas which he dubbed, 'a Pagan festival'.

We'd had many a long, bitter argument about that, and his passion for neatness had obliged me to hang up our Christmas cards like washing on a clothes line, while I preferred them propped up in comfortable confusion on the mantelpiece so that I could look at the messages written inside them.

Suddenly I began to feel quite perky again. Tomorrow was Christmas Eve. When I'd done my stint at the Red Lion, I'd go shopping in the town square market, buy myself a Christmas tree and a bundle of holly, and treat myself to a chicken and a piece of ham to boil. After all, there was no telling who might call to see me – or who I might invite come to that. Perhaps I'd better buy a pork pie, too, and open one of those jars of Mrs Pickles's piccalilli. I'd need lights and baubles for the tree as well.

I sat down and began to scribble a shopping list.

Avril came to see me a little later on, to tell me that she and Arthur would be having a real family Christmas, after all. Their son Mark, and his Jamaican wife had resolved their differences and were bringing little Steven to stay with his grandparents.

'Oh, I'm so happy for you,' I said.

Avril smiled through her tears. 'I can't think what Lady Nettlefold will say when she finds out that Arthur and I have a chocolate-coloured grandson,' she said, her face aglow, 'but I really don't care any more.'

'Why on earth should you?'

'The thing is,' she beamed, 'we'd like you to come to us on Christmas Day.'

'Thank you. That would have been nice, but I've already arranged to spend Christmas Day with Julienne and Dominic.'

'Come on Boxing Day, then,' she said quickly.

'Well, I'm not sure about that. You see, I thought I might ask Miss Cox to come here on Boxing Day. There's a Ginger Rogers and Fred Astaire film on in the afternoon, and we have a thing about old movies.'

'You and Frances Cox?' Avril lifted her eyebrows in surprise. 'Well, I knew that you weren't daggers drawn any more, but I never dreamt that Miss Cox would care for Ginger Rogers and Fred Astaire.'

'You'd be surprised.'

'Well, at any rate we'll be seeing you tomorrow night, won't we?'

'Tomorrow night?' I frowned slightly.

'Unless you've arranged something else, of course. One never knows with popular people like you, Mizz Shelton . . .' She chuckled.

'I don't get it.'

'I'm speaking about the midnight carol service in church,' she reminded me, 'and do for heaven's sake remember to wear gloves or mittens during the Processional. I forgot mine last year, and the candlegrease kept dripping on to my fingers.' She giggled. 'Just wait until you hear Lady N trying to hit the right note in that first unaccompanied verse of "Once in Royal David's City". Mr Plunkett usually gives her a reminder on the organ, but if she doesn't quite catch it, she simply bellows, "Play it again . . ."'

'Sam,' I said, and wondered why I felt like crying.

I felt as mellow as an owl when I left the Red Lion on Christmas Eve. No wonder, I thought, after a couple of stiff gin and tonics and a swig of Polly's cooking sherry.

215

Funny how Christmas got through to one in the end, when everyone started kissing and exchanging presents.

'Eeyah,' said Polly, planting a wet kiss on my cheek, 'you might as well have 'em now, I suppose. Those tablemats you wus awn about.'

How on earth I'd manage to carry my groceries and a Christmas tree as well I had no idea, as I jaunted along to the square and got caught up in the crowds milling round the stalls.

As I sailed past Waldorf Winninger's antique shop, I caught a glimpse of him placing his 'Mature Shop Assistant required' notice into the window. At the same minute a large, red-faced lady fairly hurtled out of the shop and slammed the door behind her muttering, 'Well, of all the cheek!'

I'd never seen the market place so busy before as people milled round the stalls, doing their last minute shopping. There was a sense of urgency and happiness abroad under the lowering sky. Then the street lights came on one by one, springing to life like mop-headed chrysanthemums, making warm stepping stones of colour at my feet and shining down on striped awnings and the upturned faces of children.

The Salvation Army band was grouped near the sparkling Rotarian Christmas tree by the entrance to the newly-furbished Red Lion Hotel where, tomorrow, Mrs Amor and her enterprising new chef would serve traditional Christmas luncheons to a packed dining room, helped by a contingent of smart waitresses gleaned from the local employment agency.

'Looks as if we're in for snow,' Buddy, the crippled news-vendor said as I stopped to buy a paper. 'The sky's full of it unless I miss my guess.' He grinned. 'I hope it does snow. I like white Christmases.'

He shrugged his shoulders to ease the weight of his bag full of papers. 'Well, a happy Christmas to you, love,' he said cheerfully as I slipped a pound note into his sack. 'Hey, you've forgotten your change!'

'No, I haven't. A merry Christmas to you, too, Buddy.'

I queued for ages to buy a chicken, a pork pie and a hunk of farmhouse Gloucester, and the greengrocer's stall was a free-for-all of bulky women pushing forward to buy oranges and apples, nuts and boxes of sticky dates. I was elbowed aside three or four times before I managed to grab the attention of a harassed assistant.

'Sprouts and potatoes, please,' I gasped, 'and I'd like a small Christmas tree and a bunch of holly . . .'

'Sorry, love,' the woman said, 'we've sold right out of Christmas trees and holly.' Then she smiled at me sympathetically. 'You've left it a bit late, love, but you could always get one of those tinsel trees from Boots.'

'Yes, I suppose I could. Thank you very much.'

As I started to walk across the road towards the bus queue, I heard a familiar voice at my elbow, and looked up to see the Commander smiling down at me.

'Hello, Sally.' His arms were full of parcels too. 'You look a little downcast. Is anything wrong?'

I told him about the Christmas tree and holly. 'It's my own fault, I might have known everything would be sold out at this stage of the proceedings.'

I hadn't meant to tell him about Hugo's dislike for Christmas in general and of Christmas trees in particular. Perhaps it was just so nice to be with a friend in the bustling market square.

I laughed, 'Maybe it's just as well they have sold out. I'd never have got on the bus with all this lot plus a tree.'

'If you're heading for home,' the Commander said, 'my car's parked just round the corner.' He seized my heavy bag of shopping. 'Allow me to carry that for you.'

'But you can't possibly carry that and all your own shopping,' I protested. 'Why don't you give me that big box before you drop it?'

We did a parcel juggling act as we walked down the side street to the car, laughing as we did so.

'That's my wife's present,' he said, 'a housecoat. I hope she'll like it. Perhaps I've chosen the wrong colour . . .' He looked worried.

'I'm sure she'll like it,' I said because that seemed the right thing to say, and because I'd always believed that presents, whether one liked them or not, should be accepted in the spirit in which they were given. If the Commander gave me a puce housecoat with orange flowers and a khaki collar I'd think it was beautiful; that or a monk's habit with a rope girdle.

'Kay might not care for it,' he said levelly, 'you see she isn't very well at the moment.'

'I'm sorry,' I said as he unlocked the boot and stowed away the shopping, 'but how does she cope with that big house?'

'I'm afraid she doesn't cope with it any longer.' He backed the car then put it into forward gear, and I knew as we headed for the coast road that he wanted to talk about his wife, the way that I had wanted to tell someone about Hugo's dislike of Christmas trees with needles. 'We have a housekeeper and a daily woman nowadays.'

I noticed the tense way he gripped the steering wheel, and this was a Commander Bruce I had never seen before – a man with problems who needed someone to talk to.

'If only I could get Kay interested in life again,' he said. 'If only I could convince her that life is worth living after all. But you don't want to listen to my troubles. Oh look, it's beginning to snow!'

'So it is!' I watched the windscreen wipers making fan shapes against the whirling goose-feathers. 'We're going to have a white Christmas, after all.'

'I've just remembered, I promised to call in at The Hollies to make sure that the electricians have left everything in order there. I wonder, would you care to have a look at the house? I don't believe you've been inside it before, have you?' He smiled.

'Only once,' I said, 'but that was a long, long time ago.' I told him about Amelia taking me there when I was ten to meet Miss Berry, and I noticed that his hands had relaxed on the steering wheel as I talked, and all the time I was remembering that Rebecca had described him as a 'knight in shining armour.'

A mile from the Bagdad Corner turning, he nosed the car down a side road leading to Tootington another way. 'Well, here we are.'

'Gosh, so soon? I mean, I hadn't realized that there was a short cut to the village.'

He switched off the engine and we sat together in the little warm world of the car looking at The Hollies.

The For Sale notice had gone from the garden. The house looked safe now, I thought, and warm and waiting, with its pinkish bricks and stoutly-tiled roof, wide, welcoming front steps and tall chimneys.

'It's a lovely house, isn't it?' I said breathlessly as he opened the car door and we walked together up the path.

Inside, he snapped on the lights, and we stood in the hall with its broad staircase and panelling.

218

'Miss Berry's drawing room was through that door on the left,' I said eagerly, 'and her dining room was simply splendiferous, with a door leading to the conservatory. You know, I think the old people will love that conservatory. Perhaps they could bring their own pot plants and take cuttings, and have you thought that we might put some garden chairs in there where they could sit when it's too wet to go outdoors?'

'You love this house, don't you?' Howard said quietly.

'Yes, I suppose I do.' I smiled up at him, 'I loved it the minute I saw it all those years ago.'

'Your enthusiasm's catching,' he twinkled. 'I must confess that I had never thought about the conservatory before. But you're quite right, it would make a splendid winter garden.'

'Wouldn't it be marvellous,' I said, 'if you could get your wife interested in this place? Perhaps what she needs most is people to make her come alive again . . .' I felt the colour rush up into my cheeks. 'Oh, I'm sorry, I shouldn't have said that.'

'Don't apologise, my dear,' he held out his hand to me. 'You're quite right, as it happens. Kay does need people.'

I put my hand in his for a moment. The warmth of one human hand, I thought, is worth a thousand kind words.

'Don't worry,' I said, 'everything will come right in the end.'

He smiled. 'Do you remember the day of the village fête? You said that food given without love has no nourishment. I've thought about that a great deal since then. Now I know that nothing given without love has any value.'

He let go of my hand. 'Thanks to you, Sally,' he said softly, 'this house will be a real home again one day. Come next spring when the furniture vans begin to arrive.'

'Come next spring,' I said, my eyes shining. 'Oh yes, that will be something to look forward to, when all these empty rooms are filled with people. Poor house, it has been empty for such a long time. It needs people to make it come alive again.'

'Everyone needs people,' Commander Bruce said slowly.

We faced each other uncertainly, and I knew beyond the shadow of a doubt that I was in love with him, that I'd loved him from the moment we met. I only hoped that he would never know how I felt about him. 'Perhaps we'd better be going,' I said, 'before we get snowed in.'

'Yes, you're right.'

He locked the door of The Hollies behind us, and tucked his

hand under my elbow as we walked together through the falling snow.

And now it was time to get ready for the carol service, lighted candles, woollen mittens and all.

I looked at the Christmas cards crowding the mantelpiece; so many cards that they had overspilled on to Amelia's sideboard and bookshelves. More cards than I had ever received in my life before. There was even one from Lady Nettlefold, and next to it was Rebecca's charming card simply inscribed, 'With love to my dearest Sally'.

Above it was Amelia's *Light of the World*.

How in the world could I have ever felt lonely, and yet . . .

Strange how one longed for one bright star above all the rest; that special shining star to anchor one's heart to an unshakeable sense of security and belonging, no matter how remote, how distant.

Ah well, I thought, pulling my woolly hat well over my ears, no use dreaming that kind of dream. Far better to get on with the business in hand. I sang the first snatch of 'Once in Royal David's City' to get my tonsils in working order, then I opened the door.

It wasn't a very big Christmas tree, but the bunch of holly was enormous, all glossy with masses of glowing berries. I laddered my tights on one of the prickly leaves, but I didn't care.

There were two boxes of lights and baubles lying on my doorstep as well, tied with pink ribbon. No puce housecoat with orange flowers and a khaki collar, just a small Christmas tree with lights, and all that holly, but then, I figured, the Commander knew I didn't want a housecoat.

Tears stung my eyes as I carried the Christmas tree indoors, then the lights, the baubles and the holly.

I opened the card attached to the tree with trembling fingers.

'For Sally,' it read, 'who makes me smile with my heart'.

And suddenly my bright star was there, smiling down on me, and my world seemed like a shining treasure-trove, with diamonds above and below me, and the sound of church bells spilling into the cold, clear air around me.